GHOST CAVE

A Mystery by Helen Currie Foster

This is a work of fiction. All incidents and dialogue, and all characters, with the exception of some well-known historical and public figures are products of the author's imagination and are not to be construed as real. Where real-life historical or public figures appear, the situations, incidents and dialogues concerning those persons are used fictitiously and are not intended to depict actual events or to change the entirely fictional nature of the work. In all other respects, any resemblance to persons living or dead is entirely coincidental. Although Texas has significant prehistoric and historic rock art, Cloud Ranch and its rock art sites are entirely fictional. Coffee County and Coffee Creek exist solely in the author's imagination, located somewhere in the Texas Hill Country between Dripping Springs and Fredericksburg.

Printed by CreateSpace, An Amazon.com Company
Available from Amazon.com and other online stores.
Available on Kindle and other devices

Library of Congress Control Number: 2014921945
CreateSpace Independent Publishing Platform, North Charleston, SC

For Larry, Sydney and Drew

Chapter One

Delicate Dance

Alice slowed down at the lights in Fredericksburg, then headed west again, remembering the curiosity she had felt, mixed with a little trepidation, before her first appointment with Ollie, two months earlier. Lean, unsmiling, imposing, in starched jeans and polished boots and carrying his gray hat, he had stalked into her law office in Coffee Creek, Texas, shaken her hand, and looked intently at her for what seemed an hour. She had stared back at him. Then they sat down at the tea table in her office and began the delicate dance of two humans who are discussing the imminent death of one of the two humans, and the disposition of a lifetime's worth of accumulated property.

Ollie had sat in her office as the August afternoon sun moved past the shaded west window. Slowly the picture unfurled: what Ollie had seen in his doctor's eyes on the previous visit, what Ollie wanted to do for his ranch, and for his daughter, Mary, and for a young man named Allen. Ollie made it clear he wanted both confidentiality and control. "I might change my mind about things," he said. "So I don't want expectations out there." He wanted the cave paintings on the cliffs protected so nothing could disturb them, wanted Mary to be able to live at the ranch for her lifetime if she chose, and wanted the same for Allen. When Alice asked why he would do that for Allen, Ollie was silent for a second. "Well," he said, "I promised my brother, before he died. Allen was his stepson. He knew Allen was a little . . . limited. He's right, too. Allen can't seem to grow up. Thought it might help him for him and his mother, Leanne, to live at the ranch after my brother passed. But Allen kinda went off the rails last spring when she died too. Still, now and then Allen can be a good hand. I don't want him left with nowhere to go."

He also wanted the plan to include a trustee to manage the conservancy assets, including the ranch itself and the initial fund to protect the rock art. For his other assets, he wanted the bank to manage the various accounts. Alice asked how Mary, his only child, would feel about this. Ollie said simply, "It protects her." And he wouldn't explain beyond, "I don't want her worried or pressured. This way everything gets done, and I don't mind paying the bank fees." He looked at Alice. "Hell, I'll be dead! Bank won't mind, and I won't either. Besides, Mary has charge of all the medical decisions under that medical thing you had me sign, right? That's enough."

Before her first appointment with Ollie, when he first phoned Alice, Alice had called in her secretary, Silla. "Why in the world is he coming to me for legal work?" Alice asked. "Why not someone in Fredericksburg?" She was wary of inadvertently taking on a client with a history of serial run-ins with prior lawyers.

"Well, of course his wife, Cassie Ney, grew up here. She ran that antique store in the old Ney house on Pecan where she grew up. Coffee Creek Old Style."

"Ollie just said she died a few years ago."

"She disappeared ten years ago."

"What do you mean, 'disappeared'?"

"Supposedly she just disappeared. Apparently on a trip to the border." Silla lifted a skeptical eyebrow.

Ollie had later told her about Cassie's disappearance. And too bad for Ollie, Alice supposed, but maybe it simplified his estate planning. All in all, Alice thought with some satisfaction, she had successfully translated her client's desires into a solid structure she considered creative but sound. She wasn't sure how many years or months Ollie had left to live and knew that she, and he, would feel better when the one remaining document was executed and the last domino was in place.

West of Fredericksburg, with the land steadily rising, Alice found the gate to Cloud Ranch. "Named for my mother. She was a McCloud," Ollie had said. "Mary's named after her." Alice pressed the gate code into the box, waited for the big bars to swing open, and bounced the truck across the cattle guard. The gate clanged shut behind her. Before her, the caliche drive led straight up a steep limestone ridge rough with cedar, then began switchbacking left and right, higher and higher. She downshifted to second to make the last turn; then, abruptly, the truck nosed over and she was headed down the other side of the ridge. She slammed on her brakes.

The view took her breath away. Ollie's ranch, at least the part she could see, was a big bowl rimmed with hills. Straight ahead to the west lay a quilt of fenced pastures, ending at foothills on the western horizon and steep rocky cliffs to the north, on her right. From those infolded rocky cliffs the small creek emerged into a valley that glinted with narrow water. The steep road down the limestone ridge where she sat crossed the creek on a low-water dam, creating a blue-green pool. A set of rapids left the pool and cascaded sideways toward the south, to her left, then meandered below the southerly ridge as it curved west. Alice gripped the steering wheel and started switchbacking down the equally steep creek side of the limestone ridge, almost standing on the brakes as she made the last turn. The unpaved road briefly became concrete as she crossed the dam. Tall feathery cypress trees lined the far side of the blue-green pool. As Alice drove up the bank on the far side, a great blue heron grawked from the top of a cypress and flapped away.

The dusty gravel drive bent left and wandered along the creekside into a pecan grove. There she saw the ranch house. Ollie stood out front with another man. They stood stiffly, like they'd been arguing, faces set, arms crossed on their chests. Alice parked and slid down out of the truck. Ollie, stooped but still tall, in his usual starched jeans and a chambray shirt, stood next to a dark-haired, soft-bellied twenty-something man with a discontented face. Whatever the dispute had been about, Alice could feel Ollie's personality settle over the scene. Ollie had the upper hand over Mr. Softbelly.

"Ms. Greer, this is my late brother's stepson, Allen Debard," Ollie said, stepping forward to meet her. as she approached. Alice shook hands with Ollie, mentally giving him several points for clarity of genealogy.

"How do you do," she said to Allen.

"Ma'am," he muttered, glancing briefly at her, then down at his boots.

Ollie said, "Allen is just heading for town, right, Allen?"

Allen looked up at Ollie's impassive face.

"Yessir." But Allen did stare again at Alice before leaving. She stood in the sort of discomfort she felt when someone was silently chastised in her presence, while Allen slammed the door of his old blue Bronco and gunned it across the creek, leaving a roostertail of water and then a cloud of dust as he swerved up the switchbacks toward the highway. Alice felt sorry for him; he was having trouble measuring up to Ollie's standards, and she knew, from Silla, how he'd lost his mother the year before. Now she felt compunction remembering her laughter when Silla described his mother's demise. What had Silla said? "The wreck sure messed up Sunday lunch at Sonny's Barbecue. The way Leanne hit the pits, they had to give up on the brisket. All they could serve for lunch that day was ribs and pork chops."

Ollie watched the Bronco top the ridge for a moment, then turned to Alice.

"Let's go. We'll take my truck," he said. "Don't mind Allen. He's a good hand, but . . . like I said. Limited." She scampered to keep up with Ollie as he strode to the truck. Alice left her old briefcase locked on her front seat, taking only her phone and binoculars, and clambered into Ollie's battered Ford F-250. Ollie was a Ford man, like his father and grandfather before him—despite, or maybe because of, the mocking words of Johnny Mercer's 1936 "I'm an Old Cowhand." Ollie too was riding the range in his Ford V-8.

Ollie drove fast. Alice glanced at him, wondering why he was in such a hurry. They left their own roostertail of white dust, heading first west then northwest along a rocky track that skirted fences and then headed straight toward the tall cliffs that bounded the north side of Cloud Ranch. Ollie rejected Alice's effort to get him to talk more about the cave paintings and their locations, and just said, "Let me show you. Then you'll understand."

Chapter Two

Dark Place in the Rock

They drove in silence. The track climbed farther and farther back into the hills.

Ollie stopped, finally, at the foot of a steep bluff: a tumble of limestone rockslide at the bottom, then steep slabs of limestone with a few trees in the cleft rock, then cliffs soaring up to blue sky. Looking halfway up the bluff at the distinctive fans of dull green-yellow needles on little black-trunked evergreens, Alice said in disbelief, "Are those piñons up there?" She knew there were piñons in the southern Guadalupe Mountains of far west Texas but couldn't believe there were any this far east. Some bird must have dropped a few seeds.

"Yes. It's high enough for piñons here. Now, can you climb?"

"Yes, sir." She followed Ollie along the bottom of the bluff and then up a rockfall. As the rockfall grew steeper she had to hold her binoculars against her chest with one arm and hold branches with the other. She could hear the rancher coughing and grunting ahead of her and felt momentary panic at the thought that he might die right here—how would she ever lug him out? On they went, sidling along what started as path and slowly rose into a ledge until it became a small, level place. They were now above a small fork of the creek; she could hear water somewhere below.

"Now we have to climb," said Ollie. Alice's eyes widened. "I guess you thought we were climbing," he said. "That was walking." He grinned at her and turned back toward the rock slab. Alice looked up. Looming above stood twenty feet of slanted limestone, leading to what appeared to be a deep ledge with more cliff far above it. She slung the binoculars across her front and followed Ollie up. The handholds and footholds weren't bad if she watched carefully where he put his hands and feet. Alice tried not to think about the return trip.

Following Ollie, Alice inched over the top of the slab and onto the ledge, face down, grimly gripping the last handholds. One she had crawled forward onto safe rock, she lay there for a moment, her heart pounding. Then she looked up and gasped.

Before her, reaching ten feet up the cliff face, figures were dancing on cream and golden rock. Never had she seen such an array of dancers. Alice had secretly classified as tedious the rock art photographs in her college anthropology text. Yes, found in scenic places; yes, reflecting hard work by unknown humans—but the photographs seemed static, boring. These pictures, however, were ravishing. Simple lines indicated dancers bent over, dancers arched back, circling across the rock. Higher up, leaping deer, graceful as could be. A bear, standing with raised claws. She could faintly see colors on the dancers—pale rose, more gold, some green. The dance was magnificent, was all of life itself. She wanted to stand and dance. She wanted to be there.

Ollie was watching her. "Think they're worth protecting?"

"Oh," said Alice. "Oh, oh, oh. This is a treasure."

He looked at her for a minute. "Here's the deal, Ms. Greer. There's more. And you need to see it, but I'm worn out. I can't climb to the next spot. Are you game?"

Alice looked where he pointed. Just left of the little golden cliff face where they sat was a rock slot with a few small trees growing in it. "Go on in there. Follow the water." He grinned. "I'll wait for you right here." He pulled a pack of Marlboros out of his shirt pocket. "I'll be enjoying a smoke." He pointed at the binoculars. "You better leave those; you'll want your balance."

Alice dutifully laid down the binoculars, shaking her head. "You'll want your balance," she muttered. She started up the slot, holding onto branches and pulling herself through, climbing as the rock slot climbed. Then there was only air. The slot stopped, with the cliff bending around toward her right. Alice looked past her toes at the drop—at least fifty feet, she guessed. Now what? And what water? Above her right shoulder the bluff rose high to the deep autumn blue of the sky. Alice peered along the cliff to her right. She could hear the gracious plashing of water somewhere. She could see an improbably green spot on the other side of the rock face—pine trees, grass. Nothing but sheer rock below it. Perhaps fifty feet away. How to get there? She looked up again at the rock face to her right, at the creamy tilted limestone. This time she saw another shelf six feet above her head. Good grief, she thought. What kind of client service did I sign on for? It looked like she could get there if she climbed up that tilted rock slab. Alice crawled up the slab, grabbing a small pine that had rooted into a cleft in the rock, and pulled herself up onto the shelf. Now the way was clear: the shelf was about fourteen inches wide, fairly smooth, and led straight across the cliff face to the little forest.

Alice shuddered. She hated heights—what Jordie had euphemistically called "exposure" when he took her hiking in Scotland on their honeymoon. He'd laughed at Alice's preferred technique: use both hands, both feet, and her rear end to slide down anything "exposed."

Now, on this little shelf, Alice decided, crawling was the better part of wisdom. No macho walking along the shelf for her. She crawled across, grateful for jeans and hiking boots, happy to have her right elbow scrape the rock, carefully looking ahead and practicing "gaze discipline," not letting her eyes stray below. At the end, the shelf opened onto a gentle pitch with some grass and a few trembling alders and pines at the downhill edge of the slope—above another sheer drop. Alice inched up onto safety, held a tree, grabbed the next tree, pulled herself up onto hands and knees. And there was the water. Fed by a small clear seep, with its rippled surface hinting at water rising from hidden channels in the surrounding rock, there was water in a small stone fountain, with pebbles in the bottom. A cliff spring. Only a yard across, it was life in the midst of rock. The pool had fed the wind-blown, bird-dropped seeds and started a garden on the lap of the cliff. Alice's heart slowed. Still on her knees, she dabbed her bandana in the small fountain and wiped her face. No, she thought, and dipped her hand three times to the water and to her forehead. Alice had begun blessing herself this way when no one was present to see (part of a recent effort to reclaim some part of her faith), and here there was no one to see.

But Ollie had said, "There's more." Was this it? Surely the spring was enough, with its clean smell and clear voice. Clinging to the bunch grass and slim tree trunks on the slope, she lifted her gaze beyond the little sanctuary, toward the cliff face, and there she saw a dark place in the rock. Oh no. A cave. Must she? And when she lifted her head further, and saw the awaiting drawings in and above the cave, her heart pounded. Here was the home of fear.

Over the centuries irresistible fingers of water had pried open the cliff, making a shallow cave not much taller than Alice. A rockfall of shattered limestone blocked one side of the cave. But from a crack in the back of the cave, edged with iridescent green moss, a trickle of clear water slid across the cave floor and down toward the round spring. The arch of rock face slanting back into the cave and then soaring up above it held an image, the very shape of which transfixed Alice: a tall form with arms and legs but no head, all in white. Slightly below loomed another figure—but in black and with a head. Above them both writhed a snakelike shape.

Alice leaned back, now looking farther up this arch of rock. Paintings on it extended at least twenty feet above the cave's entrance. The white figure floated up toward the snake, and other black figures, with black lines like ribs, were strewn below, all with heads. A huge figure, clearly a mountain lion, leapt up on the left. Alice took a deep breath to slow her heart. This white figure floating up—was it this that was so frightening to her? No, no. The snake shape above? No, Alice prided herself on being unafraid of snakes, unlike most people she knew. The mountain lion? It was so real she could almost feel its hot breath as it leapt up toward the top of the arch. But her fear did not seem to rise from that either, or any of the pictures. The shapes startled more than scared her. So what was it? She tried to focus.

Her fear came from the mouth of the cave. A faint cold breath flowed out and disturbed the sunny, fragrant air around the spring. She felt deep reluctance to move any closer. And she felt she was running out of time, with her seventy-eight-year-old ailing client behind her, on top of a stiff climb. She now remembered she should take pictures. She groped for the cell phone in her pocket. She began photographing the cave pictures, emailing them back to her office computer, making them part of Ollie's file. The cell phone balked but finally made its odd pretend click and whirr as it announced that each picture was taken and sent. Spring. Arch. Snake, mountain lion, white floating figure, black figures below. What was on the arms of the white figure? Little bags? She squinted but could not quite tell. She crawled a few feet closer. Could she not stand up? No, she feared she would trip and roll past the spring and off the cliff. "Are you woman or mouse?" she muttered. "Mouse, without a doubt."

Oh, come on, Alice, she argued. Stand up!

No. She would crawl. She inched closer, to a place where she could see the little black figures better. The closer she got, the more detail came into focus—arrows? spears? Then her eyes were drawn up almost irresistibly to the white figure that headed up, up, up toward the top, the snake looking on. Alice herself was flying. She breathed in and floated up—she was almost there—leading with the top of her head, light coming into the top of her head, sun pouring into the top of her head, she was flying, flying, flying, her arms were wings, her feet were pushing off the earth, she was soaring free—

"Ms. Greer! You okay?" Ollie's hoarse shout intruded. Whump. She fell to the ground. No, she hadn't fallen; she was still on her knees; she'd never left. Alice shook her head. What a totally odd sensation. She looked down at her hands. Normal, no feathers for fingers. She wiggled her toes in her hiking boots. They felt like her own feet.

"I'm fine," she called. "I'll be right back." Yes, that was her own voice—nearly.

She looked up but now the pictures were silent, and old, and handmade. She looked toward the dark mouth of the cave and thought, I should at least look further, but—

"Ms. Greer, we ought to be getting back." Ollie's voice sounded strained.

"I'm coming," called Alice. She checked the GPS app on her phone, inserted a note as to the location, and zipped the phone into her pocket. She crawled carefully, backward, toward the spring. She touched water to her tongue and then, with her hand, brought water three times to her forehead. Now for the narrow shelf. Still on her knees, she edged backward. It felt safer to back down it than to crawl away from this place headfirst. She started down, craning her neck to check direction, gravel biting her knees, sun and shade changing the temperature of each breath she took. Now she was at the halfway point, where the cliff bulged out a little, making the shelf smaller. Alice wriggled her tail around, leaning just a bit on the rock. Past the bulge she crawled backward a little faster, carefully slid down the tilted rock slab at the end of the shelf, scrambled down into the rock slot, and finally stood on the platform by Ollie.

Chapter Three

Did You Fly?

Ollie looked bad. His face had a greenish cast under the gray cowboy hat. He was bent over, face intent, hands on his hips.

"Ollie. What can I do?"

"Nothing. I've just gotta go back down. Give me a minute here." Ollie straightened up, squared his shoulders. He looked slightly less green.

"Oh," said Alice. "I have to get these pictures too before we go." She looked up above Ollie at the golden slab and dancing figures. She switched her phone to camera mode and squeezed off several shots. "What are you doing with that thing?" Ollie asked. His voice was nearly normal. "I'm taking pictures with the camera on my phone and emailing them to my office," said Alice.

"How's it work?"

Alice walked him through the steps, showing him the pictures she was sending to his file. "It's a little slow out here because there's not much cell coverage. But now they're all online, and if I need them for your file, they're there. Even if I lose the phone, I'll still have the pictures."

"Humph," Ollie said. "Pretty slick. Mary made me get a new phone"—he tapped his jeans pocket—"but I never thought about using it that way."

"Actually it's pretty useful," said Alice. "Only occasionally do I need my big camera, but frequently I need a quick picture for a real estate dispute or need to send photos to a client's insurer—you know, the fence is down, the county garbage truck hit the client's gate, the electric co-op accidentally whacked down their favorite live oak. It's very handy. Sometimes I use the GPS app to check field notes on a survey or a legal description." She kept watching Ollie. His color was much better.

"Okay," he said. "Let's go back."

Alice bit her lip, recalling the steep climb down. Should she go first in case Ollie fell? Try to break his fall? "Ollie, let me start down first."

"No," he ordered. "I'm used to it. And I'm gonna put your feet in the right places." Honestly, thought Alice, cowboy gallantry at seventy-eight with lung cancer. But I love it.

Ollie's gray hat disappeared over the ledge. "Okay," he grunted. "Back on over. Not too fast. I'll place your feet."

Alice hung on her stomach on the side of the ledge, legs dangling, inching back. She felt Ollie's hands on her ankle, poking her toes into the first toehold. She straightened and let him guide her left foot into the second toehold, farther down. In an elegant ballet Ollie backed down, using whichever hand was free to put whichever of Alice's feet was dangling, until they were down. Then he turned and faced east, watching intently. Alice turned. Far off she could see a plume of dust coming down the dry limestone ridge from the direction of the highway. "Come on," he said. "Let's go."

Ollie backed up the truck and slipped it into gear. To her surprise, he turned away from the ranch house, heading farther west for a few minutes, then south, then east on another ranch road that ran along a pasture and then back toward the house.

Alice looked at him, eyebrows raised. "Different route?"

"Think that's Allen coming back. He doesn't need to know where we've been. He's a little upset. One reason is he's afraid I may sell the last of the cows."

"Ah."

"Sometimes I think Cloud Ranch should return to its roots. Look the way it did before the Europeans came. No cows. Wild animals. Native grasses. Allen doesn't know that or he'd really be upset. Anyway, no need for Allen to know where we've been," he said, looking at her. "Or anyone else."

"Does Allen know about the trust? Or the power of attorney? Or the life estate?"

"Only what he needs to know and what I want him to know, and that's not much of anything, yet."

"What about Mary?" Alice was worried about Ollie's refusal to let his daughter in on his plan.

"Same. I didn't tell her anything much. The way we have it set up, she gets to stay at the ranch, and she gets nearly all the money under my new will, right?"

"Yes," Alice said. "Everything but what you left to the Men's Wild Game Committee at your church, and to that orphanage up in Hill County."

"Right," said Ollie. "And you set up the trust so I could change my mind about putting the ranch in it? The conservancy and all?"

"Any time," said Alice. "You're the trustee, you know."

"Good," said Ollie. "No need for Allen and Mary to worry about this yet." He looked at Alice. "And I do not want Allen knowing I took you up to the cave pictures."

"You mean Allen's never been there?"

"No. He thinks he knows this place inside and out, but he hasn't been up there."

They jounced over the rocky road. Alice was puzzled: how could Allen live here and not know?

"Aha." Alice sat up taller. Now she understood. "Ollie, can you not see the paintings or the cave from the ground?"

"Right. You can't see either set. I've stood down there on the ground a hundred times to check. The first set, the cliff face stands far enough back that you can't see it from the bottom. The second set, the cliff turns a bit, as you found out going up that little shelf. And besides, looking up from the ground, the slope with the little trees blocks you from seeing the pictures—or the cave. So nobody knows, unless they know. Unless I tell them."

"And you haven't told anyone?"

"Well, of course Mary knows. But she's only been to the second set once. She's terrified of heights. And Cassie knew. She and I used to go up to the first set a lot, just to sit and look. We went up to the cave a couple of times too. Cassie called it the ghost cave, said she could still feel the spirits of the people who had come up there, the dreams they'd had."

"Ah." Alice understood that. Powerful soaring dreams.

"The only other person I ever let go up to the cave where you went today was my daughter's husband, Doyle, back when he was courting Mary, and only because he pestered me so long. I let him go up for a few minutes. He claimed to be studying the Indians that used to live here. But he hasn't asked again. Must've lost interest. I don't think Doyle talks much to Allen, and I doubt Mary's mentioned the rock art to Allen. Allen's real interested in the arrowheads and stuff on the ranch—he doesn't know I know about his little arrowhead collection in the bunkhouse, but it's okay. In fact, that's another reason Allen's pissed at me right now. I've told him to quit digging."

"You mean there are more, um, archeological sites on the ranch?"

"Oh, yeah. All along the creek, in the cave areas below the bluff, you'll find stuff. Little bits of pottery, arrowheads. Those are cave shelters, like in that Mousterian or whatever part of France I went and saw that one time with Cassie. I used to let the Boy Scouts come out, dig around some. They found some pretty good stuff. Not rock art, though, not down low along that part of the creek."

"Heavens,"said Alice, wondering what the Rock Art Conservancy would think about decades of Boy Scouts excavating arrowheads from who knows how long ago. And Mousterian? It didn't sound right but she'd look it up later. "So, Ollie, were you the one who found the cave? Up on that shelf?"

"I think so. At least, no one in the family ever mentioned it to me. I knew about the first group of paintings, and used to sit up there and smoke and look out at the world. Then I found that little rock shelf. Don't know why I felt compelled to inch up it, but I did. And you saw what I found."

Alice sat silent, thinking of the moment when she was flying—flying.

Ollie looked sideways at her. "Did you fly?"

"Yes."

"Did you go into the cave?"

"No, I was trying to get the nerve up when you called me."

"I haven't been up there in—a real long time. Years and years. My knee won't let me crawl any more. The cave—I haven't been in for a very long time. And when I did, I nearly got surprised by a rattler."

"You didn't say a word about snakes!" said Alice.

"Well, it's pretty cool today," said Ollie.

Not much consolation.

Alice said, "I'm beginning to see why those Rock Art Conservancy people have been so enthusiastic about the trust. At first I thought, These people get offered every hot rock spot in Texas; we're going to have to sweeten the pot with a lot of money for access and upkeep for them to accept trusteeship. But they seem very excited."

"Yeah. The funny thing is I only took that conservancy guy Bender to the first set. He thought those paintings were so beautiful, he couldn't get enough of them. Practically hyperventilated. Then I told him about the black-and-white figures on the second set and his eyes got real big. He looked at the ledge—I could tell he wanted to go. But no way could I get him to walk up that shelf to the second set. Or crawl. Finally he said he was actually extremely scared of heights and wanted to come back with somebody who had ropes, or whatever. So they still haven't made it to the cave. They're supposed to come out next month."

Alice remembered Ollie saying in August, when they were working on the conservancy trust, that Bender thought these paintings might reshape current teaching: they were similar to the best-known rock art sites in Texas, down on the Devils River and the Pecos River, but were located much further north. She mentally rechecked her trust document with its description of the rock art to be protected. She thought it would serve, but vowed to review it again now that she had actually seen what Ollie called "both sets." And she thought she might call Bender when she got back to the office.

Alice thought of one other thing. "Allen and Mary and Doyle did cash those nice checks you sent them in August, the ones you wrote from the trust account?"

"Yep."

"Good," said Alice.

"I know," said Ollie. "I remember what you said."

Alice had told Ollie that once checks from the trust were cashed, it could be harder for the check recipients to challenge the trust, or the contemporaneous will. Doyle wasn't a beneficiary, but she had thrown him in for good measure, asking Ollie to write him a check as well. "Ollie," she had explained, "one challenge a disgruntled heir can make to a trust is that the person who created the trust lacked the required mental capacity at the time he signed the trust document. So I like to have the trust send checks to people early on. A person who cashes a check from the trust, signed by the person who created the trust, has a little more of an uphill fight to claim that the person who signed that check also lacked capacity to create the trust. Looks tacky."

"Right," Ollie had said.

"Not that 'tacky' is a legal term," said Alice.

Chapter Four

Sense of Entitlement

When Ollie and Alice pulled up in front of the ranch house, the blue Bronco was back. Allen stood there, knees locked, arms across his chest. He stared at Alice, then lowered his eyes. Gee, she thought, you really don't like the lady lawyer? Why not?

"Where were you?" said Allen, ignoring Alice. "Mary's inside. You just missed Doyle. He was here when I got back but said he was going out to the west pasture. Claimed he was gonna check the fence out there. There's nothin' wrong with that fence."

"Oh, I was just showing Alice around," said Ollie easily. "We haven't seen the house yet. And she hasn't seen your place, Allen."

Allen grunted.

Ollie nodded toward a small stone building next to a pole barn north of the ranch house. "Allen lives there. We call it the bunkhouse but it's got a kitchen and everything."

"What do you do, Allen? Do you work on the ranch or in town? Or both?" asked Alice. You're being obnoxious, Alice Greer, she thought, making this poor lad admit his fecklessness.

"I work here. I help run this place, even though Doyle doesn't seem to think so. I never see him fixin' fence out here. No brush scratches on his truck. What does he know about ranch management?"

Ollie cut him off. "Doyle loves this place."

"Yeah. But he can't pull wire or handle a come-along," muttered Allen.

Ollie said, "Alice, how about I get you some coffee and look at what you brought." Alice noticed that Allen was not invited. Allen noticed too. He spun on his bootheel and headed for the bunkhouse.

Alice went to the truck and unlocked her briefcase. The old combination lock balked, for the first time in living memory, but finally popped open and she extracted the labeled folders for the draft power of attorney and the two exhibits. Alice furrowed her brow. The trust asset exhibits were in the wrong folder, with the power of attorney. Had she done that in a hurry yesterday afternoon? Alice was strict with herself about folders—she had learned the hard way that folders and disciplined filing were the only way she could stay organized.

She walked with Ollie into the cool dimness of the old ranch house, a relief after the sunny dust outside. Ollie stalked past her into the kitchen and Alice followed. She smelled slightly burned coffee. An old electric percolator winked its red light from the tiled counter.

Alice looked around. Gray Formica table and matching chairs, vintage

1963. Original wooden cabinets, windows looking out on a small flower garden and pasture. She admired an antique pie safe on one wall, and an antique German kitchen cupboard holding unusual antique kitchen implements on another wall. Above the kitchen table someone had framed watercolors of the ranch, the creek, the dam, and a man in jeans and a gray hat climbing atop a corral fence. Alice thought the paintings showed real skill—and were clearly done by someone who knew Ollie. That had to be him climbing up that fence. She moved closer and peered at the signature. "M. M. West." Mary, then. Someone had put a pint jar of pink and yellow zinnias on the table—again, probably Mary. But still, the kitchen had the feel of a kitchen in a house with no woman occupant. Now why is that? wondered Alice. What is it, exactly? The feel of a house with an old man living alone? Habit, silence.

From the table she looked out the window at the drive, while Ollie got down two heavy white mugs. "Sugar? Milk?" he asked, pulling an open can of evaporated milk out of the refrigerator (the ranch version of "milk," Alice knew, and a very good thing to have on hand). "Just milk," said Alice. Ollie's coffee looked too fierce without something to tame it. Besides, she actually liked evaporated milk in her coffee. She found it reliably creamy but not guilt-inducing.

Ollie grinned. "Chicory coffee from Louisiana. The kind my mama made. That'll make your hair curl."

Alice automatically patted her hair. Still straight. She was glad to see Ollie smile. "Ollie, you feel okay?"

"I'm fine. Let's look at that stuff you brought."

"Okay, then. On the power of attorney, it has two parts, as we discussed. The first part tracks what you wanted for the income-producing assets," Alice said, pulling Ollie's copy from the folder of non-trust exhibits. "Those are the ones you wanted the bank to manage if you become incapacitated."

Ollie scanned it. "Bank accounts," he read, scanning the numbers. "Securities accounts, looks like those are complete. Looks right."

Next she pulled out his copy of the conservancy exhibit. "On these conservancy assets—that's the ranch and the nest egg providing some income for the Rock Art Conservancy—you wanted a trustee to manage them if you are disabled. And the conservancy trustee has to manage the ranch in a way that protects the rock art. No building, development, mining, logging, or other encroachment can be allowed that would put the rock art at risk."

"Good," Ollie said. "I want it really tight on that."

"I think it's tight." She watched Ollie.

"Okay," he said, "and when I die, the trust plan will make those protections permanent, in the trust agreement for the conservancy? Right?"

"Yes," Alice said. "So the rock art will be protected during the life estates of Mary and Allen, and afterward too."

Ollie nodded.

"Anything else you want to add?"

"Nope."

"And then, separately, Mary handles the medical decisions if you can't, under the medical directive you signed back in August."

"Looks good. Can I sign this thing now?"

"No, we should have disinterested witnesses, and Silla will get it all set up at the office, just like we did before. When do you want to come in?"

"Tuesday. Tuesday afternoon, because I have a Men's Wild Game Committee meeting Tuesday at five over at the Methodist Church. I could come by your office to sign at four thirty."

"Perfect," said Alice. Through the window behind Ollie, she saw a truck pull up and a man emerge. Cowboy hat, dark glasses—she couldn't see his face. She watched Mary appear from somewhere close by. Standing next to the truck, they talked for a moment, Mary answering the man's questions. Doyle? Then she saw the man pull Mary to him, slowly run his hands down her back, grab her blue-jeaned rear, run his hands back up her front, all the while staring down at her face. Alice felt like a voyeur. Air must be full of pheromones. The two broke apart and the man headed one way, Mary back the way she'd come. Alice heard footsteps.

"Daddy?"

Mary walked in, face a little pink.

"Where were you, honey? I want you to say hi to Alice."

"I was doing your laundry, Daddy! Alice, it's nice of you to drive out here."

Alice smiled at Mary, whose blue eyes looked like her dad's but were anxious, without Ollie's shrewd eye crinkles, a testament to his seventy-eight years of skepticism. She'd met Mary in late August when Mary drove up from New Braunfels to sign acceptance of her role on Ollie's medical directive. Slim in her jeans, Mary was forty-five. According to Ollie, Mary moved to Dallas after college to work in museums there, had one early marriage that "didn't take," and married Doyle ten years ago after moving from Dallas to run the gallery in New Braunfels.

"Alice brought me some paperwork." Ollie handed it back to Alice and went to pour himself more coffee.

"Alice, while he does that, come out back and see the hollyhocks," said

Mary. "They're going to seed and you mentioned you would like some seedpods."

Alice followed Mary outside. The tall hollyhocks—pink, magenta, white—nodded against the rough gray fence. They were beginning to fade; some had already made seedpods. Ollie's ranch sat high enough and hence got cool enough for hollyhocks, unlike semitropical Austin, where hollyhocks would balk and refuse their critical role in a garden. Alice admired the way that hollyhocks, once established, starred in any flowerbed, refusing a supporting role. Mary snapped off some seedpods and slipped them into a plastic bag. Alice pocketed the bag and thanked her. Oh well. The gift took some of the fun out of the acquisition. Alice was an inveterate seed snitcher. Though she scrupulously observed most laws, reminding herself she was an officer of the court, she could not resist snitching rose hips and seedpods from anyone's garden. Licensed acquisition was never as satisfying. Still, she would like to have Ollie's hollyhocks growing at the corner of her house. She knew she was going to miss him when lung cancer finally claimed him. She shook her head to dismiss that thought. He was tough and should last for a good while longer—maybe longer than he wanted to—as the cancer tightened its hold.

"Thank you so much, Mary," said Alice. "I need to head back—have to stop at the fence supply store on the way home." Mary walked Alice back out to the front yard. The man with the dark glasses was now standing by Alice's truck, his back to the house, talking to Ollie. His back was rigid. Alice heard him say, "You got to be kidding. You could make really good money leasing to them. Thousands! Every year! And you lose nothing! All the property is still yours!"

"Nope. I don't want those things in my view." Ollie's face was set.

"Hi, darling," called Mary. The man who turned around was tall, and square all over—square head with short brown hair, square face, square shoulders. Dark glasses hid his eyes. He walked over and kissed Mary with a proprietary air, then settled his arm around her shoulders.

"Honey, this is Alice Greer, Daddy's lawyer from Coffee Creek," said Mary. "Alice, I want you to meet Doyle."

"Nice to meet you," said Doyle. He smiled behind the Ray-Bans, one cheek dimpling. Alice smiled back and held out her hand. Doyle squeezed her fingers, not taking the whole hand. Alice just hated that—first, it wasn't a real handshake; it was what men did when they didn't really want to shake a woman's hand. Second, it hurt when your fingers got squeezed that way. "You make house calls?"

"Only for my favorite clients," said Alice. "I did want to see this place.

It's beautiful."

Doyle rocked back a little on his boots, face shaded by his glasses. He looked east at the limestone ridge and the blue-green creek, then west at the pastures beyond the bunkhouse, then north toward the forested cliffs Alice and Ollie had just climbed. He inhaled, wrinkling his nose, as if hungry for the scent of the land. "Yes. This place is beautiful. And it could be a showplace in many ways."

Mary looked up at him, smiling tentatively. Ollie stood unmoving, poker-faced.

In the awkward silence that followed, Alice heard the sweet high notes of a bird in the big live oak by the ranch house. "What kind is that?" she asked.

"What kind of what?" asked Doyle.

"Birdcall," said Mary. "You didn't hear him, Doyle?"

He shook his head no. "Saw the eagle pair again coming in, though. Spotted their nest down past the crossing."

Alice said her good-byes and shook Ollie's hand. "See you Tuesday afternoon," she said. She got in the truck and headed for the highway, thinking about trusts and wills and real estate. In a way, her law practice was a corrective to her normally optimistic view of the world. You heard some particularly unattractive aspects of family life when you helped people allocate their money and their real estate—especially in connection with their real estate, which seemed to bring out primitive greed and a sense of entitlement in otherwise decent people.

Still, Ollie's plan seemed sound.

Chapter Five

Get a Life!

On the way back from Ollie's, Alice stopped in Fredericksburg, on impulse. She wandered into the famous five- and ten-cent store on Main Street, reveling as always in the old-time feel of the place. Counters full of children's clothes, tinware for picnic tables, toys, sewing notions—you name it, you could find it if you looked hard enough. She bought a length of oilcloth with a retro fifties pattern of cherries and checked gingham borders, long enough for the table on her deck. But will I sit out there alone? she asked herself.

She strolled slowly back toward the truck, window-shopping for Western wear, and then—again on impulse—stopped at the Altburg, across Main Street from the manicured city park and the octagonal wooden church built by the doughty first German settlers. She grabbed a little table under an elm tree in the beer garden where she could sit in her preferred anything-but-"aces and eights" position, ever mindful of the foolishness of Wild Bill Hickok. The day he broke his own rule—never sit with your back to the door—he was shot in the back of the head by Jack McCall, and died holding a poker hand of two pair: aces and eights. After reading that story, Alice felt justified in hating to sit with her back to the door. When the movers set up her Coffee Creek office with the stately antique partner's desk placed in the middle of the room, facing the west window, Alice felt herself beginning to break out in hives. She made the movers rearrange so that her desk faced the door and no one could get behind her. She liked to see what was coming.

So, sitting in the shade, her back safely to the beer garden's wall, she could assess passing tourists, who came from all over to this still emphatically German central Texas town. Idly she wondered what they would think of her. Medium everything, thought Alice: medium height, jeans, hiking boots, brownish-blond hair highlighted with talent by her Austin hairdresser. Alice was used to being quietly assessed, out here west of Austin. She was still unsure what conclusions people drew.

The burly Altburg waitress swung by, carrying huge frosted mugs of beer. "Be with you in a second, hon!" she called. Alice smiled inwardly. Why not compound her sins? She ordered grilled bratwurst and a cold lager. The waitress soon brought the sausage plate and a frosted mug of beer and set both down with a thump. Mmmm, thought Alice. No light lunch here.

Alice ate her sausage, enjoying the contrast between her own cool comfort—sitting here, beer in hand, in the shade in the Altburg beer garden—and the sunburned sweaty tourists walking up the concrete sidewalk outside the picket fence. She leaned forward, closed her eyes, inhaled the aroma of the beer.

Hops, bubbles, freshness, bitterness. Is it possible, she thought, that beer is the perfect electrolyte? Or that at least the chemicals in the bubbles rising steadily from the bottom of the brew are delivering microbursts of substances our bodies love? As she inhaled, eyes closed, considering these issues, she heard a voice.

"Alice?"

Startled, she opened her eyes and looked up. Short guy, starched blue shirt, sharp blue eyes, sandy hair: her fellow real estate and probate lawyer, David Frohbel, born and bred in Fredericksburg. She and Frohbel currently worked together on a state bar committee. They had met the first week of law school and organized a study group, which included David's brilliant wife, Isabel, who had memorably closed down Scholz Garten in Austin after first-year finals, dancing on the picnic tables in the back. Isabel, a tax genius, was heavily recruited by big-city firms, but she and David had headed back to David's hometown. Alice understood that their law partnership was highly regarded.

"Alice Greer! What are you doing in our neck of the woods?" David asked, leaning over to hug her. "Didn't mean to startle you."

"It's half of Frohbel and Frohbel! I was lost in my beer!" said Alice. "Sit down!"

"Can't stay long," said Frohbel, waving at the waitress for a beer, "but I saw you sitting there and thought, maybe one cold beer on a perfect fall day. A little hot, but perfect." His sharp eyes scanned Alice's face. Frohbel missed almost nothing. "What are you doing in Fredericksburg? Shopping like all these fabulous tourists who keep our lovely Main Street hopping?"

"No," said Alice. "Well, of course I did the five-and-dime. But I've been out calling on a client. He's elderly and I thought I'd save him a trip to town. Ollie West, over by Faison."

"I know Ollie," said Frohbel. "Heard he had some bad news from his doctor. Sorry to hear it. Of course I know Mary better than Ollie."

Alice was interested. "How do you know Mary?"

"I was best man at her first wedding," said Frohbel. "We were infants at the time. She was barely twenty-one. Married an infant, too, even if he was my own fraternity brother. Ol' Morris Johnson. Called him MoJo, of course."

Alice winced. How could you marry someone called MoJo?

"I heard that marriage didn't take."

"No kidding," said Frohbel. "I've always felt bad about it. Like maybe as best man I should have done a better job getting the groom ready for the deal. Ol' MoJo was not ready for the concept of monogamy, apparently."

"Well, did you know that?" said Alice. "I mean, in advance?"

"Well . . . yes and no. On the one hand, his other nickname at the frat house was Quickdraw."

"Ick," said Alice.

"But on the other hand, no, I didn't really know it, because what did I know about marriage? I mean, MoJo was one of those guys that all the girls just had to kiss. Actually, he was very good-looking—from Weslaco, down in the valley. I later learned he had a goal of kissing every girl he met one summer, while he was lifeguarding at some church camp, and he did it. Every single girl. But you know, when he and Mary got engaged, I thought it would be different. Thought you passed through some magic curtain and when you came out on the other side—you were married! Transformed! Didn't happen to ol' MoJo, though. Apparently he was still working on that list."

"Sounds painful, if you were Mary," Alice said. She watched Frohbel enjoying his beer.

"She figured it out pretty fast. Think they were about to separate when he died."

Alice looked up, eyebrows raised.

"Oh, he wrecked his car. He'd been up in Dallas to talk to Mary and was heading back to Austin. Hit a bridge abutment on the interstate. Apparently fell asleep at the wheel."

"Do you know Doyle at all? Current husband?" she asked.

"I've never met him. But I know I heard something that made me a little . . . well, I can't remember exactly. Can't even remember who told me. Maybe something that happened in college. But lord, if you had to believe everything you heard about what people did in college . . . we'd all be in trouble."

"Right," said Alice. She could remember several incidents from her own college career that she planned not to share, ever, with John and Ann, her precious children.

"How're things in Coffee Creek?"

"Pretty good. I'm getting the hang of the small-town thing. How's the practice?"

"Good. We Germans just keep life interesting here. Ve haff our vays. Always good stuff going on."

Alice grinned. She always enjoyed Frohbel's tales of the intergenerational deals—reflecting passion for land, and careful but determined investment—around Fredericksburg. Alice waved at the muscular waitress, ready for the bill. Frohbel got up to leave, then stopped. "Hey! Ben!"

Tall man, dark hair, jeans, cowboy shirt with the sleeves rolled up, loafers, spectacles. Odd look—sort of Hill Country professional. He'd walked in the gate, then stopped six feet from the table. "Didn't mean to horn in," he said to Frohbel. "I saw you talking to this woman." He turned to Alice. "It's got to be you, Alice MacDonald!"

"Alice MacDonald Greer, now," said Alice. They stared at each other and Alice smiled. She stood up and shook hands with Ben Kinsear, whom she had not seen in twenty years. Black curly hair still, but now with some gray in it. Kinsear turned the handshake into a half hug. Alice consented to the hug—just barely. She could smell starched, ironed cotton shirt. "Ben, can you join us?" Alice asked, then immediately second-guessed herself. What a begrudging invitation. Why was she so cautious? Why not just say, "Great to see you! Sit down! Have a beer!"

"Gotta go," said Frohbel, "or Isabel will kill me. You two stay. Good to see you!" He pushed open the wrought-iron gate and joined the crowd on the sidewalk.

Kinsear took Frohbel's chair. "What are you doing in Fredericksburg, Alice?"

"Client trip. Visiting a client who has a ranch out west of here."

"Did I see somewhere that you are practicing in Coffee Creek now?"

"That's right. Since two years ago. And what about you?"

"Oh, we moved back here five years ago." Alice thought she remembered a brief mention in the law school alumni notes. "I'm finally opening that bookstore I always wanted. I'm specializing in Texas books. Broad range of inventory—everything from vintage shoot-'em-up cowboy thrillers, to the grim history of convict labor in Texas, to geology of the aquifer systems of Texas."

"And of course, the inside scoop on what really happened at the Alamo?"

"Too dangerous to write," said Kinsear with a smile. "Much less sell!"

"What's the name? The name of your bookstore?"

"The Real Story," said Kinsear, grinning.

"Love it! Well . . . ," said Alice, sliding her chair back, "I guess I should head home."

"I just got here," objected Kinsear.

"I've got to stop at the fence supply place to get another float for the water trough," said Alice. "They close early on Saturday."

"Where are you parked? I'll walk you back." He unfolded himself and stood up.

Alice thought, why am I so skittish? So ungracious? So incurious? Why do I not ask kindly about his wife and children? Why do I act like he's some sort of—of threat? Just because he stopped in at the Altburg to say hey to two law school classmates? She and Kinsear had dated pretty seriously their second year of law school but she'd lost track of him (and everyone and everything else) the next summer, after she met Jordie. Rumor was that Kinsear had gone off to New York, made it large as general counsel to a hedge fund, and married a Texas girl from their law school class, someone Alice had never known.

Walking next to him on the way to her truck, she asked to hear more about the bookstore.

"Alice, how about coming to my grand opening? It'll be a good party. It's the Saturday before Thanksgiving."

Alice found herself saying, "Sure, I think I can do that."

"Great! I'll send an invitation."

"It's good to see you," Alice said. "Take care."

"Will do. You be careful on the highway."

Alice unlocked the truck, scrambled up onto the seat, smiled, waved at Kinsear, standing there on the sidewalk, put the truck in gear, and pulled out toward Main Street and Coffee Creek. As she reached highway speed, she heard nothing but the sound of the truck. Radio silence, she thought. I hear nothing. No voices. No dialogue. No exchange. No one else's thoughts. Just radio silence. Alice shook her head. In other words, she was lonesome. It was Saturday night. She was heading back to her own little house at the end of a long road, and there would be no one else to laugh with, hug, make dinner with. You are ridiculous, she told herself. If Jordie were here he would say, "Alice! Get a life!" He would, too, in that Scottish accent. But oh, she thought, how I miss that voice.

Chapter Six

Working on Some Energy Matters

On Monday Alice was at her office by seven. Her street was quiet, but two blocks away, on the far side of the courthouse, a steady stream of pickups was parking in front of the Camellia Diner. She trotted up onto the porch, unlocked the door, and walked into her office, in the old living room on the right. Client chairs and tea table by the window. Computer. Law degree and court admissions on the wall. Ann and John in silver frames on one corner of the desk—her beautiful children, both far away in Edinburgh for their fall term abroad. She could hardly wait until Thanksgiving, when she would fly over the Atlantic to visit them. No picture of her darling Jordie though. It was too soon to put up his picture; too soon to be forced to explain to any curious client that his helicopter went down flying back from his inspection of a North Sea oil rig. Too soon. And one frozen frame of his face wouldn't bring back one second of the things she missed about that big Scot.

Silla wasn't in yet. Alice knew she had spent the weekend competing in barrel racing at the Marble Falls rodeo, in a grudge match against the woman who had edged her out three years ago by a tenth of a second in the college rodeo championships. Silla had been tight-jawed all week, getting her game face on. The office would be much nicer this week if Silla had won.

Alice made coffee in the office kitchen and sipped it slowly while she downloaded the pictures she had emailed herself from Ollie's ranch for Ollie's electronic file. And, she thought, I believe I might print these too.

She labeled each one, remembering where she had been when she took the shot on her phone (humbly acknowledging that she had been crouched on her knees, terrified of standing up; no need to include that information in the captions). She still felt a tug from the flying pictures—the white figure, the black figure, the leaping mountain lion. Could she fly in her office? She opened the cave pictures again, blew them up, gazed at the figures rising up the rock. Again she felt herself on the little slope, staring up toward the cave and the cliff, pulled toward them and then pulled up, up, up . . . Stop it, Alice. You're in your chair. In your office. On Monday morning. She took a deep breath, pulled the phone over, and dialed Bobby Bender at the Rock Art Conservancy.

"Hey, it's Alice Greer, out in Coffee Creek. Have you got just a moment?"

"Yes ma'am. I have a big mug of coffee sitting right in front of me. So I can be civil. And articulate. Possibly even brilliant, though some would say that's a stretch. What's up?"

"I went out to Ollie West's on Saturday morning and saw the pictures."

"You did? They're beautiful, aren't they?"

"All the pictures."

Silence. "You went up that damn ledge?"

"I did."

"Well, tell me!"

"I thought maybe you'd like to see for yourself. Remind me again of your email?"

Keeping him on the phone, Alice sent Bender two of the pictures from the cave area. She could hear his computer pinging as the emails arrived. There was silence.

"Holy Toledo," he broke out. "Good God, Alice!"

"Yes?"

"These are unbelievable. Ollie gave me a general idea, but—I didn't dream, or even hope, that he had something like this up that ledge. Wow!"

"So, interesting?"

"Alice, of course that first group of pictures is remarkable, not only for their condition and variety, but for their sheer beauty. But this second area—it looks so much like the key sites down on the Pecos and the Devils River, but it's much farther north. I can't wait to get there. Except for the damn ledge."

"I hear you will have to be sedated and dragged up by ropes."

"That's nearly true. I get really anxious on heights, but if I'm roped in, somehow it isn't as bad. Had a bad fall one time out in Big Bend and kind of lost my nerve after that."

"What happened?"

"Oh, we were up in the Chisos Mountains looking at rock art and it was the same as out at Ollie's—one set of pictures, and then just a horrible little ledge you had to shinny up, sheer rock below, to get to the second set. I was about halfway across that ledge when I got to a point where I couldn't go forward, couldn't go back and couldn't figure out what the hell to do."

"How did you get down?"

"We had a couple of ropes—not technical ones. Like idiots we had gone off to Big Bend with nada for equipment. One rope broke and so did my ankle, but worst injury was to my pride. Anyway, too much about that. Ollie tell you we are scheduled to come out next month?"

"Yes. What happens then?"

"Another guy is coming with me, from A&M, and we're going to document everything—photos, logs, you name it. We'll need to go into the cave very, very carefully. We'll have a team, in fact."

"How come?"

"Well, you may or may not know about shamanistic practices in the Pecos and Devils River cave areas, but some current thinking is that the caves were important places where shamans—and perhaps others, not just shamans—would seek to enter the otherworld, in an altered state of consciousness. Their souls would make a journey, often being transformed into the person's spirit animal. Sometimes they reached this stage from drumming, or fasting, or sleep deprivation, or self-hypnosis. Or hallucinogenic drugs."

"Peyote?"

"Peyote, datura, mescal beans—could be different things. Controversy among the archeologists on that, as well as who the seekers were, and what they were seeking. But our team needs to look really carefully at the cave area, documenting every detail as we go. This is essentially our baseline study. Major precautions, major protocol. Huge deal."

"Goodness," said Alice. "Have you ever—do these pictures have an impact on you?"

Silence.

"I can tell you about one cave shelter down on the Devils River," said Bender. "We were doing some work down there and my grad student had to hike back down to the truck for something, left me there. It was so quiet. Not another human around for I don't know how many miles. I was just looking at the pictures, trying to figure out if one picture included feather bags or what the guy had on his arms . . . the next thing I know, I'm off in la-la land and I didn't come back until the grad student shook me."

"Huh," said Alice. "And did your spirit animal find you?"

"I believe I was a gray-backed fox." She heard Bender chuckle. "Was afraid of the mountain lion and the serpent, but I was a fox so I knew I had some escape talents. No, seriously, the pictures can be pretty strong stuff. You want some books about them? I can give you some titles."

"Please."

"Okay, I'll email them. Now, Alice, you want to be there when we come out? Might be a good idea."

"Sure, I'll come."

"And is everyone still cool with the trust? Family, et cetera?"

"Everyone doesn't know yet."

"Ah. Okay, just forewarn us of anything dangerous so we know to bring the Kevlar vests. But seriously, Alice, Ollie has big-time major-league pictures on those rocks; this is huge news. Very big deal."

"Could there be any more out there?"

"You mean rock art? Wouldn't Ollie know? I think he's found the mother lode, and the location indicates the kind of protected place that would mean this might be a one-off, sort of the sacred place for that area. But one thing I was wondering about, Alice. It's fairly typical to expect there would be some limestone middens somewhere nearby. Know what those are?"

"I have a vague idea," said Alice. "Aren't they trash heaps? Very old trash?"

"That's true for plain old middens," said Bender. "But burned limestone middens are remnants of ovens—underground ovens—where people baked materials at quite high heat. They're still used down in Mexico, for agave plants, and other stuff too, I understand. We may not find any more rock art quite like this, but I'm thinking that more likely than not, unless they've been disturbed, we may find burned rock middens at Ollie's, not up high but down low. Might find some mounds. Might find some pit ovens and flat-stoned hearths, and maybe points, tools, other artifacts. The kind of thing you might expect in the vicinity."

"Could they be anywhere on the ranch? Do they have to be near the pictures?"

"Nope. But given the quality and extent of the pictures, it seems likely that site was in use. And it could be even more significant than it already is if we could locate and map the middens. Alice, I'll bet you a chicken-fried steak at the Antler Café that we find middens. Might be near the creek, could be further west along that bluff on the south side of the ranch."

"I'll take that bet!" said Alice. "I win either way, win or lose, if I get a chicken-fry at the Antler Café! Talk to you later." Her stomach growled. Should have eaten more breakfast, she thought. Quit thinking of chicken-fried steak! Alice loved an occasional chicken-fried steak at the Antler Café. She preferred it with fried okra and green beans (with bacon). Her friends favored the mac 'n' cheese with jalapeños, but Alice stuck with what she piously called green vegetables. Her friends pointed out that fried okra was no longer green, that it had been transmogrified. No, said Alice, it has been transmuted, into something rich and strange. Those are pearls that were his eyes, right there in the okra, see?

Silla sailed through the front door, humming. "Hey, Alice!" she sang out, disappearing into the kitchen. Alice grinned. Silla had beaten her nemesis.

"Congratulations!" she called.

Silla stuck her head around the corner, red hair in a ponytail. "Beat her by three full seconds. Ha!"

"How'd your horse do?"

"Great. Fabulous. He read my mind, every step of the way. Took those turns like a Spanish dancer. Roared out of the last turn for home like the Dixie Limited." Silla shook her ponytail, smiling. "What a feeling!"

Silla started for the workroom, then swung back around. "Hey, how was Ollie's cave?"

"Interesting," said Alice. "I met the family. Mary, Doyle, Allen."

"And?"

"Doyle's pleasant. But he wants Ollie to lease for wind power. Ollie doesn't want to. And I could see what you mean about Allen. Immature."

She turned back to her desk, surveyed the appointments.

Monday meant Rotary Club, which meant Alice was wearing her red sweater. Red Griffin would swing by and pick up Alice in the red sweater, as she had nearly every Monday for two years. Red, who combined the narrow-eyed calculation of a CPA (which she was) with the daring of a former rodeo queen (which she also was), was the primary reason Alice had thrown caution to the wind, abandoned her normal economic conservatism, and moved her practice to Coffee Creek. Alice had met Red the same summer she met Jordie, when Alice had a student clerkship at a big Houston law firm. Alice had acquired a reputation for tenacity that won her a rush assignment the day before a deposition in a big oil-company lawsuit over a drilling failure, requiring her to decipher three just-received boxes of exhibits. Grimly pawing through a stack of dense spreadsheets with hieroglyphic calculations for fracking fluid and drilling mud, Alice called Red, the firm's adored chief financial officer, and begged her to make sense of the numbers. "Lemme at 'em," Red had said. "I speak fluent spreadsheet. In fact, spreadsheets are my mother tongue." She helped Alice work through the barrels, gallons, and equivalents, always concise and clear in her explanations, watching and waiting until she could see Alice understood. By 3:00 a.m., when Alice finally went home, she had the "handle" for the partner taking the deposition, and an intense appreciation for Red. From the first day of her Houston clerkship, Alice had admired the way Red laughed her way down the hallways, crisp in designer suits and heels, always smiling though slogging through what Alice heard was a bad divorce. Now, Red was a friend.

When Alice took a job in Austin, she and Red had stayed in touch. One day, as Alice sat at her computer high above Congress Avenue, working on a brief and ignoring the view of the blue-green Colorado River, an email from Red popped up: "Please advise. See attached. Have found place in Coffee Creek." Alice looked at the attachment in astonishment. It was a contract between the state of Texas and "Red's Rescue Ranch Inc.," showing Red Griffin as president. The contract obligated Red's Rescue Ranch to take in, board, and rehabilitate up to fifteen abused or neglected horses a year. The state paid a boarding fee and vet bills for the horses, and then, when the horses were sold, paid Red a sliding fee depending on the price. The better off the horse was by the date of sale, the higher the fee.

Alice immediately called Red. "Red! Red's Rescue Ranch?" said Alice.

"Happened about three months ago. I was staring out the window on the seventy-fourth floor of this building, looking at the skyline," Red answered. "I was wearing my red Armani suit and my four-inch heels. I looked good, I had just finished the budget for next year, and the managing partner had just told me this is the best-run law firm in Texas and that he attributed all that to me. And then I stared out that piece of plate glass and I thought, But this is not me. I want blue jeans, I want horses, I want hill country. So I called and volunteered to work weekends at a horse rescue place up in Conroe. And then I bought a sixty-acre place south of Coffee Creek. Then I answered a state request for proposals. And it looks like I won, doesn't it?"

"Yes. It does. So are you going to do this?"

"I am."

And Red in four weeks gave notice, sold her condo, and moved to Coffee Creek so fast Alice couldn't believe it. Now she was a local celebrity, chased after by the cowboys, admired for her rescue work. Alice had sat on the top rail of the corral at Red's Rescue Ranch and watched Red gentle a trembling horse that had just stumbled down the ramp of the state trailer, letting the horse sniff the cedar air of its new home, letting the horse hear her voice, letting the horse learn an environment where Red's touch was comfort, where Red in the saddle meant security and consistent handling, where horse memory could calm and the sky become less threatening.

When Jordie's helicopter went down in the North Sea, Red had helped Alice through the dreadful first weeks, helped make arrangements for the stunned teenagers and their mother to fly from Austin to Edinburgh, to deal with the fact that Jordie's body had not been recovered, to return to Texas, where life would never be normal again. In one of their monthly lunches, which Red insisted on after Jordie died, Red had looked at Alice and said, "Alice. Look at you."

"What?"

"You are wearing a brown shirt and brown shoes and brown pants."

Alice looked down. "You're right, I am."

"Alice. The world is red and pink and blue and sunny and gorgeous. It is not a brown world. Time to pull up your socks."

"But I feel brown. No, I feel gray," said Alice.

"I know, honey," said Red. "But it's time to live again. Why don't you quit commuting from Coffee Creek to Austin and just move your practice out to

Coffee Creek? Wear blue jeans, meet new people, be near me?"

"I'd starve!" Alice said. "I still have to get the kids through college."

"Pooh," Red said. "Double pooh. Jordie left those children money for college, and we need a decent real estate and trusts lawyer out here. Alice, we have land in Coffee Creek, did you know that? Real estate. Dirt. Just like in Austin. Furthermore, people die out here and they need their wills probated. Just like in Austin."

"Hmm." Alice was floored by the idea.

"You can do it. But you can't wear brown. Pull up your socks."

"I miss Jordie."

"Yes. I know. What would Jordie say about this?"

"He would say . . . well, he never liked me in brown, it's true."

"Right."

"Okay, I'll think about it."

That was the beginning. The next week Red had called Alice. "Puryear's old stone house on Live Oak is going up for sale. You should buy it for an office. Close to the courthouse." And Alice did.

Now it was Monday, two years later, and she sat at her desk in her own office in Coffee Creek, remembering the very first time Red had picked her up for lunch at the Coffee Creek Rotary Club. Looking back, she could almost see herself in her dark suit and boring white blouse and pearls, sitting at her big desk that Monday morning, wondering whether this week would again mean net outflow from her bank account, with no inflow. She had no appointments, no clients to call, no phone calls to return. No perplexed person was parking in front of her office and striding in with a problem for her to solve. In her checkbook, the last deposit slip was dated two weeks earlier. For the umpteenth time she had picked up the paperback called "How to Succeed in Small Towns," which she had bought just before resigning from her safe position in Austin. No need to read it; she knew perfectly well what it said. She needed to be out meeting people, shaking hands, volunteering. Chapter One: "Networking." She shrank at the thought. The front door had opened that morning, and the UPS man had walked in. "Package for Alice Greer. Can you sign?"

Once the delivery man had left, Alice looked at the package. It was from a women's store in Austin—one that Alice found particularly intimidating. She had never bought a single thing there. But this was clearly addressed to Alice Greer. She opened the package. A red sweater. Yes, it was a red sweater, as red as geraniums, as red as lipstick, as red as a traffic light, as red as . . . And it was very soft. It felt like silk knit. It was her size. But the neck looked low—lower than Alice would wear.

The phone rang. "Alice? It's Red. Did you get it?"

"Red! I should have known! You sent me this sweater?"

"Yes ma'am. And I am picking you up for Rotary today at eleven twenty. You didn't forget, did you?"

Alice had soundly repressed the idea of going to Rotary, envisioning a sea of bland male faces in identical suits, a place where she would make no impact whatsoever. "Oh, right," she said.

"Alice. Put that sweater on," ordered Red.

"It's beautiful," said Alice, "and thank you so much! But do you think it's appropriate?"

"Alice," said Red, "I am taking you to Rotary. In that sweater. Eleven twenty, sharp." Click.

When they got there, Alice and Red had picked up their name tags at the table. "Here you go, hon," said Madam Secretary Jane Ann Olson of Olson Title.

Alice clipped the tag, which read "Alice Greer, Greer Law Firm," to her unbelievably red sweater, muttering to Red, "I can hardly find a place to clip this thing. There's no front."

Red grinned. "Get over it," she said as she clipped on her tag: "Red Griffin, Red's Rescue Ranch." She and Alice walked into the loud chatter of Rotary. Red howdied the first people they met, with Alice lagging behind for protection. A tubby man with owl-like spectacles barred their way to the buffet. "George, this is Alice Greer," said Red. "Alice, George heads our biggest survey company, so think about him when you need a surveyor for all those wills and easements and deeds and contracts you do for your clients. George, be nice to Alice and she'll make you rich."

George was all ears. He talked to Alice all the way through the buffet line. She picked up corn, barbecued sausage, red sauce, coleslaw, unsweetened iced tea. He picked up corn, potato salad, beans, a second helping of potato salad, brisket, sausage, ribs, coleslaw, and a roll, and then thoughtfully drizzled barbecue sauce over the entire plate in a lacy pattern. "Makes it mo' bettah," George said. "Can I join you and Red?"

Red had made her way to the table in the dead center of the room, right in front of the microphone. Alice couldn't believe it. She had been eyeing the table in the corner next to the door—the table for shy people who needed to slip out of the room fast with their heads down.

"Alice, sit here," said Red. She made Alice sit facing the whole room, right by the microphone.

"Good grief," said Alice.

Red's table filled up fast. She introduced Alice to a dizzying parade of people. The names were a blur. "Alice, meet Tom, VP at Citizens Bank. He and Miranda are archrivals. Aren't you, Tom? How's the deposit race going?"

"We're neck and neck." He smiled and shook Alice's hand.

"Well, you need to know Alice so she can get all her trusts and estates customers to make you executor. Earn you some nice fees from dead people's money."

"Great work if you can get it," said Tom. "Alice, tell me about yourself."

Red interrupted. "Alice, I want you to meet a great CPA. Mike, you need to meet Alice. She does not only real estate but wills and estates too. You need her to hire you to do the accounting for those estates." Mike was in CPA garb, including the glasses, but with a crisp chambray button-down. He sat down right next to Alice.

When guest time game, Red made Alice stand up and introduced her to the entire room. Lunch went by fast; Alice learned more about ongoing deals than she had learned in two months in Coffee Creek. As they stood to leave, Mike was buttonholing Alice, going on about doing wills for a couple of his clients who didn't have them. He asked about fees.

"I can offer your folks a courtesy discount, since I'm new here," said Alice.

"Wonderful. I'll get them to call you this afternoon," said Mike.

George, the surveyor, sped to catch up with Alice and Red as they left the meeting. "Um, Alice," he said, "do you do conservation easements?"

"Of course," said Alice.

"Well," said George, "I'll give you a call."

"That would be great," said Alice.

Red gave George a big smile. "Bye, George," she said.

"Bye," said George, with a shy smile back at Red.

"Heavens," Alice said as they walked back to Red's red SUV. "That was amazing."

"Stick with me," said Red. "Just stick with me. You're gonna do fine here." From that day on, Alice had done fine in Coffee Creek. George's city rancher client had called, asking if she could help him on a conservation easement. She used George's surveys for real estate transactions. She and Mike now did a steady line of work together. He referred clients who needed help on property or estate matters, and she sent him executors who needed help on estate tax accounting. And she wore the red sweater to Rotary every week. One of these days, Red might let her wear something else.

Today, two years later, Rotary felt familiar and friendly. Even the announcements were entertaining. Red stood up and signaled the podium. "The chair recognizes Red Griffin! Yes, ma'am?"

"Everyone, don't forget, Tuesday is 'Keep Your Day Job' night at the Beer Barn," Red said, pointing at Jane Ann Olson and making her stand up. "Our own Madam Secretary is making her debut singing with the Henly Hot Hands. Come on out! See you at the Beer Barn!" Everyone cheered and hurrahed, and Jane Ann turned pink and grinned. Alice loved it. She'd never been in a Rotary where everyone either sang in a band or wanted to sing in a band. Her favorite vet played mandolin, Tom the banker played harmonica, and the head of Olson Title was going to sing at the Beer Barn. Ah, Coffee Creek. No symphony yet . . . but music of another sort.

As she stood up to leave, Alice felt eyes on her back. She turned around to see a lanky sandy-haired man staring at her.

"Aha," said Red. "Jeff Treacher, meet Alice Greer, a fellow lawyer. Alice, Jeff just moved to town last month. From where was it now, Jeff?"

"How do you do, Ms. Greer," said Jeff Treacher. "Just moved back here from Arizona. Working on some energy matters. Nice to meet you." He didn't smile, just nodded importantly and somewhat dismissively, then strode off. Alice wrinkled her nose at the almost visible cloud of aftershave he left in his wake.

"Well!" said Red. "Not too interested in the competition yet, is he? But soon enough he'll figure out he needs you."

Chapter Seven

The Real Money

The office was quiet when Alice came back from Rotary. At about two, the phone rang. "Alice, you have a call from Jeff Treacher," called Silla from the workroom.

"Alice Greer," Alice said into her phone.

"Alice, this is Jeff Treacher. Met you at Rotary this morning."

"Right," said Alice. "Saw you'd opened up your office here. Welcome to Coffee Creek. What can I do for you?"

"Ollie West is your client?"

"I've worked with Mr. West on some things."

"Well, I represent Ventopoder. The wind power company. I expect you've heard about them if you know anything at all about the wind industry."

Patronizing twit, thought Alice. Of course I know about the wind industry, as would any Texas real estate lawyer worth her salt. You will be punished, señor, for your impudence, she promised silently.

Treacher went on. "We're ready to lease Ollie's land. He told me to call you. We have a great deal going with the leases; no one has had any problem with them. I need you to get Ollie signed up and that section will be ready to go."

"I'll need to talk to Mr. West, of course." She prickled at his presumptuous use of her client's first name. "When did you talk to him?" She wanted to know, given the discussion she'd overheard between Ollie and Doyle.

"Oh, last week sometime."

Alice thought, I'm onto you. You contacted my client directly, and may have gotten his number from his son-in-law, but you aren't telling, are you? "You could send over the form of lease you're using. What is the signing bonus?"

"Four hundred dollars an acre," said Treacher.

Alice let the silence hang. "Gosh, that sounds low," said Alice.

"No one else has had any problem with it," said Treacher.

Alice wondered about that. "Well, send me what you have. I'll take a look."

"Hope we can do some business," said Treacher. "Everyone else out there is ready for this deal to make. Your client might not be too popular if he's the only reason we don't get this section finalized."

"Might not be too popular, you say?" said Alice, starting to steam. "Which of his neighbors has expressed any such idea?"

"Oh, now, I didn't mean it like that. Some of them are real eager for the money, though, like Mr. Powell. And of course they won't get any lease payments if we don't get a workable section. Cloud Ranch is key because of the highway access for our power lines. And lease payments—that's where the real money is for the landowner."

"Or where it could be, if and when Ventopoder chooses to go forward, right?" Alice hated being bullied in a negotiation—and hated worse for her clients to be. "Which they might not, even if you get the whole section leased up?"

"Well, right," said Treacher. "But of course we think this is going to be a great location."

"Please send me what you have. Thanks." She hung up. She knew the lease was likely to say that Ventopoder didn't have any obligation to go forward with construction of a wind farm, even if the neighbors were panting for a couple of decades of lease payments.

Alice sent Silla off to the courthouse. "Check for memoranda of leases. Maybe with one of these guys," she said, handing Silla a list of various corporate entities associated with Ventopoder she'd found online.

"You want copies?"

"Yes, please."

Silla got back at about three thirty. "That Treacher guy has been busy," she said. "I got one real lease and then several memoranda of leases. Looks like he figured out after he recorded the first complete lease that he didn't really need to put in all that confidential info and could just do a memorandum of lease." She shook her head. "Pretty bush league."

"Who signed with him?"

Silla showed her. Gunny Powell, four thousand acres, just west of Ollie's ranch. The Johnson clan, several parcels adding up to nearly two thousand, further west of Ollie. The Smyers ranch, a couple of parcels adding up to thirty-five hundred acres, further west still. Looked like Ventopoder was aiming for the long ridge that ran east and west along the north side of Ollie's ranch. And the cliffs on the north side of his place would be prime wind turbine locations. Alice could imagine Ollie's cold-eyed response to such a proposal. She looked over the one complete lease, with Gunny Powell's signature, containing all the provisions. The powers granted to Ventopoder were huge: broad access rights, along with power to install the turbines on concrete bases that Alice knew could extend thirty feet underground. Under the agreement, Ventopoder could also build a network of permanent roads and connect to power lines. Covenants favoring the landowner were few: Powell had negotiated very little say for himself as to location or disposition of any improvements. Alice knew from experience that, contrary to most ranchers' expectations, having the huge turbines installed on a piece of ranch land was like agreeing to have your quiet rural acres turned into a subdivision, with roads, towers, and concrete foundations. Under Powell's lease, Ventopoder had no duty to remove these improvements if the wind power use ended. It would be up to the rancher to try to get the improvements out, if he wanted the land to go back to its original state. So, he could say good-bye to the original state. Alice supported alternative energy, including windpower, but shook her head at landowners who failed to make provision for impacts on their own property.

"The clerk say anything, like why did you want this stuff?"

"No," said Silla. "They know better. I never tell them anything like that. But that new little Chatty Cathy at the counter, she volunteered that Mr. Treacher brought all those in at once last week."

Alice looked down at the documents. Indeed, they had all been recorded last week. Surely Treacher had not done every deal the same day? No, she saw as she checked the signatures that the documents had been executed up to six weeks before. Why hadn't he recorded them as he went? Because, thought Alice, he doesn't want people to know precisely what he's doing or where, at least not yet.

Alice went to the shelf and found her copy of the state utility code. After a while she called, "Silla, can you find a map of the state utility routes?" Silla came back with a printout of the state-designated transmission routes that let companies build lines to bring wind power from the windy west to more populous eastern parts of the state. She and Silla looked at the transmission route map then at each other.

"Ollie's ranch is nowhere near any of those routes," Alice commented. "And I don't think, at least on first look, that Ventopoder has the power of eminent domain. It's not an electric utility." She didn't think Ventopoder could condemn private property in order to build a transmission line for its wind power unless it made a deal with an electric utility. Maybe that explained the effort at secrecy at this early stage, while Treacher was trying to put together his parcels. Besides, though Ollie's land was desirable for turbines, because he owned the high ridge on the north boundary where the cave art was, his land wasn't strictly necessary for a transmission line; there were other ranches connecting to the same highway. She looked back at the leases Silla had copied. Ventopoder did not appear to have any obligation to actually build the wind farm unless and until it was satisfied—"in its sole discretion," per the lease—with the acreage it had put together and the economics of the project. If Ventopoder decided not to build, the ranchers would be left with only their signing bonuses. They would get real money only if the wind farm was built, once they started receiving their lease payments.

Alice pulled up Ollie's number on the computer and dialed the ranch. The phone rang and rang. Finally Ollie's growly voice answered.

"Ollie, it's Alice," she said. "Had a call today from Jeff Treacher of the wind power company Ventopoder. He says he called you about leasing and that you told him to call me."

"That's about half true. He called me and I told him I had no interest at all."

"Well, he's sending me a draft lease. If it's like the one I looked at that your neighbor Gunny Powell signed, it could pose some issues with the Rock Art Conservancy guys."

"Just tell that idiot to get lost. I told him I have absolutely no interest in having him set foot on my ranch."

She wasn't going to ask Ollie if he was sure. He was sure. "Okay. Well, one other thing. The conservancy guys confirmed they want to take a good look at the cave when they come out next month, really start mapping it. They're pretty excited. If it's okay with you, we can talk about details tomorrow. Sound okay?"

"Yeah." Ollie sounded like his mind was on something else. "I've got something I've got to do right now. Let's go over all this tomorrow afternoon."

"Right."

Ollie hung up. The email from Treacher was now on her computer screen, with a draft lease attached. Alice scanned it. Same provisions as for Gunny Powell. Looks like a cut-and-paste job, she thought; he just changed the name and land description.

Alice leaned back in her chair and considered. Maybe a Miranda visit was in order.

* * * *

Alice left the office and pulled into the parking lot at Madrone Bank with her deposit slip and the morning's sprinkling of fee checks. She walked into the lobby. Immediately the aroma of freshly baked chocolate chip cookies assailed her, and she cursed herself for forgetting Miranda's diabolical customer service tricks.

"I should never come to the bank just after you bake the afternoon cookies!" she told the teller.

"I know," said the teller (name tag: "Sue Ann"). "Just think how we feel about it. The entire office has had to start power walking on our breaks."

Alice waited for the machine to whir out her deposit confirmation.

"Who bakes them? Or do you just have a can of fresh-chocolate-cookie air freshener?"

"We take turns," said Sue Ann. "I stuck those in the oven just before you got here. They'll be out in a second."

"Was that part of your job description when you hired on? Chief teller-cum-baker?"

"It sure was. We are to have perfect cash drawers and perfectly baked cookies. Miranda told me up front that she likes to feed clients. She made sure when we built this branch that it had a kitchen with an oven, and a dishwasher. She says people make better investment decisions when they are full of chocolate. Translated: they leave their money here!"

Miranda appeared behind the teller. "Hi, Alice! How about a cookie?"

"You are single-handedly undoing six months of yoga. But if you have some time after work I would love a visit."

"Done," said Miranda. "I'll drop by after closing."

Alice thanked the teller and looked with gratitude at the total on the deposit slip. Enough to pay the office utilities and Silla. Nothing like a few checks in the mail to warm the heart of the anxious entrepreneur.

Miranda was another reason Alice was slowly making a success of Coffee Creek. Tall, slim, regal, Miranda grew up in West Austin (which she still referred to as "the navel of the world"). She dutifully followed the path of her well-to-do sorority sisters at UT—engaged and married at twenty-two, Junior League volunteer of the year, mother of two perfect children—until her picture-perfect life began to shift slowly out of focus. When there was no turnaround, she divorced and rejoined the workforce. She spent several years in private banking, moving gracefully up the ranks and carefully cosseting some wealthy private banking clients. Miranda came to the attention of Madrone Bank, which was considering opening its first branch in Coffee Creek. When they offered her the chance to build and manage the bank, Miranda jumped at it and never looked back. She loved the limestone building, loved the customers, loved her staff (whom she mothered fiercely), and loved the competition with other banks. Cookies were only part of the plan. Miranda's customers got significant attention from her in ways that constantly surprised them.

Alice was no exception. When she first dared to think of leaving Austin for Coffee Creek, Alice dipped a toe in the water by walking into Madrone Bank to open an account. Her tentative entry into the stone building was met by a whirlwind of smiles and paper forms. She emerged holding a new account card, a cup of coffee, and the memory of a couple of fine chocolate chip cookies. The next morning, Miranda called Alice's Austin office and asked her to drive out to Coffee Creek for lunch at the Camellia Diner. There Miranda interrogated her about her Austin firm, law school, Austin clients, bar activities. When silence fell, Alice found herself staring into Miranda's narrowed blue eyes, feeling thoroughly assessed.

Does she know what sort of underwear I'm wearing? thought Alice. Can she tell I'm scared to death of this whole move?

Then Miranda had said, "What can I do to help you love Coffee Creek? We need you here!"

Alice—startled—said: "Help me be part of the place. Help me learn about it."

"Deal," said Miranda.

The morning she opened her Coffee Creek office, Alice got two calls from prospective clients. Both of them said Miranda had suggested they call. She got a call from the president of the chamber of commerce, too, inviting her to the next lunch and asking if she would like to be on the speakers committee. And later that day, Miranda sent flowers. After that, they had slowly become friends as well as banker and client.

This afternoon, as promised, Miranda tooled up to Alice's office at 6:00 p.m. in an old, well-kept blue Jaguar.

"Drink," she said once she was inside.

Alice obligingly got crystal tumblers from the breakfront, ice from the kitchen, and a bottle of Talisker single malt from the cabinet behind her desk. She carefully added a teaspoon of water to her glass, "to release the taste," as Jordie used to instruct. The two women sank into the armchairs at the tea table and clinked glasses.

"Salud," said Miranda. "What's up?"

"Don't tell me anything you can't," said Alice. "But can you tell me anything about Jeff Treacher?"

"Sure. He's not a bank client and I know him from chamber. Lotta hat and no cattle. Or at least nobody's seen any cattle. I think he tries to take credit for other folks' cattle. Where do you want to start?"

"What kind of person is he? And what kind of lawyer?"

"Kind of person, I don't know. I heard he was with the Phoenix office of a San Antonio law firm before he moved here. He's leasing that office across from our bank short term, didn't buy it. And he's leasing his house short term too but with an option to buy, I heard. So, I don't know how permanent he plans to be. Otherwise—wears too much aftershave, thinks he's God's gift to women, and isn't."

"What kind of law does he do? And who are his clients? General practice, litigation, what?"

"He's apparently working with a Portuguese wind power company to lease up wind turbine sites west of here. I don't know if he really represents them, though, or if he's acting on his own account. I understand a couple of ranchers who signed up with him got pretty unhappy after they figured out what they had gotten themselves into. That's all I know and actually that's more than I know. Why?"

"I'm just trying to figure out if he's somebody I need to be careful of. Someone I need to keep an eye on."

Miranda sipped her Scotch. "I would." She narrowed her eyes. "I would never let that guy get behind me. Keep him where you can see him."

Alice thought, I can figure this out. She inhaled the aroma of Talisker in her glass. "How is everything else, Miranda? How's Roland?"

"Taking me to Santa Fe for the weekend."

"Mmmm. Good dinner reservations?"

"Yes, at Rowe Mesa Grill, and maybe prickly pear margaritas at the San Jose, and a piñon fire in the fireplace in our room."

Alice smiled at Miranda. "And a little passion."

Miranda smiled back. "Roland is fun to be around. And it's always good to get out of town for a little fun." She looked speculatively at Alice. "So, when can I start prowling for a boyfriend for you?"

Alice shook her head. "I get lonesome. But I am still lonesome for Jordie, not for any old guy."

"Watch out, Alice. I may make plans for you," said Miranda, unfolding her long legs and standing up to leave. "Thanks for the drink."

Alice watched the Jaguar pull away from the curb and thought about Santa Fe. Now, in the fall, the cottonwoods would be bright gold against dark green piñon and deep blue sky and dusty orange adobe buildings. She could almost smell piñon smoke. She let her imagination wander: cholla cactus, impossibly pink on an adobe-colored hill; the air so clear you could see nearly forever; following a trail through tall pines in the Pecos Wilderness. She thought about what Miranda had said. But she still couldn't imagine hiking up a mountain with some stranger, some man who was not Jordie.

Then she looked out the window again and thought about driving home, down the long creek road to . . . a very quiet house. Maybe Miranda had a point.

Chapter Eight

Cordite and Color

Alice drove down her long caliche driveway in the dark, watching stars come out in the clear evening sky over the ravine. She parked the truck in the pole barn. Silence, except for a solitary fall cricket. "Maybe, Ollie, I'll take one last look at your documents tonight," she muttered, pulling the briefcase off the seat. She unlocked the house and turned on the kitchen light. Pasta? Something quick. She was starving. Water boiling in the big pot, add salt, add olive oil: what sort of pasta? Tortellini, decided Alice, with cheese inside. And some fresh tomato. A real vegetable would be nice.

She chopped the tomato, grated cheese, and snipped basil. It had taken huge discipline, after Jordie died, to start cooking for herself again. One day, standing at the kitchen sink, eating a piece of cheese for supper, she'd said to herself, "I am taking the pledge. This will not do. I hereby pledge to my mother and my grandmother that I will sit down and have supper every night. I will not eat supper standing at the sink. I so pledge."

Alice slid open the big door to the deck, so she could hear the night noises. Now she heard some rustling under the deck. Possum? Armadillo? Or it might even be the pudgy skunk she had seen a few times in the early dawn light, foraging for fallen sunflower seeds under the birdfeeder. Alice had dubbed the skunk "Waddles" because of its busy, hilarious walk, but had made a considered decision to quit throwing leftover salad into the compost pile below her back deck, announcing, "Waddles, you do not need any encouragement around here."

Her cell was ringing—Ann! "Hi, darling daughter! What's going on in Scotland?" Cradling the cell phone on her shoulder, Alice lifted the tortellini in the basket out of the big pot of boiling water and set them aside to drain. Still listening to Ann, she picked up the big pot with two hands and carried it out to throw the hot water off the deck. She watched the huge arc of boiling water—and then—

"AAIEHH!" A male voice under the deck, thrashing feet—and a warning snarl from some smaller mammal, followed by the most astounding rush of skunk smell, a billowing Hiroshima mushroom cloud of steam and skunkiness.

Alice stood paralyzed with the empty pot in one hand and the cell phone squawking in the other. "Mama? Mama!"

The whoever-it-was below her was grunting and scrambling out from under her tall deck. The dark form thrashed through the undergrowth back up the hill and around the house and up toward the driveway.

Alice was seized with fury. "Call you back!" she yelled at the phone before punching the off button. Who was this damned person? Racing back inside, Alice was full of rage. I want to shoot him! she thought. Or take his picture! Or something! How dare he invade my place! She had no pistol. Wait! She did! She had the Verey pistol—the flare gun—that Jordie had brought home after he sold his boat. She grabbed it out of the top cabinet. She had a notion to shoot the flare gun and then use its light to take a picture of the marauder with her cell phone so she could take it to the police.

She'd never fired the flare gun before. It felt heavy; she hoped that meant it was loaded. Was it safe to go outside now? She could see the guy staggering down the road toward the gate. Alice raced outside, waving the pistol in the air. Should she shoot the flare right at him? No, she wanted light so she could take a picture, not to actually hit him. She fired the pistol into the air. A bright red flare went up. She shot again. Green flare. The air was full of cordite and color. She set the cell phone on camera and squeezed off pictures. The whoever-it-was galloped toward the gate. He had to climb either the gate or the barbed wire—which would it be? The barbed wire. Uh-oh—looked like he was having some trouble . . .

If that bastard parked anywhere near my property, Alice thought, I am going to run him down and get his license plate. She hauled on her old boots by the door, dashed to her truck and slammed it into reverse, then headed down the driveway. On the other side of the gate she saw truck-sized headlights flash on and turn back down the road toward the highway. He must have parked behind the trees outside the gate; she hadn't seen his vehicle when she came home.

Then Alice saw flames in her side-view mirror. In the pasture, leaping yellow flames danced next to the road. She had caught her own pasture on fire with the flares. Alice slammed on the brakes and jumped out. She stomped on the fire in her boots till the last ember gave up, then went back to get some water. No way to catch the bastard now. Alice lugged the big water bucket over, poured water on the charred grass, and stomped around some more. Thank goodness for her sturdy old Fatbaby boots.

Her cell phone was ringing in her pocket. "Mama? What in the world?" said Ann's voice.

"Well, some guy was under my deck. And I poured boiling water on him."

"I see. Like 'pouring boiling oil through the murder hole onto the castle invaders'?" That was a family joke.

"Well," said Alice, "if I had known he was there I surely would have opted for boiling oil, but all I had was my pasta water. Plus, I did not know he was there. However, he deserved it entirely."

"Of course he did," said Ann. "But what did he do when the boiling water hit him?"

"He started running, but he made Waddles mad."

"Oh no!"

"Yes, this entire place smells like the world's maddest skunk. I think Waddles must have unleashed on him."

"He deserved it! Did you see his face? Or get his license?"

"I tried to," said Alice, "and I tried to drive after him, but I caught the pasture on fire with the flare gun, so I had to stay and stomp it out."

The phone was silent. "Flare gun?" asked Ann. "Pasture on fire?"

"'Fraid so."

"Damn. So you couldn't chase him."

"Correct," said Alice.

"But wait!" said Ann. "Wouldn't he want to try to get the skunk smell off?"

"You're right!" said Alice. "I'll call you back."

Alice dialed the Quick Stop convenience store on the road to Coffee Creek—the closest place she could think of that would still be open. "Ramón, it's Alice. Alice Greer. I am just wondering, have you had anyone come in to buy tomato juice in the past little bit? Like, in bulk?"

"Hi, Mrs. Greer. Funny you should ask. Guy just came in reeking of skunk. Face was all red too. In fact, he had blisters on his forehead. Told me a skunk got him but I didn't know skunks raised blisters."

"Did he get tomato juice?"

"No, we were out. Big empty spot on the shelf. He had to settle for Bloody Mary mix. Don't know if that'll work, but the man was desperate. I'm still trying to air the place out. Lordy!"

"Ramón, did you know this guy?"

"Feel like I've seen him before but I can't recall his name. Not too old, not too young, dark hair. And those blisters. Gonna be hard for him to get a date, blisters and skunk smell."

"What about his car? A truck, maybe?"

"He parked right in front. Big truck. Texas plate. Big black brush guard on the front. Truck was a dark color—maybe green? Not sure."

"Thank you, Ramón." Alice hung up. She looked around her house. She felt the waves of adrenaline and rage beginning to evaporate and realized how wacky things were. The front of the house still smelled like a grass fire; on the back deck, a cloud of skunk scent was practically peeling the paint off the house. Meanwhile some guy soaked in pasta water and eau de skunk was careening home to bathe in Bloody Mary mix.

Alice started giggling and dialed Ann. "Bloody Mary mix!"

They laughed until they cried. Then Ann sobered up. "Mama! Have you locked all the doors?"

"Yes, ma'am," said Alice. "I have. Plus, I'll call the sheriff and tell him to watch and smell for a boiled skunk victim."

She did as promised, calling the Coffee County Sheriff's Office to report trespass. She left out a few details, feeling that the sheriff's office didn't really need to know about the flare gun. The burn ban was still in effect countywide, so she also didn't mention the pasture fire. The constable dutifully took down the information.

"Any more identification, ma'am?"

"Well, Ramón at the Quick Stop says he had a big truck with a black brush guard."

"Ford? Chevy? Toyota? What color?"

"Well, Ramón said maybe it was green. Or dark, anyway."

"So maybe it could have been the same guy at the Quick Stop as was at your house, ma'am. But maybe not. There are an awful lot of people with trucks like that."

"But they don't smell like him. Ramón says he is still airing out the store, the guy had on so much eau de skunk. Plus Ramón says he had those pasta-water blisters on his forehead."

The constable chortled. "Well, I can put down that he had some kind of blisters, if not pasta water, which I cannot confirm. You must have a pretty good arm with a pot of hot water." He paused. "Have you ever had a burglar out there?"

"Never," said Alice.

"Can you think of any reason someone would be trying to get in your house?"

"You mean beyond the usual, like burglary or intent on my person? No," said Alice. Then she thought some more. "What bothers me now is that this person was apparently already there when I got home. Don't most burglars get scared and leave if the owner comes home?"

"Yep."

"Well, this guy was standing under my deck while I was in the kitchen cooking and talking on the phone. Once he knew I was home, why didn't he leave? And why did he leave his truck hidden out beyond the fence? It was a long walk down that drive to get to my deck."

"Keep thinking," said the constable. "Is there anything you can think of that's in your house that someone might be trying to get? Maybe something you brought home with you? Because a guy walking down the road and hiding under your deck, leaving his truck like that—it does sound weird."

Alice was silent.

"And ma'am? Check your doors and windows. Keep 'em locked."

"Yes sir," said Alice. She hung up. The burglar was not after the usual electronic toys (which anyone could look through the windows and see she didn't have). She turned and looked at the bench by the door where she habitually left her briefcase. Ollie. This all had to do with Ollie West. She picked up the briefcase and locked it in her only locking closet.

"And so to bed," said Alice.

Chapter Nine

Not a Trace

"Everything's ready for Ollie," said Silla. Alice looked up. This Tuesday afternoon Silla sported barrel-racing garb—tight, flowered Western shirt with gold sparkles on the bosom, crisp boot-cut jeans, excellent black-and-white leather boots embroidered in red.

"Silla! Those boots!"

"Yep," said Silla. "Finally got my real hand-tooled Goodson Kells." Kells owned a legendary hole-in-the-wall leather store in Coffee Creek. Alice was still waiting for her own boots: Kells took more than a year to fill an order. Silla went on, "Power of attorney is all ready for him to sign, and I have Jeanie and Sue Ann from the courthouse coming by on their way home to be the two witnesses."

"Great. Thanks. Ollie's usually at least five minutes early so we should be done in plenty of time for his five o'clock meeting."

"For the Wild Game Dinner and Auction?" asked Silla.

"Yes."

"I already know what I'm bidding on at the auction," said Silla. "Goodson Kells is donating one of his hand-tooled saddles. I know I probably can't afford it, but I'm still bidding."

The Wild Game Dinner and Auction was a big deal for Coffee Creek, particularly for the men who worked the event. They planned it all year and raised thousands of dollars. The crowd had grown so big they had moved the event to the high school gym, where on the chosen night—at the close of deer season—the men offered a huge spread of barbecued beasts: antelope, deer, buffalo, elk, and "specialty" items, including raccoon. Alice had actually tried the raccoon and liked it. As owner of a local business, she had even found herself (with muffled hilarity) signing up as a sponsor. The silent auction brought hunters from all over the state, drawn by hand-carved gunstocks, elaborate gun cabinets, and all the accoutrements for luxury deer blinds. Last year the take was over fifty thousand dollars. Consequently, every charitable and school organization in Coffee Creek tried to work their charms on the Men's Wild Game Committee. Ollie had worked on the committee for years.

Alice reviewed the power of attorney one more time. Of course she found no typos: Silla was house-proud about her documents. Then she set out two crystal highball glasses on the polished Scottish tea table, one Jordie had brought to Texas when they married. She wanted to toast Ollie and salute his quiet courage and non-whiny decision-making.

Her clock ticked. Four thirty. No truck in front of her office. The courthouse ladies had arrived; Alice heard them talking with Silla in the kitchen.

At a quarter to five, Alice pulled up Ollie's contact sheet on her computer and called the ranch. No one answered. She left a message. "Silla, do we have any other number for Ollie?"

"No," said Silla. "I asked for his cell but we never got it."

At five thirty, Alice gave up and told Silla to thank Jeanie and Sue Ann and send them home. "I'm worried," said Silla. "Do you think he had a wreck? Or is in the hospital?"

Alice called Mary's cell phone. "Mary, we were expecting your dad for an appointment at four thirty but he didn't come. Do you know if something came up? I tried the ranch number but nobody answered."

Mary sounded puzzled. "I haven't talked to Dad all day. I'm up in Dallas on some meetings for the gallery."

"Can you call him? Or give me his cell?"

"Oh, I can't get Dad to use his cell—he says the coverage is rotten out at the ranch. I'll try it though. And I'll ask Doyle to try him when he gets home." Odder and odder, thought Alice. She remembered sitting frozen right here at her desk during the original interview with Ollie, when she had asked about Mary's mother. First Ollie just said, "She's dead. As of—about ten years ago."

"As of?" Alice looked up from her notepad, puzzled.

"Nobody told you, huh?" asked Ollie.

"I heard she had . . . disappeared, Ollie. But I don't know any details."

Ollie had sat there a moment, stiff and unblinking. He looked out the window and then directly at Alice. "You don't know any details. The thing is, Ms. Greer, I don't either. I don't talk about it to people, because—well, hell." He straightened his shoulders, took a breath. "I'm seventy-eight. Time to talk about it, I guess. Ms. Greer, this is the worst thing that's happened in my life. My Cassie disappeared ten years ago this October, just before Mary was going to marry Doyle. I had to drive up to Lubbock to check on my aunt, and Mary was up in Dallas for her bachelorette party. Wedding stuff. Anyway, I got home and there was a note on the kitchen table—'Gone to Laredo for paper flowers for the wedding.' I guess Cassie had this notion of decorating the ranch for the wedding with those big Mexican paper flowers that you saw back then. Cassie had arranged a mariachi band and so on. Back then it was safer—she and her friends used to drive down to Laredo and cross over to shop. Anyway, she left that note. But we never saw her again. We had police all over the ranch. Police all over Laredo. Highway patrol looking for her car in Texas. And police looking in Mexico. We hired detectives. We ran ads. We looked. We waited. Not a trace of her."

"Good grief," Alice had said. "How old was Cassie?"

"Cassie was a little younger than me." He stared out the window. "She was just twenty when Mary was born. She was fifty-five when she disappeared."

"You've never found out what happened?"

"I still don't know. Detectives asked me if she was seeing someone else. If she was unhappy at home. Looked at my bank accounts. Looked at her bank accounts. Looked for missing stuff. Et cetera. Checked the phone bills. Nothing."

Alice did not think it odd that Cassie would just drive down to Laredo, cross the border, and shop for paper flowers—she herself had made just such road trips in the past, though she certainly wouldn't now, with the escalated drug violence. But even back in the day, Alice had not gone alone. "Did she usually go down there all by herself?"

"No," said Ollie. "We called the friends she usually played with—Ilka and so on."

"Ilka Mayer?" Alice knew Ilka, did work for her and counted her as a dear friend.

"Right. She hadn't asked any of them to go. I thought she would have at least called them. But then I thought—well, Cassie may have just wanted to dash down, grab the flowers, and head back without the usual shopping and lunch and so forth."

"I could see that," said Alice. She thought of her own friends and their single-minded, nearly demented planning for their daughters' weddings, trying to create the perfect day they thought their daughters would want. "I could see someone thinking, 'Yes, it's seven hours down and back but if I just make this road trip I can buy the damn paper flowers and get it checked off my list.'"

"Yeah," said Ollie. "Maybe so. But the whole time we were searching and waiting, I second-guessed our entire married life. I know she loved me, Ms. Greer. And she adored our baby girl. I knew she'd been worried about the wedding, but otherwise at the time she seemed fine to me. So it didn't seem real, for her to disappear. For years afterward, I'd be doing something—putting up a horse, going over a bank statement, didn't matter—and I would think, maybe I'll turn around and she'll just be walking right back into the house. Or I'd be sitting there at night and think I heard her car coming down the bluff and starting across the creek. But . . . it wasn't any good living in limbo like that. Mary and I needed the waiting to end. It was like we were suspended—couldn't even grieve for her the way you finally have to grieve. So, seven years after she disappeared we filed papers to have Cassie declared dead."

Ollie had shaken his head. "I can't even say those words without feeling bad all over again. 'Declared dead.' Like we could do something about it, somehow bring her back, if we didn't file. I waffled about that filing for months. Was it right? Would it help? But one day Mary and I looked at each other and said, we can't go on if we don't let her rest. So I told my lawyer to file. Then I second-guessed myself, tried to unfile—but the papers were in, so I left it." He shook his head again, sighed. "But you know, if she walked in the room right now, it would be the best day of my life."

"Well," Alice had said, "you going ahead and taking that step makes the estate planning a little easier to draft. But I am so sorry. She must have been very special."

"She was. Nobody in the world like Cassie. Mary looks a good bit like Cassie, but Cassie was . . . deep. I don't know how she knew some of the stuff she knew. Always seemed to be able to look right into people. You couldn't lie to Cassie. I never even thought about lying to Cassie. Seemed like she usually knew what I was thinking before I thought it."

Ollie had pulled out his wallet and leafed behind the bills at the back so he could lift up the fabric flap. He handed Alice two frayed photos. One showed a tall woman in jeans and boots climbing atop a rail fence and smiling at the photographer. "I took that," Ollie said. He handed Alice the second photo, a head shot. Alice stared. Cassie was lovely, not smiling but looking through the lens and through the photographer and somewhere far into space. What was this woman thinking? Alice wished she had known her.

She notice that Ollie's story included details on precisely where he and Mary were when Cassie disappeared. Always so suspicious, Alice, she told herself. Sometimes she wished she could stop her habitual testing of reality, could take people at their word—could shed the ever-watchful, contrarian nature that saw her second-guessing almost every human emotion. But she recognized that those same traits had also been carefully honed in her legal work, and had proven quite useful.

And now Ollie—wallet, photos, crisp jeans, crinkled eyes, failing lungs—had failed to show up. Very unlike Ollie. Hopefully she would hear something tomorrow—he had trouble with the truck, or he felt bad and headed in to see the doctor, or had just forgotten the appointment. Because for Mary to have one parent vanish was very sad. To have both parents vanish would look like . . . carelessness? Or worse.

Chapter Ten

Light of the Moon

"Hey, Alice!" said Silla. "How much longer are you gonna be?"

Alice looked up from her keyboard. Silla—still in jeans, boots, barrel-racing glitter —was standing at her office door, keys in hand.

"What do you mean?"

"Jane Ann! This is the night! She's making her debut! You wanna go, don't you? You said you did! Actually, you need to go."

"Oh, right," said Alice. Jane Ann Olson produced the title work for nearly all Alice's real estate closings. "Beer Barn, here we come." Alice shut down the computer. "But I'm still puzzled about Ollie."

"Maybe he'll be at the Beer Barn?"

"Nope," said Alice. "And you know that as well as I do. Even if he missed his appointment with us, he wouldn't miss that Wild Game committee meeting. So I doubt he'll be boot-scooting around the Beer Barn."

"I know. I was just hoping." Silla touched up her perfect lip gloss with a practiced hand. "Okay, see you there. I just didn't want you to sit here staring at the computer and miss Jane Ann. She might be miffed."

"Thanks."

"Nor did I want you to go all shy on me and not want to walk into the Beer Barn. Want to ride over with me? You really coming?"

"Sure I am. But I'll bring my own truck. No need for you to run me back here."

She and Silla pulled into the last two slots in the gravel parking lot in front of the Beer Barn. Alice slid down from the truck seat and followed Silla in. As she picked her way in her heels across the gravel she checked for possible rides belonging to skunk man. Between her truck and the door she counted three dark pickups, one green, one black, one navy—all with brush guards. The constable was right.

The Beer Barn was at least a hundred years old. In prior incarnations it had served as a livery stable, then been upgraded to a feed store. In the 1980s, three Coffee Creek residents had decided the town needed a dance hall. They had put up a stage, hung some lights in the rafters, and bought a portable lighted sign for the highway side of the building—on wheels, with flashing lights and movable letters. The sign grossly violated Coffee Creek's current sign ordinance, but since it predated the ordinance it was "grandmothered," as the owners said. Today the sign read, "BEER—It's not just for breakfast any more." Alice devoutly hoped she would someday get one of the three Beer Barn Barons (as they called themselves) as clients, just to know how they decided each week what the sign would say.

She and Silla sauntered in—or Silla sauntered, wearing her new Goodson Kells boots, while Alice, in heels, just tried to saunter. She watched as Silla headed for the bar, was intercepted by a Handsome Young Cowboy, and acquired a Dos Equis without even trying, much less paying. Alice sighed and headed for the bar, signaling the barkeep. "Shiner Bock, please." Down at one end of the bar she saw Jeff Treacher, talking to a red-faced man with a cowboy hat pulled low on his forehead. They both looked down the bar at Alice. Treacher muttered something and the two left the bar, heading for a table by the wall. I'm not planning to talk to you either, she thought. She paid for her beer and turned to survey the dance floor.

"Hey, Alice!" It was Jane Ann Olson. No longer garbed in her blue title-company suit, she was spilling out the top of a Western shirt and packed into jeans with silver conchos down the sides.

"Mercy! You look—dynamite!" Alice said.

Jane Ann grinned. "Don't ask me to sit down, because I can't. These jeans are so tight I thought I'd have to ride over here in the bed of a pickup. And I stopped by Janine's Hair and asked her to do my makeup. She got a little overenthusiastic, didn't she?" Jane Ann's mascaraed eyelashes were nearly an inch long.

Alice grinned back. "Oh well! Girl's gotta do," she said. "And you did, too! What are you singing tonight?"

With some difficulty Jane Ann pulled an index card out of her jeans pocket. "Whoof! Set list," she said. "I understand that's what this is called. Okay, what do you think? We're doing a retrospective on beer hall music. I'm a little nervous, but the band sounds pretty good, Alice. We're starting out with 'If You've Got the Money I've Got the Time.' Check out the lyrics. Got some new verses, tailor-made for Coffee Creek."

"Really!" said Alice.

"And then 'Friends in Low Places.' Same thing—more, uh, tailored lyrics."

"All right!" laughed Alice. "I like it."

Onstage the band was tuning up—wasn't that her vet up there? Yes, it was the large animal veterinarian, Joe Banks, with his big hands all over a little bitty mandolin. He had helped Alice when her two donkeys, a jenny and her year-old baby, got into a fracas with a coyote. The donkeys had won, but had taken some serious hits. When Alice called Coffee Creek Large Animal Clinic in a panic, Banks rolled straight over in his big white clinic truck, handed Alice a cold beer from his cooler, soothed the donkeys for a while with his big voice and big hands, gave them shots, put in a couple of stitches, and then handed Alice a giant tube of antibiotic. "They'll be fine, Alice," he said. "Put this on twice a day for the rest of the week."

She knew he could sing because he had sung to the donkeys. He crooned the whole time he was patching them up. Alice couldn't quite tell but thought it was "Faded Love." When he finished, the donkeys practically had their heads in his pockets.

"They're in love with you," said Alice.

"Shows how smart they are," said Banks, flashing a quick look at Alice. "People underestimate donkeys all the time."

"How much do I owe you, Dr. J?"

"Hey, I'll send a bill. Come hear me sing sometime. Henly Hot Hands. We play at the Beer Barn every chance we get. And because we're so democratic, the Beer Barn generally doesn't charge a cover when we play." He looked at Alice. "Donkeys are fine. Don't worry. See you."

And now here she was. Banks was up there tuning, the keyboard guy and the poker-faced drummer were banging around, and now Jane Ann stood by the microphone, looking full of potential. She was fingering a shot glass of amber liquid and surveying the room.

"That's a lot of woman up there," said a voice in Alice's ear. She turned. Tom the banker stood next to her.

"Yes, she is!" said Alice, smiling up at Tom.

"She does all my closings," he said, eyes riveted on Jane Ann. "Boy, is she smart."

"Does mine, too," said Alice. "Tom, how come you aren't playing harmonica?"

"Oh, I play with a group in Wimberley every Thursday," said Tom. "That's enough for me. I still have a day job at the bank."

"I hear you," said Alice. But secretly Alice wished she were standing up with Jane Ann, singing close harmony. Her fantasy.

The bass guitarist, totally deadpan in true Texas roadhouse style, started laying down an irresistible rhythm line. Lead guitar laid a big playful opening riff on top. Alice's entire body jumped when the drummer cranked up.

And then Jane Ann leaned toward the microphone, cuddled up to it in a most surprising fashion, leered at the audience, and sang—suggested—intimated—"If you got the money, honey . . ." Everyone sang the next line with her, cheering.

"Hey, Alice! Let's dance!" She and Tom headed for the dance floor. He was a masterful two-stepper. She followed as best she could, letting him spin her left, spin her right. The two-step technique required the male never to look at his partner, just to guide her with his hands while his eyes were on some goal, somewhere further on. Like the Mier death march to Santa Fe? she thought. No, this is fun. And she let herself dance.

As promised, Jane Ann was singing her new lyrics. She was pointing straight at George the surveyor, singing, "You got to watch him when he puts in his stakes! Loves 'em and he leaves 'em, all those heartaches . . ." The crowd loved it. George was blushing.

Over her shoulder Alice saw Jeff Treacher cut in on Silla. Silla did not look best pleased. Nor did her partner, the Handsome Young Cowboy. He stood glaring as Treacher whirled Silla off toward the band. Silla was giving Treacher a raised eyebrow and her skeptical look while he talked up a storm. Looked like he was trying to persuade Silla of something. So far she wasn't buying, it appeared. Alice lost sight of Silla when Tom gave her a big twirl—no, a double twirl—while Jane Ann wound it up to a big crescendo on "If You've Got the Money I've Got the Time." Lefty Frizzell never sang it better. The audience roared, whistled, stomped. People were busily searching for partners. The band started up again. The lead guitar stepped into unmistakable Garth Brooks territory, the lead-in to "Friends in Low Places." Did Jane Ann really think she could do that?

"Thanks, Tom!" said Alice, panting slightly.

"My pleasure," he said, grinning.

"Hey," she said, pointing at Treacher and Silla. "Looks like Mr. Treacher's after my secretary! Wonder what his intentions are?"

"Don't know," said Tom. "Are you her keeper?"

"She's pretty independent," said Alice. "But still—what do you know about Mr. Treacher's leasing project? Is it going to make?"

"Hey, I hear he hopes so, because he gets a big bonus when it does," said Tom. "Or at least that's the word. He's not one of my customers so I can say that. Apparently that's his deal with Ventopoder—he's sort of the developer for this, not the hourly paid lawyer, if you see what I mean. What I hear is, he's counting on it."

"Ah," said Alice.

"That's the scoop," said Tom. "Or at least the scuttlebutt, which can be totally fact-free, as you know. What I hear is, he doesn't get paid unless and until he's got something all wrapped up and tied with a bow. Then he can take it to Ventopoder."

"Hmm. Well, thanks, Tom," said Alice, and started for the bar.

But George the surveyor grabbed her hand. "Alice! Let's do it!" And before she knew it, George, with Alice following as best she could, was tearing it up in the middle of the dance floor. She couldn't believe it: George led even better than Tom Brothers. George did it all with his hands—led, pushed, spun, guided. Never sweated, took minimal steps, all perfect. No bounce, no shake, just a smile. Five foot nine, thirty pounds overweight, chino pants, blue button-down oxford—he looked like an aging frat boy, but one whose big sister had really taught him to dance before sending him off to college. Alice wasn't sure she'd ever danced, or been danced, this well.

"George, you are fantastic!" she panted.

He smirked. "My one talent. Always pick the best-looking partner." He raised her hand, spun her underneath it with his other hand, let her go, grabbed her back. Jane Ann had the mike in a death grip. "Cause I've got friends in low places, where . . ." Here she and George went again, whirling in the center of the floor. Alice couldn't help laughing, breathless as she was. Jane Ann had verses naming local bankers, city council members, and the three owners of the Beer Barn. What would she do next?

With her sweaty dancers huffing and ready for more, Jane Ann lifted her chin at the drummer, who laid down the law for a Delbert McClinton cover. What had become of the Jane Ann Olson of the navy suits, the immaculate settlement statements? She was seriously rocking now, leaning into "Givin' It Up for Your Love"—she pointed the mike at the crowd. "EVERYTHING!" they roared. Jane Ann grinned back.

"A star is born," Alice panted.

"Yup, that Jane Ann has management skills," said George. "She's got this whole place movin' like a herd headed up the Chisholm Trail. What a woman!"

"Yup," said Alice, slowing to a halt, out of breath.

"Another beer?" said George.

"Thanks," said Alice. "I can't stay much longer, I've got to be up early in the morning." Which was partly true—Alice wanted to make the 6:00 a.m. yoga class. And she did need to get up and check the animals.

They watched while Jane Ann worked into another roadhouse blues. "Mercy," said Alice. "Who's going to do our closings if she starts touring?"

"Ms. Greer!" It was Jeff Treacher. He grabbed her hand and swung her out on the dance floor before she could say no. Ye gods, who was responsible for that aftershave? Miranda was right. Someone should burn the factory.

"Hey, can I call you Alice?" he said. Alice smiled her third-best smile. Prevented her from having to answer. "How are you liking small-town practice?" he said, holding up his hand for her to twirl under.

"Fine!" she said. How long was this song? Forever?

"Ever worry about security, stuff like that?" he said.

Alice stopped dead, in the middle of the dance floor. "What do you mean, Jeff?" she asked. "Thinking of a little B and E, or what?"

Treacher's expression was hurt. "Hey, hey, I'm just making conversation," he said. "Just wondering about what Coffee Creek is really like. Like, do people lock their doors—you know, that kind of stuff. I'm coming from Phoenix, which is pretty heavy metal when it comes to security."

"Well," said Alice, "probably Smith and Wesson protects a lot of premises here." She hoped that would shut him up. "This is handshake country. You can't depend on someone's handshake, you don't want to do business with them."

"Oh, of course, that's my mantra too," said Treacher.

If you think I believe that, Alice thought, you are quite, quite wrong.

As Jane Ann wound up to her finale, Alice said, "Thanks, got to run." She dropped Treacher like a hot potato and headed for the restroom. Once inside she swabbed her hands with liquid soap. "Grrr!" she said to the mirror, lathering her hands.

A stall door opened. It was Silla. She sniffed. "Do I detect a bit of . . . Monsieur Treacher in the air?"

"Mais oui," said Alice. "I saw him swooping you around out there, Silla."

"Yuck." Silla was lathering her hands. "How do you say 'yuck' in French? Anyway, double yuck. Guy's a sleaze. Do you know what he wanted?"

"No," said Alice.

"He wanted to know what we did with our originals," snapped Silla. "Like we were total country yokels. Weren't we worried about security? What did we do with client documents?"

"Bizarre," said Alice. "He asked me if we had a security system."

"So why would he want to know that?" asked Silla. "What possible interest does Jeff Treacher have in our filing system? What a creep!"

Alice peered under the other stall in the restroom. Empty—or at least no feet were visible. "I just wonder. After last night, with skunk man under my deck, I just wonder if someone is interested in Ollie's paperwork. Maybe someone just wants to know who gets the ranch, for wind power lease purposes, if Ollie dies. Or who Ollie's appointed under a power of attorney. I'd hate to think Treacher's that ghoulish, even if he has deplorable taste in aftershave."

Alice understood the bell curve but regretted that for the human animal it appeared to apply not just to intelligence but possibly to sensitivity, bedside manner, honesty, and ethical behavior. Basic decency, in other words. If so,

Treacher was, in her book, at the far end of the bell curve, out at the asymptotic line stretching just above zero toward infinity, or hell, whichever was furthest out there.

"Time for home," Alice said to Silla. "See you mañana. Have fun tonight." She headed outside to her truck, grateful for the sharp, bright moon, the sharp, cool air, the scent of cedar, and a hint of fall. Sometimes I despair of the human race, she thought. But then she thought about Jordie, who would have reveled in Jane Ann's debut at the Beer Barn, and she thought about Jane Ann's raucous good humor and dead-on delivery. She thought about pudgy George's fabulous dancing and Joe Banks's airy mandolin. Maybe we're not so bad, not all of us, not all of the time. We do make music. And we dance by the light of the moon. So comforted, she headed down the creek road for home.

Chapter Eleven

One and Only

On Wednesday there was still no word from Ollie, or about Ollie. Alice talked with one client who wanted to preserve his ranch while still letting his children build vacation homes, reviewed closing documents and held a conference call on a ranch purchase by a Houston woman, went to a brown bag board meeting for the food pantry in Coffee Creek, and then worked pro bono on terms for the new lease for the food pantry. When sunset orange shot into her office from the west window in Silla's workroom, Alice sighed and shut down the computer. Time to go. She checked the locks twice and headed home.

At nine on Thursday morning Alice was in the middle of proofreading a closing statement, brow furrowed, calculator at hand to check the tax proration, when Silla burst in the front door. "Alice? Did you hear about Ollie?" Alice's stomach knotted. Ollie?

"I heard it at the Camellia Diner. The EMS guys were there. He apparently fell off some rocks. They say—well, there were vultures. Alice, he's been dead for a while."

"How did it happen? Who found him?"

"Apparently Doyle found him. He called EMS and they drove out there and met him. From what they say, Ollie was out somewhere on the west side of the ranch. Looked like he might have fallen down the steep side of a hill. EMS thought he'd broken a bunch of bones."

"I guess this is why he couldn't get here on Tuesday." Alice felt sick.

"Sounds like it. One of the EMS guys thought he'd been dead a day and a half. Of course they had to call the sheriff. There'll be an autopsy."

"Poor Mary," said Alice. But her mind was racing: on the west side of the ranch . . . not on the north side, where the rock art was, but in the foothills trailing west toward Sonora. Why would Ollie be out there?

Alice tried Mary's phone—busy. She left a message. It was impossible to find the right words. Alice had felt herself becoming fond of Ollie, and now she felt tears welling up, hot tears. The old rancher, gray hat, crisp jeans, gallant to her always. Whose Cassie had disappeared. Who loved his daughter. And who, for whatever reason, wanted those mysterious rock paintings to live and breathe on his ranch for a long, long time.

She tried Mary again. This time she picked up. "Mary! This is Alice. I'm so, so sorry."

Mary burst into tears. "I wasn't there! I should have found him! I don't know how long he lay there, Alice!"

"Oh, Mary." Alice slowly exhaled. "Do you know what happened?"

"We really don't," said Mary. The line was quiet for a moment. "He was on the ground over on the west side of the ranch below a big hill with a steep rockslide. His truck was over there. I guess he was climbing up onto the hill for some reason, and fell. The sheriff says it must have been a pretty bad fall."

"Sounds like there was nothing you could do, Mary. Did he try to call?"

Again the line was silent. "Nobody said anything about his phone," Mary said. "So I don't know if he did or not. I hadn't thought about that."

"Well," said Alice, "this isn't the time for me to ask about such things. We've lost Ollie, and Ollie was the one and only. There's nobody like him, anywhere, Mary, and I know these aren't the right words to say, because there aren't any."

"No," said Mary.

"Will you have a service?"

"Yes," said Mary. "They told me there has to be an autopsy. We had to call the sheriff and ambulance and all. So we won't have the—his body. I think the memorial service will be next Monday."

"I'll be there. Let me know if there's anything I can do. I'm so sorry, Mary."

She looked at Silla. "Camellia Diner, huh? I thought you were addicted to those yogurt and brewer's yeast shakes in the morning. With your new regime and all." The "new regime" was from the Healthy Barrel-Racing Women website. "What took you there?"

Silla did not blush (part of her Oklahoma mind-over-matter ethic). She did bridle, somewhat. "I had a breakfast date."

"Breakfast date?" Alice could hardly imagine having to talk to anyone before coffee. It seemed indecent.

"Yep. With Adam Files."

"Do I know him?"

"He's a constable in the Gillespie County Sheriff's Office. I knew Adam in high school. He's asked me out a couple of times."

"Ah." But what happened to the Handsome Young Cowboy? Alice wondered.

"We were supposed to meet at seven when he got off shift. But he got the call about Ollie early today and was out there with the EMS. Called me and said he'd be a little late because they had to get Ollie back to town and fill out all the papers."

"Did he tell you anything else?"

"He was wondering about Ollie's truck. It was parked in an odd sort of spot. Back where you couldn't really see it from the road. And no one knows what Ollie was doing climbing up there. Apparently Doyle said Ollie might have been trying to figure out a site for the wind power turbines."

"You're kidding."

"No, that's what one of the EMS guys said that Doyle said. Said maybe he was checking out the sight lines from the ranch house when he fell."

That did not sound like what Ollie had in mind for the ranch. But she supposed he might have wanted at least to know if there was some way—some placement of the turbines—to please Mary and Doyle and still protect his rock art.

"Silla," said Alice, "when did Doyle go out there?"

"He told EMS that he came out early this morning from New Braunfels because Mary was worried. Went to the house, drove all around the ranch, and then when the sun came up saw the vultures and then found Ollie and then called EMS. And EMS called the sheriff."

"And Ollie was—too hurt to call anyone for help?"

"Huh," said Silla. "Nobody said anything about that. I think he was busted up pretty bad, Alice."

Busted up too badly to use his new cell phone, Alice thought. If there was even cell phone coverage out there on the hill where he fell . . .

Alice thought of something else. "Where was Allen? He lives right there in that bunkhouse. Didn't he check on Ollie or wonder where he was?"

"He wasn't there. Doyle gave Adam the number and Adam called Allen on his cell. He said he's been up in Fort Worth visiting his relatives."

Oh, Ollie, thought Alice. Not what I wanted for you. Lying there dying, all by yourself, looking up at the sky.

Silla was talking.

"I'm sorry, can you say that again? I missed it," said Alice. "What did you say?"

"I told Adam you are Ollie's lawyer and said he could call if there were any questions about—anything."

"Okay."

Chapter Twelve

The Confessor

Silla left at noon, heading for a stable out past Henly to inspect a new horse. Alice's calendar was bare for the afternoon—no appointments—and she found herself at loose ends. Nothing in the office seemed appealing, nothing was enough of a puzzle to make her quit thinking of Ollie. Maybe stop by the library? Or not? She grabbed a jacket, locked the office, and found herself walking two sides of the courthouse square, then up Pecan Street to the front yard of Coffee Creek Old Style, the antique store that Cassie had opened up in her own old family home, and which her former partner was still running. Alice had been there before, looking at antiques, but that was before she ever heard of Ollie, or the Neys, or Cassie. The old house was large for Coffee Creek; the Neys had settled there early, in 1880, and had some money—enough to build a modified slightly Italianate limestone house. As Italianate as anyone could build in 1880 in Coffee Creek, meaning a few parapets and a square-roofed tower on the front corner.

Alice stood on the stone steps, read the historical marker, then walked through the open door, coveting the bronze dolphin doorknocker as she did so. The dolphin's patina was golden-green, and the metal looked solid and warm and inviting. But, she thought, who would use it at my house? She considered how silly it would be to knock before she let herself into her own house.

"The ineffable Ms. Greer!" boomed a voice. Out of the former dining room came Bryce Sheridan, tall, bony, spectacled, in a violet gingham shirt and impeccable trousers.

"Hi, Bryce!" said Alice. "How are you?"

"Ecstatic now that you're here. What can I do for you today?" said Bryce. "I have new goodies. Not just from my last trip to Scotland, but some fabulous stuff from a big old house out in Colorado City. Owner was the last of a bunch of daughters and she died at ninety-nine and the heirs had an estate sale. People are so silly, the stuff they give away."

"What did she have?" asked Alice.

"The best was a bedroom suite in pink. I am not kidding, pale pink wood with cream-colored woven cane on the headboard. The dressing table has a triple mirror and all the fittings. Chamois nail buffers! Powder puffs with a Dresden china doll head for the handle!"

"Pink? Pale pink sounds—Bryce, it sounds different from your usual polished mahogany."

"Yes. It was unique, very Mae West and thirties, and I couldn't resist it. But you can't see it because I sold it thirty minutes after I got back here."

"Wow," said Alice. "Well, what else do you have that's new? What did you bring back from Scotland?"

"This time I was thinking of music," said Bryce. "That was my theme as I rolled through Dumfries and Galloway in my little van. I brought back a couple of beautiful wooden music stands. Adjustable height. Want to see?" Alice did want to see. The two music stands gleamed in the former dining room, with leaf carving on the edges of the polished slab of mahogany that held the music. Each stand's pedestal ended in gracefully carved tripod feet. Alice inhaled deeply. She could smell—could she smell?—a trace of honey. Bryce looked at her and nodded. "Beeswax. You can see they have been kept in perfect condition."

Alice stroked the wood. It felt like satin, warm satin. She sniffed again. In her mind she could see her son, John, picking out a Scottish tune on his fiddle, with Ann's soprano voice laughing through the treble parts. Oh, he's a brisk and lovely lad, he's my love for aye . . . Didn't she need two music stands? Perhaps she did.

"Where did you find these?"

"Outside Edinburgh. Little village called Currie, otherwise totally undistinguished. Nice, don't you think?"

Alice found herself asking how much, and demurring at the price, and then saying, "Don't you need a new will, Bryce?"

He laughed. Then he sobered. "Yes, I do need a will. Let's just figure out a price and these are yours."

Alice was ecstatic. Again, she saw her children, heard the music—but that was not why she had come.

"Bryce," she said, "Ollie West was my client."

"Oh." Bryce's wide flexible mouth turned down. He stared at the middle distance. "I liked Ollie a lot. I'm sick about his fall. Sick. Heard about it down at the diner this morning. He told me about the lung cancer one time, back in the summer, so I've been mourning for him in advance, if you know what I mean. You know he was my landlord after Cassie's—after she disappeared? I got to see Ollie now and then when he came into town."

"I heard he used to stay here sometimes."

"Yes, he kept a little room in the back by the kitchen. I guess Mary will be my landlord—landlady? — now?"

"I believe so," said Alice.

"Hope she doesn't want to sell, or if she wants to sell, she wants to sell to me," said Bryce. "I got a little worried when Ollie told me he might someday think about selling the place. So used to being here, you know, and it makes me feel I'm still in touch with Cassie. But, whatever."

"Do you have time to sit for a second?" asked Alice.

"Sure. Come try out these two rocking chairs. Got them in Colorado City too. Don't you love those carved ram's-head armrests?"

"Goodness!" said Alice. "They are fierce." She tried her chair, rocking back and forth, fingering the mahogany ram's heads. "Bryce, tell me about Cassie Ney. What do you think happened to her?"

"I don't know," said Bryce. "I was surprised to hear she wanted Mexican flowers for the wedding. Did you hear about that? She hadn't mentioned it to me. But I knew she had planned to have a mariachi band so maybe that's right. Still, I did think she would have told me if she was going to drive down to the border for those paper flowers. We usually discussed what we were doing and how to split our time here at the store."

"But she didn't say anything to you?"

"No. Just like I told the police. She never said a word about it and I saw her the day before she left."

"Did she ever tell you what she thought about the wedding?"

"Sure, we talked. She wanted Mary to be happy. Mary was her only child, you know. She so wanted Mary to have a good marriage. That little wedding fling right after college was a disaster. He just wasn't the right guy."

"That's what I heard," said Alice. "But was Cassie pretty happy about Mary marrying Doyle?"

"That was complicated. Cassie could get along with just about anyone, but Mary sure made it hard on her. I don't know—was Mary maybe jealous of Cassie? Anyway, I still remember the day Mary waltzed in here. She pulled her hand out of her pocket and thrust it out. That ring sparkled—not big, just hers, you know. 'Darling!' said Cassie. 'Who?' And Mary said, 'Doyle Westenheim. I'm going to marry him. No matter what you say!' And she stuck that chin out. And Cassie—she said, 'Darling, I haven't met him, but if you love him, you know we will too. Tell! Who is he?'"

Bryce shifted in the rocking chair, fingering the carving. "I felt like the original fifth wheel—so awkward. Mary said, 'He's big and quiet and sexy and he loves me, and there's nothing you can do about it.' Cassie sort of laughed and said, 'I don't want to do anything about it, if you're happy! You're a grown woman! You sound like you know your own mind! I'd love to hear you talk about him. When will you bring him home?' Which I thought was typical Cassie—charming, trying to pour oil on the waters. But nothing seemed to mollify Mary. It was like she wanted to be mad. 'I may not bring him home until the day of the wedding,' she said. Well, Cassie gave up. She just sort of shut down. I know how she felt. She said, 'Well, blessings on you both. We'd love to meet him.' And Mary stood there a moment and then spun around and headed for the front door, keys in hand."

"Yikes. I hadn't heard that Mary was hard to get along with."

"Not saying she was. But as to Cassie, Mary seemed to have a burr under her saddle. Think it made Cassie really sad."

"Did Cassie ever tell you how she felt about Doyle?"

"Hmm." Bryce pursed his lips. "She was cautious about what she said about him. She said her aunt once told her, 'Honey, don't tell me anything bad about your husband. You'll forget you said it, but I never will.' But she also didn't rave about how wonderful Doyle was. She said she was a little concerned about how little Mary knew about his past. I think she was even considering getting a detective to check him out. But I never heard another word about it."

"A detective!" said Alice.

"She said something like that. She kind of laughed, and then we never talked about it again."

"So," said Alice, "what do you think happened to Cassie?"

"I think she's dead," said Bryce. "I was afraid she was dead the minute I heard she had disappeared. Cassandra Coffee Ney West was the most responsible human I ever knew—she thought she was responsible for helping the world stay tilted properly on its axis. She loved Ollie, loved Mary. She loved Coffee Creek. She loved this old house. She loved this shop! She exemplified that saying, 'Do the small things well.' She loved rooting around for antiques, mixing up homemade beeswax polish, and refurbishing dusty old wood pieces from ranches. She loved Cloud Ranch, loved weather, loved thunder, loved wildflowers. She loved this world, Alice! So when I heard she had disappeared—I knew she was dead. Cassie would never have left all these people, all these places she loved."

"And you two were partners here?"

"Yep. She called me up one day. I was up in Dallas—back then I had a high-end antique store in West End. Selling antiques at outrageous prices to rich Highland Park people. They paid, too. I went to Europe every year, sent back containers of stuff, sold it like hotcakes. And I was bored, bored, bored. I ran into Cassie at the big antiques show in Dallas and we had a drink and talked Coffee Creek gossip and I told her I was tired of the Metroplex scene and missed Coffee Creek. Never thought I would hear myself say that. Anyway, the next week I was sitting in the shop staring at yet another French armoire and Cassie called me up and said, 'Bryce, how about getting out of big D and coming back to Coffee Creek?' She had this idea that a real antiques store would work here, because so many people from Houston and Austin would come through. And she was absolutely right."

"So the partnership worked?"

"Yes. I had the shop experience, and she knew everyone here and also in Austin. As did I, of course. We did some marketing, and decided to concentrate on pioneer and Texas pieces. But we had to branch out because Texas pieces are hard to find."

"You mean, like the saying goes, hard on women and horses and also the family furniture?"

"Yes. I suspect if you were coming out to Texas in a wagon, in, say, 1853, at some point your most cherished piece of furniture became expendable. Maybe it happened when you were wrestling your wagon onto a flatbed ferry at a river crossing on the Sabine, maybe it happened when your wagon got stuck hub-deep on some muddy track in Falls County, maybe it happened when you hit a rock and the whole wagon overbalanced and splintered everything you had carefully carried across Texas to that point. So, we decided to look at Scotland. And Czechoslovakia and Germany. There are lots of Scots and Czechs and Germans around here, so antiques from those countries—that also worked for us. We had this notion that antiques from those places might remind Texans of a memory, a family story about what they left behind."

"And after Cassie? The business is still okay?"

"Well, it's just fine. Fine. But even if it weren't . . . Truth is, Alice, I don't need the money. The same weekend Cassie called me about coming back to Coffee Creek, it turned out I didn't have to work anymore anyway. My spinster auntie up in Salado died and left all her mineral interests out in New Mexico to me. And those old pump jacks out in New Mexico just go up, down, up, down, spitting out money. Oil company sends those royalty checks like clockwork every month. So I don't need to do this antique thing, and I've . . . got other stuff I do in my spare time, just to stay busy."

Alice quit rocking and stared at him. "Gonna tell me?" she asked.

Bryce glanced at her, then back at the middle distance. "Well, it's odd, Alice. If one day you wake up and realize you don't need money, after working all your life to feed yourself, you really have to think about what you want to do. And there were some things. First, I had to figure out what to do with that money. I manage my own, which you may think is crazy, but turns out I have some ability in that direction. What I do is odd but very conservative. Rare earths, gold coins, some other more conventional investments. It's fun, for some reason. And second, I really want to write. Now, Alice, you're the first person I've told this to, and if you tell anyone what I'm doing I'll have to kill you. Deal?"

"Deal!" said Alice. "I vant to live!"

"Right," said Bryce. "Me too. Well, here it is. I've always wanted to write historical novels, and that's what I'm doing. I'm bewitched, bothered, besotted. I'm more than halfway through my first one, Alice. I rented an office on Main Street here and I come in early and work until midmorning, writing. My cover story is that I'm compiling the history of German immigrants in central Texas. That gets me good plotlines at cocktail parties. Then about eleven I come down to the shop."

"And where is your novel set?" asked Alice. She had a solid guess already.

"Scotland."

"Aha! I knew it! So your antiques-buying trip to Scotland was just cover for your research?"

"You nailed it. Yes, I was soaking it up like a sponge. Every antique shop, every pub—and there were lots of pubs, Alice—every distillery, and there were lots of those, too—every graveyard—all grist for my mill, Alice, all grist for my mill!"

"So the antiques venture with Cassie was just a lark?"

"Oh, it was fun. Glorious fun, but just fun—not a pressure cooker like my Dallas shop. Cassie and I made some money but it was not so much about that. We had built something different. I still miss her, Alice. Everyone loved to come by the shop and visit with Cassie. She never told a secret and she sure heard a lot of them. And so did I. I just felt connected, being here with Cassie. People told her the most amazing stuff. I told her she was the confessor for half the people in Coffee Creek. She knew how to do it, Alice. Served hot cider in the winter, iced tea in the summer. Gingersnaps too. Homemade, naturally. And after the confessional, people would find themselves telling her just what they were dreaming of for the living room and we'd be off and running on a new commission.

"And it wasn't just her sales approach that made her fun to watch," Bryce went on. "The woman had an amazing eye for antiques. She could look at something and it would scream 'reproduction!' to her. Or she could walk in some shop—I have seen this happen—and walk straight up to a piece and stare at it and quietly buy it and get it out of the shop and it would turn out to be the long-lost footstool of Queen Mab or something like that. I called her Dead-Eye because she was so unerring. But you know what, she was like that about people too. Dealers that were trying to sell us a bill of goods . . . she always saw it right away. And she knew it, knew she could do that."

"She knew she knew?"

"Yes. It scared her. One time she told me she wished she couldn't look into people's faces and see so much. 'Too much information,' she told me. 'Sometimes it would just be easier to trust people than to explain that I've got that feeling about them.'"

"What about Doyle Westenheim, Mary's husband?"

"She was just quiet about him, like I said. But she did mention she was going to ask someone she knew to find out a little more."

"And do you think it was a detective?"

Bryce stopped for a moment. "You know, it wasn't really a detective. That's not what she said. She said someone who knew how to look at his records. But I never did know if she really did that or, if she did, what she found out. Why, is something wrong about Doyle?"

"Did you tell the police that too?"

"I can't remember. They really didn't ask me much, though. Just where I had been when she disappeared and had I heard from her. They did check our phone records, and our sales records, but I don't know if they found anything helpful."

"And you don't know Doyle?"

"Oh, of course I know him to speak to. That's just a figure of speech, since he doesn't speak to me. Strong silent type. I know Allen, though. He's come in a couple of times."

"For antiques?"

"No, he wanted to ask about some arrowheads. Said he'd come into a collection and wanted to sell them. When I asked him who put the collection together, he clammed up. Showed me a couple of really nice little points."

"What did you tell him?"

"Oh, I don't do arrowheads. Unless they're Scottish or Pictish and I need them for my book. I sent him to a guy up on the square in Mason who specializes in arrowheads, pottery, spearheads. But I did wonder where he got those arrowheads. He just had them loose in his pocket, not mounted or labeled or anything."

"Are they valuable at all?"

"Not as much as Allen hoped, but you can sell nice points for some money, likely for cash, and maybe skip the taxes. That's the reason people around here are so quiet about Indian ruins on their property, Alice. You'd be surprised how many Indian middens have been looted, or have disappeared, and how many cave shelters have been dug up all the way down to bedrock for the artifacts. They're all typically sold into the black market. Same thing all over the world." He looked at Alice. "So, you're concerned about Ollie? How he died?"

Alice looked back at him. "Yes. I am. Just the thought of Ollie lying out there, hurt, makes my stomach knot up. Besides, the entire scene seems wrong. Wasn't he too savvy, too smart about how to stay alive on a ranch, after all those years? I've climbed with him. Wasn't he too sure-footed to fall on his own ranch? I know he had lung cancer, but he was going to do things his way."

"Well, you mean he just jumped?"

"No! Not Ollie. I think he would have stared death in the face all the way to the end. And then he would have been looking for Cassie. Behind that curtain, or wherever it is we go."

"Oh, Alice. You are a hopeless romantic."

"I know." And she surprised him and herself by bursting into tears.

"Oh heavens," said Bryce. "Oh heavens, don't do that. Oh gosh, I'll have to put it in my book. Wait, let me get my notebook."

That made her laugh.

"And don't forget—you are now in possession of tremendously secret information. If you breathe one word of my Scottish bodice ripper to the waiting world, I'll have your scalp."

"Horrible mix of metaphors. Okay. I won't say a word."

"Now I'm going to call Mary," said Bryce. "What in the world can I say?" Alice shook her head. "I had no clue, myself."

She headed west on foot toward the sunset and the courthouse square, then took the southerly route around it, past the Camellia Diner, then west again on Live Oak toward her office, thinking about Allen and the arrowheads. So, he might be digging in the cave shelters out at Cloud Ranch, looking for some nice points to sell. No overhead, no taxes, pure profit. Nice work if you can get it. And Ollie knew about Allen's little side enterprise. Or at least Ollie knew about Allen's arrowhead collection in the bunkhouse, which, according to Ollie, Allen wasn't happy he knew about.

But Ollie didn't care, did he? In fact, he planned to let Allen stay on there. Maybe, thought Alice, maybe Ollie thought that if Allen had a life estate in the ranch, he would begin to view everything about the ranch as his to preserve, to care for, not to snitch. On the other hand, maybe when Allen heard about the cave conservancy, he panicked at the thought of losing his little stash of tax-free spending money when an outsider came in to run the ranch. And that is precisely what would have happened, Alice considered, under the power of attorney if Ollie had been incapacitated. Squinting her eyes, kicking up fallen leaves on the sidewalk by the courthouse, Alice tried to see through Allen's eyes: would he think he had a better shot at cleaning out the Cloud Ranch artifacts if he could prevent that transfer to the conservancy from taking effect? After a moment she thought not. Allen probably wanted stability, wanted Ollie to stay alive awhile longer. She'd seen some sort of grudging fondness there—on both sides.

Chapter Thirteen

Be the Jefe

On Friday morning Alice sat limp and relaxed in the big soft black chair, idly taking in the motley collection of gaudy record album covers that constituted wall art at her favorite Austin hair salon. Kiss, David Bowie, Dwight Yoakam, the Cars, all at the height of their fame. Sic transit gloria mundi, she thought, admiring the singers' younger, skinnier, more daring selves. Selves without the awareness of age, of flaw, of mortality. Then she thought, hey, not a great idea to think of passing glory, particularly while getting my own crowning glory cut.

Nigel turned the chair with his foot while his cool silver scissors went snick snick, quickly here, slowly there, around her head.

"Nigel, you're from Uvalde, right? Lots of big ranches around there?"

"Yup."

"But you didn't grow up on a ranch, right?"

"Nope. Went to school with kids who did though."

"Did you ever wish you had a ranch?"

"Of course. Childhood dream. I wanted to be the jefe—own as far as I could see, and farther. Have the big gate at the highway with my initials worked in wrought iron on top. Have that gate swing open every time I pushed the button in my truck. Be the man!"

"Was there any particular ranch you wanted?"

"You know, I'd have taken anything on some water. Nueces, Blanco, Frio, Guadalupe. Or a big creek. But there was one place I saw in high school that stuck with me. When you drove up, you saw a long limestone house under some enormous old live oaks. Creek running by. When you stood on the porch you could look south practically to the Rio Grande. And all you could smell out there was country. Mesquite, heat, crickets, water. Yes, I did some fantasizing on that porch."

"You knew the owners?"

"Yep. Went to school with their son. And he didn't really care about it. I couldn't believe it."

"What do you mean, didn't care about it?"

"Oh, he doesn't even live there now. He lives in a big house in northwest Austin. Just sorta 'visits' the ranch now and then. But if I owned a place like his I would be there. Except when I needed to come to Austin for a good hit of music and Mexican food. Now, take a look at the back in this mirror." Nigel always handed her the mirror and spun around the chair so she could see what he had done.

"Looks great. You did it a little shorter?"

"Yes. Gave it a little more movement." Nigel admired his handiwork in the big mirror, fluffing the back of Alice's hair. "But, Alice, that guy was a rarity. An anomaly. Growing up in that part of Texas, most people treated land like—like gold bullion. It was just so important. They fought over it, plotted over it—hey, next time you get highlights I'll tell you the story of my mother's friend who set out to get the ranch back for her family, after her husband lost it."

"Good story?"

"Well, it's a little bloody . . ."

They hugged. "Now you look great for your meeting," Nigel said.

Alice smiled to herself as she left the refreshingly funky, weirdly honest world of the salon and turned her truck toward downtown Austin. Funny how she always felt better, felt right with the world, after the burly, ever-smiling Nigel cut her hair. But now to business: she had a planning meeting at the state bar building west of the capitol, and particularly wanted to see if the committee member from New Braunfels had shown up.

Alice fought her way into the parking garage, blessed her stars as she spied and grabbed a spot, and headed for the elevator. "Ain't it awful?" she heard a voice say. Turning, she saw her buddy Endicott Ernst from New Braunfels.

"Endicott!" she said with relief. They crowded into the elevator together. "I hoped you'd be here. Yes, sometimes when I fight this traffic I wonder why it took me so long to decide to move out to Coffee Creek."

He nodded. "I feel the same way about New Braunfels. Why'd it take me so long?" Ernst had left a large San Antonio probate practice and hung out his shingle in much smaller New Braunfels—just up the interstate from San Antonio, but a different world.

The elevator doors opened onto a sea of suits, all milling around white-clothed banquet tables looking for their name tags and meeting materials.

"I need coffee! Where's the coffee?" said Ernst. They struggled through the suits to the coffee urns.

"Hey, can we sit for a second? I want to pick your brain a little," said Alice. Clutching their coffee, they made a beeline for two corner chairs, out of the traffic pattern.

"So what's up? You look bothered."

"I've got a client—had a client—who died out at his ranch last week."

"Was that Ollie West?"

"Yes, how did you know?"

"Made the New Braunfels Herald-Zeitung. Because of his daughter, Mary. She runs a gallery right downtown on the square. Sorry to hear about him, Alice."

"Thanks. I got really attached to Ollie. What I wanted to ask you is, did you by chance do the wills for Mary and her husband? She told me that she and Doyle had wills already. I thought maybe they got them done in New Braunfels."

"Yeah, I did, and it was a while back. Not very long after they got married. He's the one who called me, made the appointments, and so on. Only saw her twice, once to review the draft, and then when she came in to sign. He told me what they wanted. Pretty straightforward. They have no kids—well, you know all that."

"By straightforward you mean she leaves to him and he to her?"

"Pretty much right."

"Yeah, I understand." Alice smiled at Ernst, liking the delicacy of "pretty much right." He was telling her what she needed to know without telling her confidential client information she was not allowed to hear from him. "I'm not asking for any details," said Alice. "Just wanted to know sort of generally."

"Does she come in for everything from Ollie?"

"Well, there's a conservancy trust for the ranch because of some archeological sites." She figured the trust existed already, and the will was about to become public knowledge. "And some bequests. Mary gets income from the rest, for life."

"But she doesn't own the trust or the assets?" said Ernst.

Alice smiled back. "So, how did Doyle find you? Did you know him already?"

"No, we were at UT about the same time. Different fraternities though. Ran into him at a Longhorn alum function in New Braunfels."

"He's still working in San Antonio for a defense contractor?"

"Yeah, he has a job with an outfit that develops and sells security systems. It's on the north side of San Antonio, so that's not much of a commute for him. Very high-tech, secret kind of stuff. Or at least that was the impression he tried to give me."

"He does come across as someone who—who's very conscious of the impact he wants to make on people. Fair way to put it?"

Ernst looked up at her, then back at his coffee cup. "This is not a client confidence," he said. "This is just rank gossip. You asking about Doyle puts me in mind of a story I got from one of Doyle's old frat buddies at UT, after I did those wills. I run with this guy three days a week, in New Braunfels. Anyway, he said Doyle had quite a rep back in the day. He ran a poker game at the frat house."

"Poker?"

"Oh, come on, Alice. You're such a goody two-shoes. Half of us made our books and tuition that way, playing poker at the house."

"Huh. I had no clue."

"But apparently Doyle was pretty sharp—Doyle won a lot. Anyway, you may or may not remember, but the summer before Doyle's senior year, this other frat brother of Doyle's drowned, out in Lake Travis. He and Doyle were out there at night, after one of those big Greek parties at Windy Point. Somehow they capsized their sailboat and Doyle made it in but the other guy didn't."

"Yikes," said Alice. "What happened to the other guy?"

"Doyle said he didn't know. He said the guy was pretty drunk and fell off, and Doyle tried to dive for him but the water was too murky and of course it was dark, too. Doyle came back to the dock and tried to get help but they didn't find the guy until the next day."

Ernst looked at Alice. Alice looked back at Ernst. "Kind of thing could happen to anyone," said Ernst.

"I guess so," said Alice. But she was thinking of Mary.

"There was an inquest, case closed, no hassle for Doyle. But my running buddy says there was idle scuttlebutt that the kid who fell off the boat had been winning big too. So some people wondered if they had a system cooked up. None of that made the paper, of course. And, Alice, there's not a shred of evidence to back that up. Not even sure I should have mentioned it."

"Do you know the name of the young man who died?"

"Gotta look back in my memory bank for that, Alice. Or better, call my buddy. Hey, the chair is signaling us. We'd better go plan this seminar. Look, I just wanted to mention that old tale because . . . you know how some clients, you just love 'em, and some clients, you're real glad you got the job done and it's over?"

"Yes," said Alice. "I know exactly."

"Well, he can be very pleasant, and yet ol' Doyle seemed kind of all about ol' Doyle to me."

"Mmm."

During the planning meeting, Alice tried to pay attention. But her mind kept running in a circle. The income Mary got from what Ollie had passed along to her via his will was generous. But Mary could not pass along either the ranch or the corpus of the testamentary trust that kicked in when Ollie died. Alice had done what Ollie had wanted, and the effect was to put the assets where Doyle could not get them, whether anything happened to Mary or not. Even if her will left everything to Doyle, he would not get the ranch or the bulk of the securities.

Ernst's frat-house poker story might or might not have legs. Plenty of kids got drunk at Lake Travis and occasionally one of them drowned. Moonlit night, lots of laughter, lots of beer, pretty girls, pretty boys, the sailboat far from shore, rocking in the water . . . Anything could happen. Ernst had said there was not a shred of evidence that Doyle had done anything wrong.

She furtively checked her phone, holding it below the mahogany conference table. There was an email from Mary. "We're going to have Ollie's memorial service on Monday," she had written. "The coroner still has him, but I want to go ahead with the service. It will be at Coffee Creek Methodist at eleven." Alice quickly wrote back that of course she would come. She expected most of Coffee Creek probably would as well.

Alice, pay attention! she ordered herself. She tried to listen to the proposed continuing legal education courses, suggested a couple of topics, doodled on her notepad. Her eyes crossed with boredom. If she could just quietly disappear from the room, rematerialize in the front seat of her truck in the parking garage, and head out of Austin and back to Coffee Creek . . .

Hallelujah. The meeting ended. Alice smiled at everyone and dashed for the door. Ernst caught her at the elevator. "I think I remember that guy's name," he said. "First name was Howie, I remember that. So maybe it was really Howard. I'll check with my buddy on the rest."

"Thanks."

Chapter Fourteen

Spirits of the Old Highland Men

After what seemed weeks of Indian summer, Monday finally brought fall to the Hill Country: brilliant blue sky, a snap of chill in the morning, and cedar elm leaves, turned overnight to solid gold, fluttering to the ground. Ollie would have loved it, thought Alice, heading down the creek road to town.

The Methodist church parking lot was packed. Alice squeezed into the next-to-last pew, along with Silla and Miranda. Alice looked at Silla. She was wearing her new Goodson Kells boots. A little rodeo for a funeral, but then . . . Alice leaned toward Silla. "The boots?" she whispered.

Silla looked down at the black-and-white boots, the red stitching. "For Ollie. He believed in my barrel racing."

Alice then surveyed Miranda: bright fuchsia suit, black alligator heels, black velvet hat. And a handkerchief clenched in her hand. The banker's eyes were pink. "I loved that man," Miranda whispered, staring straight ahead.

Alice sat dry-eyed, toying with the program for Ollie's service. The Men's Wild Game Committee members were listed as honorary pallbearers. Alice glanced around the sanctuary. Yes, the committee members were also serving as ushers. And their faces were grim. They were honoring one of their own: Ollie, the archetypal men's committee member; Ollie, who always showed up for meetings, driving up in the dusty ranch truck all the way from Cloud Ranch; Ollie, who knew how to smoke venison and make venison sausage and who quietly delivered coolers-full to that Hill County orphanage every December; Ollie, who could with a single terse sentence persuade the Men's Wild Game Committee to donate more funds to the food pantry or to buy backpacks for the poor kids at the elementary school. Ollie, with his gray hat, pressed jeans, pressed chambray shirt, tobacco-stained fingers. Ollie, with the unblinking look, the hard but warm handshake. Ollie, who never said he'd be there but didn't show up, who never ducked the tough task when people asked him to do it, who didn't advertise his heartaches and disappointments, or his likes and dislikes. Now all his friends were here, helping people to their seats, honoring Ollie.

The organist shifted from lugubrious to more lugubrious. Family members filed in from the right front entrance to the sanctuary and took their places in the front pew. Mary looked pale but stood with head high, next to Doyle. They weren't touching. Hmm, thought Alice. Not holding hands. I would have been holding hands, with Jordie, I would. The only other relatives appeared to be Ollie's frail bent auntie from Lubbock, white hair swept up to her crown, leaning on her cane with one hand, and with the other holding the arm of a younger woman who Alice took to be her daughter.

Sitting on the hard pew, Alice's mind returned to the picture of Ollie lying on the hard dusty ground, staring far, far away at the hard blue sky—dying alone. And now he lay in a refrigerator drawer at the coroner's lab, subjected to who knew what indignities (Alice here drew a mental curtain across the picture). Not what I had in mind for you, Ollie. But, honestly, lung cancer, or the end game of lung cancer, was not what she wished for him either. Ollie, what were you thinking as you lay there? wondered Alice. What would you tell me, if I could have come to you, could have leaned over and listened? What would you want me to do?

The service began. Alice, still dry-eyed, listened to the excerpts from Psalms, listened to the reading from Romans, listened to a short homily. Her eyes stayed on Mary's head. She's not leaning on Doyle, thought Alice. Not looking at him. And he's not looking at her.

The pastor nodded to one of the committee members, who walked up to the podium. He stumbled a bit over the beginning of his speech, but then hit his stride. "Ollie West is the kind of man we all wanted to be," he said. "Ollie could be counted on. Ollie had wisdom. If he thought your idea was unwise, he could let you know that—in private or in public—in a way that left you some pride. And he did it in about two words. No harangues. That man had several loves. One was his wife, Cassie. One was his daughter, Mary. One was his piece of dirt, out there by Faison. But a fourth love was secret—doing acts of secret kindness. And that's what you all may not know about. Did you know that Ollie paid college tuition for a young man at the Hill County orphanage? He did, and never told a soul. I only learned that from the director of the orphanage, yesterday. Did you know that Ollie was the go-to man for the social service committee at the food pantry when some poor guy in Coffee Creek came for help to get a car repaired so he could get to work? I didn't know that, and only learned it from the food pantry folks yesterday. Who knows what else he did? And he didn't want it told. So that was his fourth love, to try to make something good happen for some person—often some person he had never laid eyes on—because of a secret kindness he had done. I believe Ollie took joy from that. You know and I know," he concluded, "that we could use a lot more folks like Ollie. But they don't come along too often. Ollie was the kind of man we all want to be." And with those plain words he nodded at Mary, nodded at the minister, and walked back down to his pew.

Alice sat as still as a stone, as still as a hill, barely breathing, thinking of Ollie. Into the whispery silence abruptly broke the skirl of pipes. A piper slowly walked out of the same door at the front of the sanctuary that Mary had used.

Kilted, erect, in ruffled white shirt and sporran, black ribbons on his pipes, he stood before the altar and piped the pallbearers to the front, where they all stood, hands folded, facing the congregation. The tune was not "Amazing Grace," staple of funerals. Instead, it was "Scotland the Brave." Alice had learned the words for Jordie. "There where the hills are sleeping, Now feel the blood a-leaping, High as the spirits of the old Highland men. . ." Oh, thought Alice, oh, Jordie, Jordie, Jordie. She could see a different piper now, under the great dome of Edinburgh's St. Giles' Cathedral, marching with measured tread down the aisle, herself standing and then following behind the piper with John and Ann, and Gran, Jordie's mum, and Jordie's brother and sister. There, as here, they had no casket. Nothing she could touch, nothing to lay a flag on, nothing to lay a flower on. Just—no Jordie. Nothing but the bagpiper's notes, flying like streamers, flying like banners, red, gold, green, blue, up into the height of the cathedral, unfurling around the stone columns, like joy on a summer day. All the joy that was Jordie! And then the notes died away, there. But were still playing, here.

Alice's face was wet. She groped blindly for her purse, face set, and felt Silla push something into her hand. She mopped, then looked. Pink bandana. "Thank you," she whispered. Silla hugged her.

Mary and Doyle walked down the aisle, behind the bagpiper, with the auntie and her daughter close behind. Alice caught a glimpse of Mary's closed, pretty face, eyes down, following the piper.

The congregation shuffled, began to move out of the pews. "Are you going to Mary's?" asked Silla.

"Thought I would," Alice said. "It's not that long a drive to New Braunfels. Want to come?"

"No, I'll watch the office," Silla said. "I've got a bunch of stuff to finish for you anyway. But please tell her I'm thinking about her."

That's a pretty sentimental speech for Silla, Alice mused.

"I loved that man," Silla said suddenly. "He made me feel—I dunno, like I could cut five seconds off my barrel-racing time the next time out of the gate! He made me feel—like I could beat that Ginnylou Hammer from Blanco at the next rodeo! He made me feel like he thought I was great!"

"Yup," said Miranda. "Ollie could make you feel pretty darn good without saying a thing. Something about the way he crinkled his eyes at you."

"Are you coming to New Braunfels?" Alice asked Miranda.

"No, it's my day to close up at the bank. Tell Mary I'll come visit her this next week."

"Okay," said Alice. "Okay, I'm off." In the crowd ahead of her she saw

Ilka Mayer, white-haired, straight-backed, holding court. Alice adored Ilka. She had handled four closings for Ilka, who at seventy-five still bought, leased, developed, and sold real estate in New Braunfels and Coffee Creek. Today she was wearing—it appeared to Alice at this distance—an honest-to-god leopard-skin pillbox hat. And black elbow-length leather gloves. Alice angled her shoulders and slid through the crowd.

"Ilka!"

"Alice, darling."

"Are you coming to Mary's?"

"No," said Ilka. "I will stop by later. Today's too much of a casserole deal. But you, young Alice"—she poked Alice in the waist—"you come see me. Got some real estate business to talk with you. Give me a call."

"Yes'm. I will."

Chapter Fifteen

A Sense of Puzzles

Alice carefully parked her truck next to the silver-green spikes of a yucca, its pink flowers nodding in the fall breeze, just past the Westenheim driveway in New Braunfels. Mary and Doyle's stone bungalow sat downtown, one block off the Comal River. Pretty chic, Alice thought to herself. Or maybe "chic" is not what the good burghers of New Braunfels call their neighborhoods. Must ask Ilka. The street was lined with post-funeral traffic, come to pay respects to Ollie's only daughter. Alice could smell what her Homer- and Shakespeare-loving anthropologist friend termed the "funeral baked meats" wafting through the air as several people moved purposefully toward Mary's house, carrying their offerings. She evaded the yucca and headed up the sidewalk, following a leather-jacketed man carrying what smelled like barbecued brisket in a huge pan covered with foil. The woman trotting ahead of him carried a basket. Alice thought she could smell homemade yeast rolls. She herself had a small offering—homemade macaroni and cheese, with jalapeños she had smoked herself. Alice stepped onto the porch, which opened directly into the living room.

She walked to the kitchen, clutching her macaroni and cheese, and looked for a spot on the counter, already crammed with casseroles, plates, bottles of wine.

"Hey, I'm Janet Levine, Mary's friend from the gallery," said a tall dark-haired woman, straightening up from the refrigerator.

"Alice Greer, from Coffee Creek. I'm Ollie's lawyer," said Alice.

"Mary wants to say hi," said Janet Levine. "She told me to tell you that. She's in the dining room, through that archway."

"That's macaroni and cheese," said Alice, "and don't worry about the pan."

"Right. Thanks," smiled Levine. "That's a help."

"I don't know why we always want to bring food," said Alice.

"Neither do I, but we do," said Levine. "It's about all we can do, so there you have it."

Alice peered into the dining room, but Mary was barely visible behind the well-wishers. She wandered back to the living room, wanting another visit with the pictures. Again, thinking about Mary, Alice felt a sense of puzzles, of hallways with mysterious doors at the end. Looking back down the hall she glimpsed a study with bookshelves. She walked back, curious. An enormous partner's desk took up part of the floor. Against the wall, polished gun barrels gleamed through the glass of a tall gun cabinet.

"My office," said a voice behind her. Alice turned. Doyle Westenheim, smiling a small smile. The smile did not quite reach his eyes. He sure isn't offering to show me his guns, is he? thought Alice.

"Quite a collection," she said.

He stood sideways inside the door, one arm slightly extended down the hall, indicating the way out of his office. "Mary is the other way," he said. "Down the hall in the dining room."

Well, at least he didn't frog-march me down there, thought Alice, glancing back at the gun cabinet. My, he was well armed. Reminded her of what Ilka once said about Jeff Davis County. "Smaller than Israel but better armed."

Alice waited in line in the dining room. She recognized the older couple from Coffee Creek talking to Mary. "Damn shame about Ollie," said the man. "Most sure-footed guy I knew. In every way! Never knew him to fall, trip, wreck the truck, whatever. Ollie never put a boot wrong. In anything!"

"Oh, honey," said the woman. "You remember when he and Cassie had that dance at the Beer Barn for their anniversary? Years ago."

"Oh, yeah. You made me wear my bolo."

"Remember when Cassie got us all doing the Cotton-Eyed Joe?"

"I do."

"Well, that's how I want to remember Ollie. Dancing up a storm with his Cassie." She hugged Mary and they left.

Now it was Alice's turn. She could find no words about Ollie without tearing up, and just hugged Mary, saying she would see her Tuesday morning. Alice retraced her steps through the living room, stopping at each picture. Bookshelves ran along two sides, below the windows. The bottom shelf held some big albums, with orange longhorns on the spines. University of Texas yearbooks. With a guilty twinge in her gut, Alice sidled over and pulled out a yearbook. She looked up the Ws in the index, found Doyle's name, and flipped to page 796. There he was, with his fraternity brothers. Amid the smiling brothers he stood: serious face, big shoulders, same unblinking stare. Alice looked at the caption, checking the names. Doyle Westenheim . . . there was a Randall. Howard Randall. Could that be Endicott's Howie? This yearbook listed Doyle as a junior. Was there a later yearbook? She put the first volume back and tugged out the next one, a year later. Same procedure: she checked for Westenheim in the index, found the fraternity pictures. No Howard Randall. She then checked the index for the name Randall. Howard Randall was definitely missing. Maybe he flunked out. But maybe he had drowned in Lake Travis. Those are pearls that were his eyes. Wait, that face seemed familiar. Sandy hair, hollow cheeks. She stared at the photo, and then at the caption. Jeffrey Treacher. How about that. Mr. Treacher and Mr. Westenheim. Same fraternity. She closed the yearbook, reshelved it, and straightened up, looking at the shelves.

"Need anything?"

She turned her head. "Oh, hi, Doyle. No, just looking at your books. Always fun to see those." She smiled. "See you tomorrow."

Didn't mention Treacher to him, did I, she thought, walking back to the truck. I need a while to think about this. Doyle and Treacher have known each other for all these years. Well, so? UT's a huge campus. So you get out of there knowing a lot of people. Especially if you're in a fraternity. So—so what?

Yes, but still, thought Alice, Doyle failed to mention to her that his old fraternity brother Treacher was going to call her about the wind power lease. And Treacher didn't mention when he called that his old fraternity brother Doyle was Ollie's son-in-law. And of course, Mary and Doyle didn't meet until much later. Or was that so? Did Mary know about Treacher or not? Alice headed out of New Braunfels, looking for the loop that led back to Purgatory Road, then Wimberley, then Coffee Creek, then home.

Chapter Sixteen

In His Right Mind

On Tuesday morning, Alice drank three cups of coffee before she even got to the office. She'd called Allen and Mary last Friday to set up the meeting, and Mary was bringing Doyle. Silla put everyone in the conference room, where Alice kept a big whiteboard where she could diagram trusts and wills for her clients.

Alice watched from the window by her desk as her three guests arrived in three cars. Mary pulled up in her little Morris, Doyle in a black SUV with "US Security" in a black and green logo on the side, and Allen in a shiny, shiny pickup. No aged Bronco. Silla, glancing out the window, said to Alice, "Hey! Look who's already spending the money! Or maybe that's the last of what he got from Leanne."

Once they got inside, Doyle was poker-faced. He pulled out a chair for Mary and sat next to her, his arm curved protectively around her shoulders. Allen made a point of sitting at the end of the conference table, several empty seats away from Doyle and Mary. He looked defiant but did finally remove his cowboy hat. Finally he said a tentative hello. Mary smiled; Doyle ignored him.

Silla offered coffee. No one accepted. Bad sign, thought Alice. She took a deep breath and smiled her best "sympathy in the face of this terrible loss but we must go on" smile. "Thank you for coming, especially at a time when I know all of you are still dealing with Ollie's death," she said. "I know this is not easy. You each have sets of the relevant documents before you. Let's go chronologically. Let me just run through the dispositions that Ollie made back last August. At that time, he had several goals. He knows—knew—Mary loves the ranch, so one goal was to keep the ranch intact, but without burdening Mary financially or operationally with having to run the place. Another was to be sure Mary could live at the ranch all her life, if she wanted. Another was to be sure Allen could live at the bunkhouse, as well." She glanced at the three faces. Allen looked surprised but pleased. Doyle looked surprised and displeased. Mary just looked anxious.

Alice went on. "Now as you may know, Ollie felt very strongly that the rock art on the north ridge should be protected. He asked the Rock Art Conservancy to take a look, and that organization agreed that the cave paintings at Cloud Ranch are, without doubt, archeological treasures. That figured strongly in the arrangements Ollie made."

She pointed to the sets of documents placed before each of them. "Ollie essentially put his property in two pots back in August, by his plan of trust. In one pot, he put the ranch, subject to the two life estates I mentioned, and enough money to fund protection of the caves and rock art. In the other pot, he put income-producing property, including brokerage accounts." She held up her copy of the trust document. "That's the first document in your set."

"What do you mean?" interrupted Doyle. "What do you mean, he put the ranch in a trust?"

"It's a common device. Ollie created a trust holding certain property. While he was alive, he was a beneficiary of the income it produced, and also the primary trustee. In other words, he ran the trust for his own benefit at that time. Also, he made sure that upon his death, Mary would have a life estate in the ranch, allowing her to live there with her spouse. And Allen also now has a life estate permitting him to live in the bunkhouse, if he wishes. Ollie also wanted the other pot of assets—retirement accounts and securities accounts and cash—to be available as income for Mary during her lifetime. He could have changed his mind about the trust during his lifetime, but he did not make any changes before he died. At the same time, he signed a new will." She held it up. "Second document in your set."

Three faces stared at her. "You mean I don't have to leave just because Ollie is dead?" said Allen.

"That's right," said Alice, "he wanted you to be able to stay on, Allen. I will have to say, though, if you or Mary die, that is the end of your life estate. It does not extend to your spouses after you die. However, Mary, if you have children, they too could still stay in the ranch house."

Mary looked at her lap. Alice knew that Mary and Doyle couldn't have children. Alice glanced at Doyle, but he was staring at the documents on the table.

"All three of you know Ollie was a generous man. He has also directed that fifteen thousand dollars go to the Men's Wild Game Committee, and that another fifteen thousand dollars go to the children's home in Hill County. He wanted Mary to have all of his and Cassie's personal effects, including china, crystal, jewelry, clothes, the art and furniture at the ranch house, and the horses. Allen, he directed that you should have his Ford ranch truck in addition to the right to live in the bunkhouse. Doyle, he left you the collection of antique maps of Texas in his office, and his guns. Everything else, he left in trust with the income to go to Mary during her life—everything but what was already in what I will call the rock art trust."

"I would trade it all just to get him back," Mary said quietly.

"Well, wait a minute," said Doyle. "You mean Mary can live out there, but she can't sell the ranch? Or manage the ranch? Or lease the ranch?"

"Right," Alice said.

"But who is making decisions about the ranch, then?" demanded Doyle.

"The Rock Art Conservancy will manage the ranch so that the trust corpus can be preserved. They are supposed to allow research and visitors to the rock art, to the extent that can be done without harming the rock art."

"This can't be," said Doyle, voice tight. "This can't be. You can't tell me that someone else besides us is making decisions about the ranch. Who are these rock art people? Bunch of tree huggers? What do they know about ranching?"

"But Doyle," said Mary, tugging softly at his sleeve, "it's what Dad wanted. And we can be out there whenever we want."

"The rock art trust agreement includes an operating agreement to handle details like that, Doyle," said Alice. "That's Exhibit A to the trust. Mary, you are free to keep horses and pets out there, live there, enjoy the entire ranch, subject to the protection for the rock art. The operating agreement requires consultation on a number of items between the conservancy people and Mary, to work out the details. They'll be in touch with you, Mary."

Mary nodded.

"Mary, everything else—other real estate, Ollie's cash and securities accounts at Madrone Bank—is inventoried at about eight million dollars." Mary looked up in surprise. "Yes, it's a good bit. That includes not only everything your dad put away but also your mother's money. She was a pretty shrewd investor, it seems. That account has grown a good bit since her death." (Not really accurate, thought Alice, since who knows when she died, but saying "since she was presumed dead" sounded so cold.) "All of that, at Ollie's death, became irrevocably part of the trust under his August plan of trust, with you as the beneficiary. Like I said, that trust will pay you income all your life. At your death, if there's anything left, and of course unless you have children, the corpus of that trust will go to the children's home in Hill County."

"I . . . don't . . . get . . . it," said Doyle. He leaned forward, staring at Alice. There was no humor, no flexibility, in his voice. "You mean to tell me Ollie's signed a new will that means Mary can't even manage her own parents' money?"

"Ollie wanted to put all the liquid assets into a trust where Mary would get all the income. That part of the trust became permanent at his death. She can certainly consult with the trustee, which is Madrone Bank, about any details," said Alice. "He signed the new will at the same time."

"Doesn't he think his own daughter has good sense?" said Doyle. "This is ridiculous!"

"Mary's father's expressed intent was for Mary to have income without having to worry about it. He certainly thought a great deal of her capabilities.

In fact, Mary, he said he wanted you to be able to start your own business, such as your own gallery, if you felt like it, and the trust expressly addresses additional expenditures for that."

"Who's the executor under this new will?" demanded Doyle. He seemed totally focused on the will, ignoring the trust mechanism.

"Madrone Bank," said Alice.

Doyle exploded. "You've gotta be kidding. I'm not letting some lamebrain cookie-baking banker tell me how to run things at Cloud Ranch! You're not gonna probate that will. Obviously Ollie was off his rocker from chemo or radiation or something. I can't believe he would've treated Mary in such a humiliating way if he was in his right mind! This is the will we're going to probate!" He slapped a blue-foldered document on the table. "I got this out of the safe at the ranch. This is the will your dad signed twenty years ago, Mary. Everything goes to you in this will. And this is what we are going to probate. Your dad was apparently a complete fruitcake when he signed this other one," Doyle said. "And any other documents he signed!"

"Doyle, are you saying you don't believe Mr. West had sufficient capacity in August when he signed the new will and created the trust?"

"Ollie West in his right mind would never have signed the ranch over to a bunch of tree huggers. He would never have deprived Mary of all her rights in that ranch."

"But Doyle, I like the way he did this," said Mary. "I think he was trying to take care of me, and I like that he's letting Allen stay in the bunkhouse."

"That's a decision you and you only should make," said Doyle. "You can let Allen stay on the ranch. But it should be your decision, as the owner. We're going to challenge this will. I don't believe the man was competent."

"Yet I believe all three of you cashed the gift checks he made out to you last August when he created the trust, at the same time he executed the will," Alice said. Looking far calmer than she felt, she pulled copies of the three cashed ten-thousand-dollar checks out of her folder. They were drawn on the "Ollie West Trust Account." The check to Doyle Westenheim bore Ollie's large angular signature. The endorsement on the back read, "Deposit only. Doyle Westenheim."

"That's not my signature!" Doyle barked.

"Honey, don't you remember? I called you at the office and told you Dad had given us each a big gift check and you told me to deposit it right away."

Doyle's face reddened. "You . . ." But he said nothing more. Uh-oh, Alice thought. He stood up, still staring at Alice; he picked up his hat and the old will, still staring at Alice; said, "Come on, Mary," without looking at his wife; and strode to the door. Mary took a moment to get up, looking first at Doyle, then at Alice, then at Allen; then, without a word, she picked up her bag and slid past Doyle, who stood in the conference room door. Alice saw that the two had left all the other documents on the table.

Blocking the doorway, Doyle, red-faced, said, "I'm telling you one more time. What you're doing is wrong. You will not file this will for probate."

Alice cleared her throat. How had her meeting spun out of control this way? "Doyle, Ollie West is my client. I am acting pursuant to his instructions. The August will reflects his intentions. I'm filing it for probate this week pursuant to state law requiring the filing of the will."

Doyle turned without a word and walked out the door. She saw him out the window, walking to his black SUV, head up. Mary hurried behind, trying to catch up, talking, her face turned toward him. Finally she tugged his sleeve. He turned and looked at her a long moment, then looked down the street, turned, got into the SUV, and backed out into the street, never saying a word. Mary stood still on the sidewalk in front of the office, watching him leave. When she turned, her face was a mask, white and still. She slowly climbed into her own little car and backed into the street—going the other way.

Alice glanced at Allen, who still sat at the conference table, spinning his hat. "Guess I'll go now," he said. "Thanks." He walked out too.

Alice turned to Silla and raised her eyebrows.

Silla raised hers back. "Nice."

"Need something to take the bad taste out of my mouth," said Alice.

"Sour? Bitter?" said Silla, picking up the three stacks of paper.

Alice considered. "Just bad. Bad." Gotta get out of here, she thought. Might be a good time to talk to Ilka. Clear my mind.

Chapter Seventeen

Like Hector

Later on that Tuesday afternoon, Alice pulled between limestone pillars into Ilka's gravel drive on the west side of New Braunfels. The driveway was invisible under a sea of leaves. She drove under enormous ancient live oaks in the general direction of Ilka's big stone house, marveling at the sinuous strength of those horizontal branches.

Ilka was standing on the bottom step of the front porch, one hand leaning on a cane, the other waving wildly at the bushes in front of the house. She was obviously reading the riot act to an old man in a straw hat holding giant loppers. Both ignored Alice as she walked up.

"I can't stand those crepe myrtles whacked up that way! It's mutilation!" Ilka thumped the cane for emphasis. "Mutilation!" Startled by the thump, a bantam chicken raced out from the bushes by the porch and zigzagged between Ilka and the old man. "And another thing! Don't trim the bushes ROUND! God didn't grow 'em ROUND! You got to maintain their natural SHAPE!"

Ilka wheeled, leaning on the cane. Different voice. Husky. "Hello, darling." She extended a cheek for Alice to kiss. She smelled like . . . Alice knew she would think of it in a moment. Something from long ago. Sophisticated. "Come inside for tea."

Up the steps she stomped. Alice followed. Inside, the big entrance hall stood open to the porch. The air was cool. Alice inhaled potpourri of old house, old linen, old books, sunshine in a clean old kitchen.

The tea table was laid. Ilka's round oak table was centered in front of the open double doors. "I put it here so I could watch Raymond," said Ilka. "Damned if he doesn't try to prune my bushes like some sort of garden for a 1950s issue of Southern Garden, every single fall. I can't stand it. Sit here, honey." She stomped off toward the kitchen.

Alice, not sitting as instructed, peeked into each of the rooms opening off the hall. To the east, a living room with bright modern oil paintings and old, old furniture. To the west, a dining room with heavy mahogany table, heavy buffet, sparkling crystal in the glass-front cabinet.

She wanted to see the kitchen. The solid oak swinging door was ajar, showing gray and yellow linoleum shining in the sun. She inched in. White wood cabinets and old wooden windows looking south. A stove on legs—from the 1930s, it appeared.

Ilka was pouring boiling water into a silver teapot on a silver tray with a silver tea strainer. The tray held little ivory napkins, hemstitched and bearing the initials "I. M." "Honey, you carry this tray," ordered Ilka. "I'll bring our coffee cake. Or teacake, since it's teatime." Carrying the tray, Alice remembered: Bellodgia, by Caron. That's the perfume Ilka was wearing. Elegant, like the upstairs of a wonderful old house, with the faint scent of sweet William.

They settled at the tea table. Ilka poured. Bone china, thin and old, the glaze crazed. Like Ilka's face and hands, thought Alice. The cake stand held something Alice had never seen—a pale smooth yeasty-smelling cake with thin cinnamon topping, only two inches tall. "Kuchen," said Ilka with satisfaction. "My great-grandmother's recipe—Big Oma made it every Saturday, let it rise, and baked it early Sunday." She cut a slice for Alice.

"Oh, goodness, Ilka," said Alice. "What is that?" The yeast dough, ivory and fragrant, left a mysterious fragrance in the air.

"Cardamom," said Ilka. "So, you like?"

"May I have Big Oma's recipe?" said Alice.

"Of course, honey," said Ilka. "But you'll have to copy it out—my arthritis is acting up."

Alice drank tea and looked out the doors, down the drive. The bantam was pecking by the porch. Lop, lop, sang Raymond's loppers.

"I really do have some business to talk with you." Ilka owned several parcels in downtown New Braunfels. She launched into an explanation of why she wanted to buy a run-down service station. Alice's brow furrowed. "No, don't worry. Tanks are gone. Dirt's all cleaned up. It's an old stone building, great character. I want to develop it for retail, then lease it."

Alice nodded, then glanced sideways at Ilka, who was grinning at her, shaking her head.

"What's worrying you, honey?" said Ilka. "I sense a disturbance in the force."

Alice had not quite formulated an opening sentence when Ilka leaned toward her.

"Hey," said Ilka, "I'm a real estate person. I read faces, shoulders, heads and arms. I know when someone likes a property, wants the property, is dying to accept an offer on the property, and so on. Your shoulders are hunched and your brows are pinched. What's up?"

"Humph," said Alice. "I hate to be transparent. I need a poker face in my business! For dealing with crazy clients and obstreperous lawyers and judges with calcified brains—or calcified hearts!"

"That's foolish and shortsighted. So many lawyers follow that poker-face folderol. Do they teach you that in law school?"

"Yes, actually," Alice admitted, remembering moot court. ("Miss MacDonald! When you do not have the floor, do not make faces at the arguments advanced by opposing counsel!")

"What a waste," said Ilka. "I'm disgusted with the entire approach. You think I have a poker face? No ma'am. Wouldn't think of it. But don't let your face just react to a situation. Honey, what you have to do is use your face. Use your face to get done what you want to do! You've got to be thinking how you use that face!"

"Tell me what you mean."

"Say I have a broker bringing me an offer on my client's ranch. Broker has a buyer from Houston. Offer is too low. I have choices. I could look disappointed, which of course I am. Instead I want to look interested, focused on finding the chink, the improvement. And helping the broker to want to improve the offer. I tilt my head. I crinkle my eyes and look at the broker. 'I'll take that offer to my people if you want me to,' I say. 'But you'd be better to improve that offer before we do. Let's talk about that. Come sit down and let's consider.'"

"Huh," said Alice. "How do you actually remember to do that, though? I feel like the first thing I think is going to show up right on my face."

"Here's what I always do," said Ilka. "Works like a charm. Before I talk to this person, before we even are standing in the same room, I plan. I think, where do I want to wind up with them? Then I think what my face needs to do to get there. Then and only then do I start talking to them. But you know, honey"—Ilka leaned back in her chair and squinted at Alice—"you're gonna need a different strategy, because I don't think you have the facial self-control I do."

"So what do I do?" demanded Alice.

Ilka tilted her head, and stared dispassionately at Alice. "Hmm." She tilted her head the other way. "Okay. Here it is. You have these good eyes. I mean, they are big and brown. Quit thinking about your mouth, and think only about your eyes when you are dealing with someone tough. Get those eye muscles working! Think only of where you want that horse to go, and guide him with your eyes!" She nodded, sure she was right.

What? Alice thought. How do I do that?

Ilka grinned again. "I can tell by looking that you don't believe me. You don't think you can manage folks just by guiding with your eyes! But you will be astounded when you try it. It's biblical!"

Alice broke up laughing. She was hopeless—Ilka had seen right through her. "What are you talking about, biblical?"

"It's some Psalm, I don't remember which one. Honey, that's my advice. Best I can do for you, with that lack of face control. But I swear it'll work or at least improve you some. I want you to try it three times this next week and report back."

"Yes ma'am," said Alice.

"But that's not why you're still sitting here, is it? Not Big Oma's teacake either. Or my fascinating conversation. Or the exciting prospect of another deal with me. What's up?"

"I've got a puzzle, Ilka. His name is Doyle."

"And which Doyle do you mean?"

"The one who married Ollie West's daughter. Mary, of course."

"Kind of a sad story. What's bothering you? He's not running around on Mary, is he?"

"Not that I know of. Why?"

Ilka looked out the front doors. "Not that she's not attractive, because she is, but when you see them together, even though he's very attentive, I just don't feel any—any real buzz on his part, you know what I mean. You've probably seen how they are together. He acts very manly and possessive. Maybe too much. But to me, it feels like . . . all show. It was a good marriage for him because of her daddy's ranch, but I have sometimes wondered since then if—for him—that's all it was."

"How long have you thought that?"

"Oh, honey, for goodness sake. I went to their wedding and you could see it there. She was looking up at him adoringly—no, not quite that, more hopefully—and he was just . . . making all the right motions, but I couldn't feel any vibrations. Even though he spent a lot of time holding on to Mary. I wasn't sure it was real. Of course I'm just a dirty-minded old lady." Ilka sat up straight. "Alice. Are you telling me something's wrong about Ollie dying that way?"

"I don't know that there is anything wrong about it, Ilka. But I find myself puzzled by Doyle and Mary. And I was standing right there when Ollie was telling Doyle he had no interest in leasing his land, I think for those big wind turbines, and Doyle tried to argue with him about that. Ollie just said something like 'Nope, Doyle, not doin' it. It's not happening. So let's drop it.'"

Ilka said, "I heard there was leasing out near Ollie's."

"Yes," said Alice, "they're still trying to put together a configuration that some power company is interested in. Because of Ollie's location at the end of a ridge, next to the highway, I suppose it would change the configuration for the wind farm. Though there are other ways to get there; he's not the only parcel next to the highway. I'm not sure how close they are to getting a package leased up."

"Well," said Ilka, "if Doyle really cares about getting those lease payments, this is the time to try to get something signed up. Of course, I understand Ollie's position—he probably would not want those power lines or anything else crossing his ranch. He probably could care less about wind power. Or, to be exact, if Ollie wanted windmills for power he would put them up himself."

"What's the story about Doyle, though, Ilka? Why do you say it's a sad story?"

"Oh, honey, you know about the Westenheims, surely? You know the story of the poker game?"

"No."

"Well, back in the Depression, Doyle's grandfather gambled away his family's ranch. It was somewhere in South Texas, I think. Then he blew his own brains out, but only after the other guy had taken his ranch. Really stupid."

"To blow his brains out?"

"To blow his brains out too late. If he'd been a little quicker he could have saved the ranch for the family—lose the poker game and then kill himself fast before the other guy could get out to the ranch. You can't collect on a gambling debt like that, at least not from a dead man."

"What happened to the family?"

"Moved somewhere else in South Texas. Victoria, maybe. Doyle's mom grew up believing she should have been the princess on the ranch. She told Doyle that about every five minutes. He got a scholarship to UT and then was in the military I think for a while and then came back to Texas to work with some defense contractor in San Antonio, selling security systems. And, of course, married Mary."

"How did he meet her? Doesn't sound like their paths would cross, what with him in the security contracting business and Mary running a gallery."

"No clue, honey, but meet her he did and before you could say jackrabbit we were all invited to Ollie's and Cassie's for the wedding. Because the wedding was most certainly at Cloud Ranch. As anyone who was there would tell you—no way they could forget it, given the timing and the circumstances."

"You mean about Cassie, right? Ilka, Ollie told me about Cassie. You knew her, didn't you?"

"I did. I loved her. I still miss her."

"What do you think happened?"

"I don't think she went to Mexico. And I don't think she would have left Ollie ever. Or Mary."

"Well, is she dead?"

"Yes, I think she's been gone a long time. Felt like a little glow went out of the world."

"But you don't know what happened to her?"

"Oh, my imagination has told me things, but they can't be repeated. So, don't ask."

"Well, you say don't ask. But someone last week told me that back when Doyle was at UT one of his fraternity brothers disappeared off a boat out at Lake Travis and drowned. Did Cassie ever ask you about that?"

Ilka frowned. "She didn't. I don't know about that. What does that have to do with Doyle?"

"It was nothing but gossip, Ilka. Somebody said there might have been a crooked poker game. At the fraternity house."

"I don't know about that. Never heard it from Cassie."

"Well, how did she feel about Doyle?"

"Honey, I don't know. She didn't say. Like I say, my imagination has told me things, but that's not enough facts for me. So, they can't be repeated."

"I don't have enough facts either, Ilka. I just feel . . . my innards do not feel right about this. I get a knot in my stomach thinking about Ollie. I really liked that man. He had an appointment with me late Tuesday afternoon at four thirty and I kept looking for his truck to drive up. For him, on time was five minutes early, you know."

"I know," said Ilka. "And he thought everyone should be that way."

"Right," said Alice. "But he didn't show up and when he didn't, I just had the worst feeling. Called his house but no answer. Called Mary. Didn't know what to do."

Ilka leaned back and stared at Alice. "Did you tell me what that young man's name was? The one who drowned?"

"I think it was Randall. Howie Randall. Or Howard Randall."

"Randall." Ilka lifted her head, stared west toward the sunset. "That reminds me of something. Something Cassie said. I may have the name wrong, though."

"What did she say?"

"She'd had a visit from someone named Randall. A girl, though. At Coffee Creek Old Style. Oh, Alice, I'm an old lady. I may have this all backwards. I think a Randall comes into this somehow and it was a girl, and Cassie called me later and said she needed to check on something a bit more. But I do not remember anything else about it. Not even what it was about. Haven't thought of this in over ten years, I know."

"Did the girl live in Austin?"

"No. That was the thing. She was on her way west, I'm thinking Denver. That's what Cassie said. And that's about all she said."

"Okay," said Alice. She still felt puzzled, discomfited.

"Hey," said Ilka. "Let me show you something. Come on."

Ilka thumped her cane toward the living room. Behind the door, she stood waiting, then silently pointed at a small painting. Alice stared. Bold colors, black, green, red, gold, with a face staring back at her from the swirling color. No signature.

"Is it Mary's?"

"Yep," Ilka said.

"And—is it Cassie?"

"Yep. I winkled that out of Mary. Begged her to paint Cassie for me, after she was gone. Mary told me that was the most painful painting she ever did. I don't think she ever showed it to Ollie."

Alice stared at the face in the swirls. "Did she say why it was so painful?"

"No, I didn't think I could ask her that."

"Is it because the face is asking us something?"

"I don't know, honey. Or was it Mary who was asking her mother something? It's a puzzle, isn't it? I really wanted Mary to paint her, thought it would help Mary, but when I saw it I thought, that wound won't heal."

"Does it make you feel any better, having this picture of Cassie?"

Ilka laughed. "When you are as old as I am, you know you lose everything, honey, even the best and the brightest. Especially the best and the brightest. It's like Hector being killed before the walls of Troy. The ones you love the most. The ones the world needs the most." She patted Alice's shoulder. "Honey, I'm not going to tell you to quit worrying. But I am going to tell you to be careful driving home."

"Okay."

They hugged and Alice headed out to her truck. The front of the house was quiet. Alice heard Raymond lop-lopping around the side of the house. "Bye, Ilka. Don't forget I need to copy Big Oma's recipe. I'll come back and do that."

"Bye, Alice. Don't forget to be careful on the way home. And don't forget what I told you about your eyes."

"Okay!" called Alice, laughing. "The eyes have it!"

She put the truck in gear and bumped off under the spreading live oaks, toward the stone pillars. She headed the truck west out of New Braunfels towards US 281, toward the red and gold sunset, thinking that since it would soon be dark, she'd prefer not to go up Purgatory Road and Devil's Backbone but would stick to the four-lane north–south highway. Safer.

Chapter Eighteen

Quite a Piece of Driving

Driving toward US 281, Alice heard the piper's notes still ringing in her head, the piper playing for Ollie. And the other piper, that cold day in Edinburgh, piping for Jordie. She thought of Mary, white-faced, walking down the aisle. First Cassie, then Ollie. She thought of Ollie, lying in the dust, lying there all night, then all day, then all night again. And she hadn't known. It was no way to go, she thought. Possibly better than a hospital room, with fluorescent lights and beeping monitors. Possibly better than the cold North Sea, which took Jordie and wouldn't let him go, so that he couldn't even lie in his beloved Scottish soil. But what is a good way to go? she wondered. Would lying there staring at the stars, staring at the sky, be so very bad?

She merged onto US 281, heading north. The west was dark now. It was deep twilight all around her, the time of evening when it is hard to see colors, hard to see shapes. She settled into the right lane, thinking about Cassandra Coffee Ney West. Cassie, where are you? Dead and cold and gone? Or still hovering over us somehow? Or alive and living in San Miguel de Allende? Alice thought Jordie stayed near her for a while after his helicopter went down. In fact, that night, before she knew anything was wrong, she'd woken up and thought he was in the room with her, passing his hand across her forehead, smiling at her, but not talking. Then the phone rang, at 4:00 a.m. It was the oil company, telling her Jordie's chopper was down and they had been searching for wreckage, but had found nothing.

US 281 required attention, required her to stay awake. Alice fiddled with the radio, looking for her Austin public radio station. Blues night. She'd like a little Pinetop Perkins right now, a little Sonny Boy Williamson, something with some edge, some lewdness, some laughter—something alive!

Across the median, oncoming traffic was light. She checked her rearview mirror. Very little traffic, one truck coming up behind to pass her.

BAM!

Alice's head jerked. Her truck flew into the median, aimed at oncoming traffic. Alice grabbed the wheel, hanging on for dear life, pulling to the right, trying to hold the truck in the center. Bouncing down the median, lights unsteady, she saw ahead the gray and gaping black of the overpass. She pumped the brakes, pumped, pumped, gripping the wheel, and hauled the truck to a stop twenty feet from the concrete abutment. Alice sat, stunned and panting, heart racing. Now there were lights behind her. She turned her head, tried to open the door. Someone opened it. "Ma'am? Are you all right?" Alice looked up. A crew-cut man in jeans and flannel shirt stared at her. She looked behind her truck, saw a little hybrid, lights on, door open. Okay, so this wasn't the battering truck. "Ma'am, are you all right?"

Alice swung her legs out, took a deep breath, stood up. "I think so," she said.

"That was quite a piece of driving, ma'am," said the man. "You were flying down that median. I was scared to death you were going to lose it and cross into the southbound lane. Amazing, what you did."

"Well, thanks," Alice said. "What happened?"

"That big truck just rammed you," said crew-cut man. "Took a run at you, it looked like, and hit you right on the right quarter of your rear end. Then he took off. Big truck, dark, maybe green, had a big brush guard on the front. Went too fast, I couldn't get anything off the license except it was definitely from Texas. Might have had a G on the plate, but I can't be sure." He reached into his back pocket, pulled out a wallet, pulled out his card. "Here's all my contact info." He handed her the card. "I teach accounting at Texas State, live in Blanco. That's where I was going when you did your fancy driving down the median. I'd be glad to help you if you need it, with the insurance or whatever. Or the police."

"I'm Alice Greer from Coffee Creek," said Alice. Hand shaking, she rummaged in her purse, watched her fingers tremble as she tried to hand him the card. "My card."

"Well, look," he said. "Just call me if you need me to do a statement, or talk to anyone. You sure you're okay?"

"Yes." She took a deep breath. "Thanks." They walked around and stared at the back of her truck. The right side of the bumper was mashed in; the right side of her tailgate was so badly dented the top hinge was showing.

"That's expensive," said crew-cut man.

"But drivable, don't you think?" said Alice.

"Think so. Want me to follow you into town?"

"No, that's so nice of you, but I don't want you to have to go all the way to Coffee Creek."

"Well, I'm worried about that guy!" said crew-cut man. "How do you know he's not going to try it again? Do you know him?"

"No," said Alice. "I don't."

"Do one thing for me. See my cell phone number on that card? You've still got to make it all the way to Coffee Creek. Whoever's driving that truck, it sure looked like he did this on purpose. At least call me if you think you see him on the road. And call the sheriff! You know how to do that? Phone charged?"

He and Alice checked out her cell phone. Plenty of juice. Alice promised to call if there was any problem. Crew-cut man insisted he was going to be right behind her until he had to turn off the highway at Blanco.

The truck started up without a hitch. Alice carefully pulled out of the median onto the highway, followed by the little hybrid, which stuck to her bumper all the way to Blanco. She flashed her lights and waved as her rescuer exited to the east, then checked her rearview mirror every fifteen seconds on the way up 281. Now it was full dark: blackness, lit by occasional brilliant headlights. Alice realized her hands were clamped like claws on the wheel. She shook first one hand, then the other, trying to loosen up. Ahead, in the oncoming traffic headed south, she saw a dark truck slow down. She passed it. Was it turning onto the median? Yes. In her rearview mirror, she saw the truck bounce up onto the highway, now heading her direction. Alice sped up, flicking her eyes back and forth to her mirrors. The dark truck was ten lengths back, but speeding up.

She grabbed her cell phone and dialed 911, using the speakerphone. A white sign flashed past: one mile to the turnoff to US 290 and Coffee Creek. Her speedometer said eighty. Eighty-five. Eighty-seven. She couldn't drive this fast in a middle-aged pickup truck. The dark truck moved steadily closer.

"Coffee County, Coffee Creek," said the laconic voice.

"It's Alice Greer. I'm just about to turn off 281 onto 290. I'm being chased by someone in a dark pickup. Please help me!"

"Yes ma'am. Where are you?"

Alice braked and swerved onto the entrance to 290, speeding as fast as she dared. "Just hit 290 from 281. Can somebody come help me? I've got to drive!"

"I've got an officer out there on 290," said the voice. "Keep this line open. What are you driving?"

"Tan Toyota pickup," Alice said. "GDM400."

Alice pushed her truck as fast as she could, flying over the first big ridge on US 290, feeling like she was in the wrong movie. Jordie! What do I do now? The dark truck was gaining on her. She saw another overpass ahead. That's his game, she thought, to smash me onto the abutment. His headlights were closer. She felt one BAM on her bumper and stomped on her accelerator. I can't drive this fast! she thought. Blue and red flashes ahead—here came help. The truck vanished from her rearview mirror. What had he done, turned off his headlights? Was he still there? She couldn't see him at all. She started to slow down, watching in the rearview mirror as the sheriff's car crossed the median and fell in behind her. She slowed further. The sheriff's car turned on its right blinker. She took a deep breath, told the dispatcher the sheriff was behind her now. She turned her right blinker on and pulled slowly off onto the shoulder. The officer took down her explanation. "Where'd he go?" asked Alice.

"I think he turned off his lights and pulled off to go south down County Road 32 back there. It goes back toward Blanco," said the officer. "But there's only one of me on this stretch of 290 and I didn't want to leave you out here alone. Did you see his license plate?"

"No," said Alice. "He had his brights on so it was very hard to see anything at all." She gave the officer the contact information from crew-cut man.

"Good," he said. "I'll give him a call tomorrow." He looked at the back of her truck. "Looks like he left some paint on you, maybe," he said. "But it's too dark to really tell. I'd like to get a paint sample. You have a garage or pole barn?"

"Pole barn," Alice said.

"Doesn't look like it's gonna rain tonight, but still, let's be careful," he said. "Why don't you come down to the station tomorrow morning and let us get a paint sample? And park under your pole barn."

"Okay," said Alice. She was very tired. She looked up. He was watching her.

"Ma'am, I'm going to follow you home," he said. And he did.

"Lock up," he said. And she did.

And for the first time, Alice MacDonald Greer contemplated getting herself some firearm other than a flare gun. Skunk man had made her furious. Rammer man scared her.

Chapter Nineteen

See You in Eden

Alice's eyes popped open at four on Wednesday morning. The BAM! and the careening feel of her truck heading for the abutment rushed back, making her sit straight up, heart pounding. Now that really makes me mad, she thought. Bang up my truck, wake me up, and make my neck sore. She sat for a moment. Try to go back to sleep? No. She went outside on her deck and checked the stars. Spring mornings were grand, when Scorpio waved its tail above the southern horizon. But she loved best Orion the hunter, out scouting the night skies in the fall, with faithful Sirius panting along next to his glittery scabbard. She sniffed the air. Drying leaves; fall. She heard a screech owl call its questioning "whirr?" somewhere downhill near the creek. She had first met Ollie in August; now it was October. He should not go into winter without—without some sort of vindication, Alice resolved. Even if it turned out that, in fact, he had fallen down that hill all by himself, and just died.

On the way into town she stopped at the sheriff's office. "Yes, ma'am?" asked the brown-shirted constable at the front desk. Alice asked for the officer who had helped her last night on US 290.

"Officer Hinojosa is not on duty this morning."

"He told me to come see you all and have a paint sample taken from the back of my truck," said Alice. This is going to be hard to explain, she thought. "Because someone rammed my truck last night out on 281."

The constable's eyes narrowed. "No fun," he said. "Is Officer Hinojosa writing up a report?"

"I don't know," said Alice. "What do I do about this paint sample thing?"

The constable got up and walked out with her to the truck. "Make you mad, wouldn't it, have someone hit you like that," he said. "I do see some black paint in this dent." He went back inside and emerged with another officer following him. "This genius technician will get that sample, ma'am." In five minutes the sample was taken, sealed, and labeled, and Alice was on her way.

Silla had already started the coffee. "Ha! Beat you in this morning!" she said.

"I had a good excuse," Alice retorted. "Had to get the sheriff to sample the paint on my tailgate." Silla stared at her. "Well, I stopped by to see Ilka on the way back from Mary's, in New Braunfels," Alice began, "and it got dark, so I thought it would be safer to go up 281 than Purgatory Road."

Silla nodded. "Makes sense."

"Well, it wasn't so safe." She told Silla what happened.

Silla stared out the window at Alice's truck. "That's creepy," she said. "Good lord. Why, do you think? Who, do you think?"

"I don't know," said Alice. "Maybe the same truck as skunk man? And it was dark last night. But of course I don't even know what color that was. They both had a big brush guard on the grille, but that's not much help."

"No, that's your stud macho brush-guard thing," Silla said. "Lots of those out here."

"Hey," Alice said. "Tell me one more time about what happened to Allen's mother. That accident, when she hit the pits at Sonny's Barbecue. No one ever figured out why her car came off the road like that?"

"Nope," said Silla. "There was an investigation. The people inside the restaurant said they looked out the window and her car was just flying down the hill toward those big brick pits. Broke her neck. She was dead at the scene. Nearly hit two pit tenders, but they dodged."

"Lucky they got out of the way," said Alice.

"Yeah, they were old football players, still had a few moves. But I don't think anyone ever figured out what happened to Leanne. Usually she had Allen drive her but she didn't that day. There was talk that the steering linkage was messed up. And something went wrong with her air bag—it didn't work right. I heard the sheriff got after Allen about that, but he didn't know anything, as usual. Why?" Silla stared at Alice. "You're not supposing Allen messed with her car?"

"I've been thinking," said Alice. "I've been thinking about Doyle not wanting us to file Ollie's will."

"Surely he won't talk Mary into that."

"Well, what I'm thinking is, it's our obligation to file it whether anyone wants us to or not. So let's file that sucker in Gillespie County. This morning."

"Any time," said Silla. "I've got the documents all ready to go. Ollie's original will is right here. Just need you to sign the affidavit."

Alice looked over the documents and signed them. Silla made copies for the file and to send by mail to Mary and Allen as beneficiaries—"Make an electronic copy too before you leave," called Alice from her office—and picked up her keys and her coat. "I'm heading to the courthouse."

"Excellent," said Alice. "And do you have your cell phone? Will you call me as soon as it's filed?"

Silla headed out. Mary and Allen should have their copies by Friday. Restless, Alice made some calls to the title company about next week's closings, then stared around her office. She couldn't settle down. She took a couple of aspirin for her neck, stretched it this way and that, stared out the window, checked the news on the Internet.

You are acting worthless, she scolded herself. You are not being productive. Her rebellious self raised its eyebrow. "Well, something is bothering me," Alice said. She realized she'd spoken aloud. "Oh, good grief," she said, and grabbed her keys and phone, slammed and locked the front door, and headed out the door toward the courthouse, then cut up toward Pecan Street.

She trotted up the stone steps of Coffee Creek Old Style. No cars in the parking spaces in front—maybe she could catch Bryce alone. "Bryce?" she called into the hallway.

"Ms. Greer! Come have coffee. I just made some more."

They walked back to the kitchen. Alice inhaled. "Mmmm, mmmm, mmmm."

"You get my very best Viennese roast," Bryce said. "Cream with that, Alice?"

They settled into chairs at the tall windows in the old living room. Bryce clinked her cup. "Cheers," he said. "What's up, Alice? Your brow is furrowed."

"Okay," she said. "Here it is. Did Cassie ever mention a Howard Randall? Or Howie Randall?"

"You mean in connection with Doyle? Or Mary? Is that the context?"

"Probably. Not sure."

"Howie. Hmm. Randall." Silence. "You know, Randall's ringing a faraway little bell. Maybe. Something about a little table."

He got up and disappeared into the office. Alice could hear drawers opening and closing.

"Triumph," Bryce said, waving a clothbound notebook at her. "This is Cassie's daybook, where she kept running notes on commissions and customers and sales. Let's take a look."

Alice took the book from Bryce. She opened it. It was her first time to see Cassie's writing. A faint scent came from the book. She looked at Bryce. He nodded, lifting one corner of his mouth in a reminiscent smile. "Yeah," he said, "you smell it too. She always wore the same perfume. I loved that stuff. Not sure I know of anyone else who wore it."

"Do you know what it is?" asked Alice. Alice was passionate about perfume but also very picky. She did not like heavy scents. Cassie's was elusive and made Alice want to lean a little closer to the book.

"I don't remember the name, but she got it in Paris, every time she went. Place with a funny name. Of course I don't do French."

Alice looked down at the book. Cassie's writing was different from what she had imagined. It was more upright, more definite.

"Go to the end," said Bryce. "If it was something toward—toward ten years ago, it'll be at the back. She was nearly to the end of the book."

Alice flipped to the back and began leafing slowly toward the front. "August tenth, Sarah Randall. Connell sewing table. She'll pick up." There was a phone number. "What does this mean?"

"I think this would mean that she had a call from Sarah Randall on August tenth and that Randall wanted the sewing table from the Connell estate sale and that she's going to come pick it up."

"Do you know if she did?"

"Well, we can look at the receipts." Bryce disappeared again.

"Yep." He waved a file at Alice. "She did pick it up. August thirteenth. Not very expensive—just seventy-five dollars for a nice little sewing table. I think I remember her. She wasn't very old. Looked like a UT student, actually."

Alice wrote down the phone number. "San Angelo area code," she said. "Probably a cell phone, then."

"You going to tell me what this is about?" asked Bryce. "Or do I crank it into my bodice ripper? You haven't asked how that's going, either."

"How is your bodice going?" Alice played along.

"Rippingly! RIPPINGLY!" roared Bryce.

Alice rolled her eyes. "You remember anything at all about this young woman? You did see her?"

"Yes, one time. Don't remember if it is when she looked at the table the first time or when she came to get it. But I do remember. Student, blondish. Not very happy. That's what I do remember. She did want the sewing table. But she seemed kind of sad. Not excited over buying her first antique, you know?"

"And Cassie dealt with her, not you?"

"Right. Cassie was very sweet with her. I remember thinking she was being extra sweet. That's pretty damn sweet, you know. But I wasn't part of that. They talked a good while. I remember that but I must have been doing something else."

Alice stood up. "Gotta go."

"Not before I show you the linens I picked up at the antiques fair in Boerne."

She fingered the concentrated handwork of the past century, hours of work by anonymous women—hemstitched dinner napkins, embroidered pillowcases, frail linen handkerchiefs with delicate initials. Whose lives were represented there? She wondered as she walked back around the courthouse square and down Live Oak to her office. The message light blinked.

"Filed," said Silla's voice.

Good. Alice tried the number from Cassie's book. She had little hope of results, after ten years. But after four rings she heard "Hello?"

"Hello, this is Alice Greer, in Coffee Creek, Texas. Have I got Sarah Randall?"

"Yes . . . ?"

"This will sound odd, but I'm calling about a table you bought at Coffee Creek Old Style about ten years ago. From Cassie West. Does that ring a bell?"

"Yes. I still have my table. Why are you calling about it?"

"Kind of a long story. Is this a good time to talk?"

"It's okay."

"And do you mind my asking—where are you? This number I called is a San Angelo number, right?"

"Yes, it's my old Texas cell phone number and I've never changed it. I moved to Denver but still have that Texas phone number. But right now, I'm in San Angelo, visiting my folks."

"My daughter did the same thing when she went off to school," said Alice. "She refused to give up that 512 area code. So it's a local call for her mama. Well, let me tell you why I called. I'm a trusts and estates lawyer in Coffee Creek. My client was Ollie West, Cassie's husband. Did you know him?"

"No."

"But you remember Cassie?"

"Of course. She was very nice to me. We talked . . . about the little table . . ."

Alice thought there would be more, but Sarah Randall didn't go further.

"Was it a special purchase for you? I ask because Cassie made notes about it."

"Yes. It was the first antique—really the first piece of furniture—I ever bought. I was living in a furnished freshman dorm, all particleboard and plastic. I guess I just wanted something real with my name on it. I was out in Coffee Creek just before the end of summer school and I saw that little sewing table and I loved it and I could afford it. So I told Mrs. West I wanted it and I picked it up on the way home to San Angelo."

That made sense, thought Alice. She could have driven from Coffee Creek right out US 290 and US 87 to San Angelo.

"But why are you calling me? That was—like you said, ten years ago!"

"You're right," said Alice. "Well, did you know that Cassie disappeared?"

Silence.

"I never knew that. What happened?"

"I don't think anyone knows. She left a note about going to Nuevo Laredo for paper flowers for her daughter's wedding."

"Oh!" said the girl. "You know, we talked about the wedding."

"Yes?" prompted Alice.

"She said her son-in-law—the groom—was Doyle Westenheim."

"Right."

"I knew who he was. So we talked."

"Can you tell me what you talked about?"

Long silence.

"It was a long time ago," said the girl. "It was because of my brother."

Alice said, "Was your brother Howard Randall? Howie?"

"Yes. Where are you going with this?"

"Did you tell Cassie what happened to him?"

"What do you mean?"

"I heard he drowned. I am so sorry. Out at Lake Travis. At night. At a fraternity party."

"Yes," said the girl. "But I don't believe it."

"You don't?"

"My brother was on the swim team in high school in San Angelo. Swam the four hundred freestyle. I don't think he would drown. Look, I don't want to dredge all this up. I'm home visiting my folks."

Alice said, "I would not call if I didn't think it was important to someone. Listen, if I jumped in my truck I could be there in a couple of hours. Could you maybe meet me for coffee in Eden? You know that café just east of San Angelo? Would that work? I just want to talk about this and I don't think it'll take more than half an hour. I'm doing it for Ollie."

Silence again.

"Okay," said Sarah Randall. "I'm a little stir-crazy at this point. You know what it's like when you go home."

"I do," said Alice. "Okay, watch for a tan Toyota truck. Let me give you my license and cell phone numbers." She recited them both. "See you in Eden."

Chapter Twenty

Creepy Feeling

Alice locked up, raced to the truck, and headed west toward Fredericksburg, then turned northwest up US 87. After she got out of Fredericksburg, the road was empty and she cranked the truck up to eighty. Road trip. She did love a road trip on a wide-shouldered road heading west, with Enchanted Rock looming far off to her right and then the hills smoothing out, big sky all around. When she saw the faint blue hills beyond the Concho, she knew she was nearly to Eden. Slow down, Alice, or you'll miss it, she warned herself. She pulled into the parking lot at the little truck stop that constituted most of downtown Eden. A car was parked out front; she saw a young woman watching her. Alice got out of the truck.

Slowly the young woman opened her car door, stepped out, took off her dark glasses, stared at Alice.

"Alice Greer. Appreciate you coming."

"Sarah Randall," said the young woman. She paused a second before shaking Alice's outstretched hand. "I'm not sure about this whole thing, but we'll see."

The Eden truck-stop décor mixed old with even older. Old Formica tables, old metal chairs with red padded vinyl seats, old high school banners on the bare wood walls. Even the menus were old. They both moved toward the table in the corner and sat where they could see the door.

"Funny how this is my favorite table," said Alice.

Sarah Randall looked at her. "Mine too," she said.

The kitchen door swung open and a young woman hurried over. "Coffee," said Alice. "And tell me about the coconut pie. Whipped cream? Meringue?" The waitress was young, straight out of high school, Alice guessed. But she knew how to sell pie.

"That pie," she said, "is made by my Aunt Grace, who makes the best coconut pie in the world. It's meringue. You are limited to two slices per customer. We have to save some for our regulars. You want a piece?"

"Hey, I've had that pie before and it's excellent," said Sarah. "Only I like the apricot better."

"Yes, but we're out of apricot. It's past apricot season," said the waitress.

"Coconut pie and iced tea," said Sarah.

"Coffee and coconut pie, one slice to start with," said Alice. The waitress left.

Alice leaned forward, staring at Sarah. "What I was hoping is that you would tell me about Cassie, what you talked to her about. I know it's a long time ago."

“I thought about it driving out here.” Sunglasses pushed up on her ponytailed head, she looked down at the table. “We just were talking about the wedding, you know? She was excited. When she said ‘Doyle,’ I had to ask. I wanted to know the last name. And when she said ‘Westenheim,’ I guess she could see something in my face. She did have this way of looking at you.”

“That’s what I’ve heard,” said Alice. “I wish I’d known her, but I didn’t.”

“So, she asked me if I knew him. And I said yes. I didn’t want to say anything bad because for goodness’ sake this guy was marrying her daughter! And the wedding was close, I think. Couple of months, maybe. But she asked me and I told her about Howie.”

“About the party at the lake?”

Sarah heaved a long sigh. “I told her what Howie had told me. And what I told my dad. But he didn’t want to hear it. So I begged her not to tell it. And if I tell you, I have to beg you not to tell it. That’s why I’m not sure we should even be talking.”

“I promise you. I wouldn’t ask if I didn’t think it might be really important.”

“Howie was my big brother. I was still in high school while he was at UT. I got to go to Austin one time just to visit him. He let me come to a party at the frat house, but was very protective. That’s the first time I saw Doyle. Anyway, a week before he died I was in Austin again for a girls’ softball tournament. Our high school made the regionals and we were playing in Austin. Howie came to the game and after it ended we got to talk a few more minutes. He seemed really worried, really down. Finally he said he had to come home and talk to Dad. He needed to tell him something. Of course I asked what. He said there was this poker game at the frat house, and that Doyle was the dealer, and he and Doyle were making some money in this game. He said Doyle had a system and he was part of the system. And then he said, ‘I can’t believe I let myself get in this mess.’ I asked him if it was cheating, if the game was crooked. He nodded. ‘Howie,’ I said, ‘you can’t do that. You know you aren’t that kind of person. You’ve got to get out of that.’ ‘I know,’ he said, ‘but I don’t know how. I don’t know what to do. I need to talk to Dad about it. Do I tell the other brothers, or what? And I don’t want to get thrown out of school.’”

“Yikes,” said Alice. “The poor guy. He must have felt sick.”

“He was so worried,” said Sarah.“ He told me he wasn’t sleeping, couldn’t study—and it was midterms. I think he thought dad would help him figure out the best way to go forward. So he was supposed to come home two weekends later, and he told me he was going to talk to Dad and then figure out what steps he was going to take. And I told him that in the meantime, he needed to figure some way to dodge any more poker games, like go hide in the library or something until he could talk to Dad. He said that was his idea too. I think he felt better after we talked. At least he said he did. He said he felt like he could talk to Dad and then get this handled."

"And then came the party at the lake?"

"Yes. The party at the lake. We were all at home in San Angelo when we got the phone call. Howie had not come back in from the sailboat. Doyle had. And we drove in the middle of the night to Austin, out to the lake. Floodlights, police boats. They didn't find him until the next morning."

Alice sat, stirring the cold coffee, ignoring the pie, unable to think of anything but Howie's parents, standing on the rocky lakeshore. Waiting. "Oh, Sarah," she said. "How horrible."

"It broke their hearts," Sarah said. "Mine too, of course, but I had that secret. I knew he was going to get out of this mess. I knew he was going to come home and talk to Dad and get it all straightened out. So I did not think he would have gotten drunk, fallen off a sailboat, and drowned. Not Howie. He wasn't perfect, but he was no coward. And he did have this bruise on his head—Doyle said the wind came up when they were trying to get the sail fixed and maybe Howie caught the boom. But nobody made anything of it."

"Did you tell your parents about what Howie told you?"

"I did. Well, I only told Dad. I talked to Dad first. He was horrified and begged me not to tell Mama. He thought it would make things even tougher for her. And there was absolutely no evidence that—of any foul play, or anything like that, except that bruise, and the police didn't raise any questions. Dad was a county commissioner here at the time, so he didn't want Howie's name muddied, especially when . . ."

"When he was dead, and it wouldn't bring him back?" Alice asked.

"Right. When it would do nothing but ruin his name, and stir up a big mess, with no real evidence."

"Did you tell Cassie all this?"

"I did tell her. You know, it was two years after Howie died, because he was a junior then, and I was a junior in high school when he died. And when I met Cassie, it was the end of my freshman year. I did tell her about the poker game, and Howie's worries, and how he was going to come home and talk to Dad. I started not to tell her all that because Doyle was after all going to marry her daughter, but she kept encouraging me. So I told her."

"What did she say?"

"She said thank you. She smiled at me. She said maybe it was just a terrible, terrible accident and that she thought Howie was lucky to have such a caring sister. Made me cry! Anyway, I liked her. And I got the table and that was it."

Alice asked, "Did you ever talk to Doyle about it?"

"No!" said Sarah. "Emphatic no on that. He didn't seem like the rest of Howie's friends. Seemed a little too old for college, you know what I mean? And he did come up to me at Howie's funeral—the whole fraternity showed up for that, of course. Doyle got me alone and tried to ask, kind of, what I knew, when I last talked to Howie. In fact those were his words—when was the last time I talked to Howie? It was sort of in a context of what would my last memory be of Howie, the last time I saw him. But I had a creepy feeling. So I didn't say anything, just said Howie was sweet to come to my ball game in Austin and I would remember that. My big brother."

"And you haven't ever seen him again? Doyle?"

"No. I've been in Denver since graduation. Never saw Doyle again and don't want to. I've never talked to my mother about this, which is a wedge between us. She doesn't really know it's a wedge, since she doesn't know the reason, but it is. The shadow of Howie."

She lifted her head, stared at Alice. "So, you said this could be important. Why?"

"Ollie's dead," said Alice. "Cassie's husband. He fell off a rock bluff, at the ranch. Doyle is the one who found him."

"Oh," said Sarah. "I see." She furrowed her brow, looked out the window.

"Maybe Ollie just took a fall. He was seventy-eight," said Alice. "But it just got me wondering about Cassie. So I went by the shop and found your name in the daybook. And called."

"I still don't connect the dots," said Sarah Randall. "Why were you looking for my name?"

"Someone I know mentioned Howie's death when they were talking about Doyle," said Alice. "And I was very fond of Ollie."

The waitress came back with more coffee and iced tea. "You haven't finished your pie!" she said, horrified.

"Could you box it?" said Alice. "I have to take mine home." Shaking her head, the waitress picked up the pie plates.

Alice said, "One more blast from the past. Did you ever meet a Jeff Treacher at the fraternity house? Was he there too?"

"Jeff Treacher. Yes, Howie said he was part of the poker-game crowd. Kind of smarmy, tried to make a move on me at the party Howie let me go to. Ick."

"That's the one. You ever hear of or see him again?"

"No."

Alice left all her contact information with Sarah Randall, and, though it felt funny, shook her hand again. Not a hugging situation, thought Alice. She picked up the little pie box and they headed out to the parking lot. Not a cloud in the sky.

"No rain," said Sarah. "It's been really dry out here."

"Yup, Coffee Creek too. We need a good hurricane to hit somewhere west of Corpus."

"Out here, we like a nice tropical storm on the west coast of Mexico, not on the Gulf side," said Sarah. "That's what usually gets us some decent rain. I've got to stop by the ranch on the way back into town and check the tanks, check the horses. That's what I told my parents I was doing, anyway. So it'll be true."

"Well, thank you," said Alice. "Thanks for driving out here to meet me, and letting me talk to you about this. I don't know if I feel better or worse, but now I know what Cassie knew ten years ago."

She realized she hadn't said anything to this young woman about her truck's rear end being bashed out on 281. Should she?

"I need to show you something," Alice said, walking to the rear of her truck. "See that? Someone hit me really, really hard, out on 281 last night. When I was coming back from New Braunfels to Coffee Creek."

Randall looked at her, puzzled. "What does that have to do with any of this?"

"I don't know," said Alice. "Doyle Westenheim lives in New Braunfels. But I don't know who it was who hit me. I guess all I'm saying is, take care. I'm not telling anyone I talked to you, without talking to you first. And you should probably do the same."

"Hey," Sarah shrugged. "I've handled it for ten years."

"Yes, but watch your rearview mirror."

Alice watched her leave, then climbed back into her front seat, thinking about Doyle Westenheim, and Howie Randall, and Cassie West, and Ollie West. And Mary?

Chapter Twenty-One

Treed

At four on Thursday morning she woke with a start again, and not because of her alarm clock.

What was it? Why was she stark staring awake at four in the morning? Was she doomed never to sleep until daylight again? Images of rammer man and skunk man crowded back into her head. Then a thought filled her mind: If skunk man couldn't find what he wanted at her house, wouldn't he look at her office? She sat still on the bed for a moment, wondering if she were crazy. Well, if so, maybe no one would notice.

Alice got up, pulled on underwear and black jeans and a too-big but warm black fleece of Jordie's labeled "Firth Rowing," and after some thought, got out her hiking boots. Her running shoes were way too conspicuous with their reflective stripes. She sniffed the cool night air, stepped into the truck, and raced out the drive to the creek road and headed for town at an unsafe speed. When she got close to her block, she slowed to a crawl. Coffee Creek lay silent under the starlight and its few streetlights. She parked on the street parallel to but a block north of her office, and cut through the yard opposite her office. Heart pounding, she stood in the dark beneath the live oak tree in the yard across the street from her front door. Parked up the street from her office was an unfamiliar camper truck. The entry light was on in her office. And a small light jiggled inside her building. Actually right inside her office, to the right of the entry hall. Alice felt fury rise up inside till her forehead felt hot. How dare someone root around in her stuff! Or her clients' stuff!

She slipped back to her truck, turned on the engine but kept her lights off, and swung back around the block, creeping to a stop in front of the dentist's office next door to her office. But now what? She had no weapon except the flare gun, which was still in her truck. She had no flashlight except the little one under the seat. She started to open the door and remembered the dome light would come on and expose her. She switched it off and very cautiously pushed open the driver's-side door. No light! It worked! She slid out, trying to be as quiet as a . . . Oh, thought Alice, how did the Comanches do it? Soft moccasins on rock and they got you before you knew they were there. But she had on hiking boots, not moccasins. And what could she do if she did capture the invader? She had no tomahawk, no knife, and no ability to use them even if she'd had them.

Alice retrieved her little flashlight and crammed the flare gun into the capacious pocket of Jordie's fleece. She crept toward the side of her office. Inside the west window of her office she could see a flashlight still jiggling around. Should she throw open the front door? The back door? Call the police? Undecided, she had just gingerly opened the wrought-iron gate to the backyard, ready to head for the back door, when a mighty roar erupted from inside. Good God! Alice thought. Sounds like the Hound of the Baskervilles in full throat.

"Stop! Down!" she heard. The back door slammed open and the wildly waving flashlight staggered out followed by a leaping dog and the sound of ripping cloth. "Get off me!" yelled flashlight man, but the dog growled and snapped. Flashlight man pulled away and ran for the pecan tree at the rear corner of Alice's back yard, apparently unsure where the gate was. Alice yanked the gate shut again. Out on the street a metal door slammed on the camper.

"What the hell?" said a male voice.

"Sunny!" yelled a female voice. Silla? Footsteps pounded toward Alice.

"Silla?" said Alice. "Is that you?"

"Alice!" said Silla, trotting around the side yard, followed by a male companion. Alice opened the gate again and the three of them ran through the gate into the back yard. Under the pecan tree at the back corner, Sunny circled the trunk, eyes on the branches, growling a deep-throated growl. The branches thrashed above.

"Sounds like Sunny has that guy treed," Silla said. "He's safe for a moment." Twigs fell on the three staring up in the branches, as flashlight man edged around to the other side of the trunk somewhere above them. "Alice, I'd like you to meet Johnny Madill. He placed first last night at Lampasas."

"How do you do," said Alice. It was the Handsome Young Cowboy.

"Ma'am," said Madill.

"First in calf roping," said Silla.

"Congratulations," said Alice.

That seemed to explain why Johnny Madill had emerged from the camper carrying a beautifully coiled lariat.

"I thought we'd just stay in Johnny's camper," said Silla. "Didn't want to bother Mama. But of course I had to put Sunny in the office."

"Of course," said Alice. Sunny, a large male Labrador retriever, had adored Silla for eight years now and could not tolerate other male animals—human or otherwise—near her. This was sometimes useful to Silla in her dating career. When she tired of some rodeo rider, Sunny was no longer left behind in Coffee Creek but became a conspicuous and constant companion. When Silla met a new contender, Sunny was left behind in Mama's backyard.

"Ma'am, do you want that guy down from your pecan tree?" Madill fingered his lariat.

"Yes," said Alice. "I would like to know who was messing around in my office."

Silla held Sunny's collar.

"Come down, sir!" ordered Johnny Madill. "I have the dog by the collar." Silence from the tree. A branch cracked. More thrashing as the man looked for another branch. Another crack.

"Get down, sir!" said Madill.

Scuffling came from the far side of the tree. "He's going to jump over the fence," cried Alice. The pecan tree branches extended into the dentist's office next door. A branch broke as the man fell heavily into the dentist's yard, got up, and started running back toward the street.

"Huh," said Johnny Madill. He jumped up on Alice's picnic table. The lariat flashed. Alice couldn't see the loop land—but she saw Madill leaning backward, then jumping down and rapidly snubbing the lariat around the table. He trotted back out of her gate and around toward the fallen man who lay in the grass next to the dentist's driveway, struggling to get the lariat off his legs. Madill sat down heavily on him.

Sunny pranced, barking happily. Alice cheered. "Nice work, Johnny," said Silla. Headlights came around the corner and a spotlight hit the scene. Sheriff's car, peering between Alice's office and the dentist's.

A constable emerged from the car. "Hi, ladies. What's going on?"

"That man was in my office," said Alice. "Mr. Madill is sitting on him."

"Let's see who it is," said the constable, waving an enormous Maglite. The procession—constable, Alice, Silla, now with a firm grip on Sunny's collar—moved toward Madill, now comfortably ensconced atop a man who was facedown, still struggling feebly in the grass. Whenever the man tried to roll from side to side, Madill crooned, "Yippee ti yi yo, hold on, little dogie." He seemed to have wrapped the lariat around the man's legs and arms.

The constable shone his big flashlight full at the man, who tried to bury his face in the grass. Alice stared at the lanky, sandy-haired man.

"Treacher! It's Jeff Treacher!" said Alice. "What were you doing in my office?"

"I can explain," said Treacher in a muffled voice. "Was in early, at my office. Saw your light on. Feared you had a burglar."

Alice looked at Silla.

Silla rolled her eyes. "I turned the light on in the entry when I put Sunny in there," she said. "But I double-checked all the locks when I left."

"Want me to run him in for unlawful entry?" said the constable.

"Yes, I do," said Alice. "I most certainly do." Her clients' papers were sacred. Nobody was going to snoop in her office unmolested. Besides, she'd never seen someone captured and arrested in this fashion. Especially a lawyer she distrusted. It had broadened her legal experience.

"Okay, sir," said the constable. "Get up."

"Can't," said Treacher to the lawn.

"Okay, sir," the constable said to Madill. "Could you release him somewhat?"

Johnny Madill stood up and rearranged his roping job. The loops went around Treacher's rear, holding his hands down. Madill rolled him to his side and pulled him to his knees. "Now you can get up, little dogie," he said.

The procession marched toward the big sedan marked "Sheriff." "Sir," said the constable to Madill, "I'm alone at present. Would you mind riding with the prisoner in the backseat, while he's trussed up? It's just a block to the jail."

Alice and Silla said, "We'll walk."

Alice, Silla, and Sunny were at the front door of the jail before the patrol car slid up. They went inside and Alice watched as Jeff Treacher was booked for breaking and entering and trespass and marched into the cells.

"Very satisfying," said Alice. She was starved. She was suddenly desperate for coffee. All of this excitement had occurred without coffee. "Let's go get breakfast!"

Alice, Silla, Sunny, and Johnny Madill walked across the street to the Camellia Diner. It opened at five sharp and the lights were on. "Coffee," they all said, heading for the corner booth.

"Comin' up," said the birdlike gray-haired waitress. "Comin' up hot."

"Well, that was weird," said Silla. "What made Jeff Treacher do such a ridiculous thing?"

"I don't know," said Alice. "And where was he when—when Ollie—?"

"Why don't you ask the sheriff to ask him that?" said Silla.

Silla, Madill, and Alice watched the waitress set steaming mugs of coffee before them. "Biscuits are comin' out," she said. "What can I get you?"

"Biscuits and gravy," they chorused.

Silla had scooted closer to Madill in the booth, Alice noticed. "Did either of you two notice anything skunky about Treacher?" she asked.

"You mean smell or character?" asked Madill.

"Well, you were sitting on him," said Alice. "Did he smell like a skunk, at all?"

"Not that I noticed," said Madill. "Just some really excessive aftershave. Why?"

Alice told them about skunk man. "Flare gun!" said Madill. He looked at Alice in wonder.

"I know," said Silla. "Can't believe she doesn't have a real gun out there, all by herself. Or even a dog." Silla patted Sunny, who was lying across Alice's feet under the table. "Alice is not yet fully prepared for ranch life," she said.

"But surely Treacher was not rammer man," said Alice. She told Madill about the adventure on US 281.

"Messing up your truck," said Madill, shaking his head. "Bad business."

"Do you think he was after Ollie's will?" said Silla.

"Not sure," said Alice. "But we've already filed it, so tough luck if that's what he was after. I intend to find out, though."

Chapter Twenty-Two

A Lot to Lose

On Thursday afternoon Silla stuck her head through Alice's doorway. "Adam Files called," she said. "From the Gillespie County Sheriff's Office. They want to talk to you."

"I want to talk to them too," said Alice.

"Good," said Silla, "because I told him you were here and he's on the way. With his boss."

Alice barely had time to slip her client's documents into a folder before she saw two men striding up her office sidewalk. Alice's brain registered crisp, tan uniforms, badges. Both were now standing in the hall, next to Silla, looking at her intently. "I'm Detective Matt Kubecka, Ms. Greer," said the fiftyish man. "Gillespie County Sheriff's Office. This is Adam Files." Curious about Silla's recent date, Alice glanced at a serious-faced slim young man—brown hair, brown eyes, tentative smile.

"Hi," said Alice. She stood up, shook hands. "Please sit."

"We hear you have had quite a week," said Kubecka. They must have checked in with the Coffee County Sheriff's Office then.

"Yes. Skunk man, rammer man, and flashlight man."

"Skunk man?" Apparently Kubecka and Files had not heard about skunk man, so Alice told that tale as well.

"Ms. Greer, we'd like to talk to you about Ollie West."

"Yes."

"Do you know anyone who would have profited from his death?"

Wow, he really just asked that question! thought Alice. All my life I've wondered if they really ask that question. "Do you think he didn't just fall, all by himself, then?"

"We have the autopsy report back. His injuries are consistent with a bad fall. But it looks like he may have been moved. The medical examiner says he may have been moved after he died. But maybe it was before."

"How can you tell?"

"Two different types of lividity marks on his back. But it's not definite. Looks like he fell, lay there a good while, and then was moved. We're not sure whether he was dead or alive. But he didn't move by himself."

"That's horrible," said Alice. "Being so injured . . . and being moved . . . wouldn't it be agonizing?"

Kubecka looked at her, nodded. "Also, his clothes show some signs that he was dragged or moved."

"So perhaps he didn't die falling off that particular hill? The one where he was found?"

"It's possible," said Kubecka. "But back to my question. Do you know anyone who could have profited from his death?"

"There's a disagreement," Alice said slowly, "about the will. Ollie signed a new will in August. He also executed a revocable trust. Instead of leaving everything outright to his only child, Mary, he put his assets into two pots. One part of the trust held the ranch and some money to protect the ranch and the rock art. One part held the other assets, to pay him income while he lived, and to pay Mary income during her lifetime. A very handsome income, it looks like. And she would also have a life estate in the ranch. So would Allen Debard. You know who that is?"

He nodded. "Debard would have a life estate?"

"Yes, Ollie wanted him to be able to stay on at the ranch. But only for his life. It didn't extend to his spouse, if he got married. Same was true for Mary—the life estate was for her life, and her children's if she had any, but didn't extend to Doyle."

"Why did he do that?" said Kubecka.

"Because there is very important rock art out there in the ridge above the ranch. Ollie wanted that rock art preserved, and last August he put the whole ranch into a trust. And now that he's dead, that trust will be managed by the Rock Art Conservancy of Texas."

"Lord, this is complicated," said Kubecka.

"Well, I could diagram it for you," said Alice.

"But did everyone know about Ollie's changing his will and signing this trust thing?"

"I don't think they did," said Alice. "We had a meeting here just this past Tuesday morning, to go over Ollie's will and the dispositions he'd made. Doyle, Mary, Allen. None of the three seemed to really know about the August will. Or that he had put the ranch and other assets into a trust. And it is true that Ollie wanted confidentiality. As he said, he didn't want any expectations created. In case he changed his mind."

"How did they react?"

"Well," said Alice, "at the meeting, Allen seemed surprised about the life estate. Maybe he had been afraid that when Ollie died he'd get kicked off the ranch. Mary said she sort of liked what her dad had done. Doyle seemed—very upset. He said he wanted to probate the old will. From twenty years ago."

"Tell me more."

"Silla was there. She can tell you too." Alice tried to report what was said at the meeting. "Doyle thought Mary should be the one to make the decisions about Cloud Ranch. And the way Ollie has it set up, Mary can absolutely have some say about how the ranch is managed, but once she dies, the ranch is not something she can pass on to anyone. She lost that right when Ollie died without changing the trust arrangement."

"Despite the will?" Kubecka asked.

"Yes." Alice explained the structure again. "The will didn't change what occurred with Cloud Ranch. It was already part of the trust."

"But these three didn't know about it?"

"No," Alice said. "I don't think so. They could have figured some of it out, because back in August he sent them each checks drawn on the trust account. But maybe they didn't notice. And Ollie wanted it quiet. After all, he could have changed his mind at any time about how he was leaving the money. But he died, so it didn't change."

"Huh," said Kubecka.

The room was quiet.

Files cleared his throat. "The second pot, that holds all the other assets in a trust for Mary—"

"Yes."

"What happens to that pot of money when Mary dies?"

Smart boy, thought Alice. Maybe Silla should show some interest in him.

"It goes to an orphanage in Hill County. It's a pretty good chunk of securities."

"But if there hadn't been a trust, or a new will, under Ollie's old will, would that have gone to Mary as well as the ranch?"

"Yes."

"So Mary gets plenty to live on and can live at the ranch, but she doesn't really own those assets? Can't leave them to anyone in her own will?"

"Right," said Alice. She told them what Ollie had said about protecting Mary.

"So," said Kubecka, "Mary has a lot to lose by the new will. I mean, in a way she has the assets; she has the money from the securities, and she has the right to live at the ranch. But she doesn't really have them. She can't sell them or bequeath them. That right?"

"Yep," said Alice. "Well, if she had children the outcome would change some. But surely you don't think Mary would ever—"

Kubecka pressed, "Does Mary have a will? Do you know about Mary's will?"

"Only hearsay," said Alice. She passed along what Ernst had told her.

"So did you file this new will? After Doyle said he did not want you to?"

"Of course we filed it," Alice said stiffly. "The law requires it."

"So, if I understand you," said Kubecka, "Doyle conceivably loses because he can't inherit the ranch or Ollie's money if something happens to Mary."

Alice stared at him. He should draw his own conclusions.

"What about Allen Debard?" Kubecka asked. "Sounds like he got nothing under the old will."

"True."

"And now he gets a life estate and can live at the ranch?"

"Yes. He can stay in the bunkhouse apartment, where he lives now."

"The timing is what puzzles me," said Kubecka. "You say this will was signed in August, and the trust was created in August. Why now?"

"You mean why would Ollie die . . . now?"

Kubecka nodded.

"Well," said Alice, "there is only one thing I know of. Ollie was supposed to come in on the Tuesday afternoon before he died. He was supposed to sign a power of attorney that would have provided for both management of the conservancy trust assets and management of his other assets, in case he became disabled. You know he had lung cancer."

"Right," said Kubecka.

"But he didn't show up for the appointment," Alice said. She told the officers about calling Mary, in Dallas.

"So how would that power of attorney have changed anything?" asked Files.

"Well," said Alice, "I'm not sure it would, really. I mean, Ollie made the real changes when he created the trust and signed his new will, though he could have revoked either at any time. But I suppose that if you didn't know or understand about the trust, you might view the power of attorney itself as the document that would result in the family at least temporarily losing any ability to control Ollie's property—the ranch and everything—if he lost the ability to manage his affairs. Which they knew was a distinct possibility, given his illness."

The officers looked at each other. "Like the opportunity to lease?" asked Kubecka.

Alice just looked back at him.

"What about people outside the family? Any enemies?" asked Kubecka.

"I don't think so, really. Although you could ask Jeff Treacher that."

"The lawyer who broke into your office? Is he going to be disbarred? Pretty hard to believe he did such a harebrained thing."

"Have you asked him why?"

"According to your sheriff's office, he's trying to get counsel and he's begging to talk to you. Says he can explain everything."

"Mr. Treacher is trying to lease up a block of ranches out west of

Fredericksburg for a wind power project. The rumor I heard is he gets paid if the whole project leases. Ollie was not interested at all. Treacher suggested to me that the neighbors would not be happy if Ollie didn't join in and lease."

"Which neighbors?"

"Look," said Alice. "I don't know if any of the neighbors really cared at all. Ask Mr. Treacher, would you? He mentioned Gunny Powell. But I hate to spread rumors just on his say-so, honestly. He apparently had his own reasons for wanting to get the deal done. But again, that too is just rumor. So you should ask him what his deal is."

Files was getting it all down.

"I have a question for you two," said Alice.

"Yes ma'am?"

"When Ollie was found, did he have his cell phone with him?"

Files and Kubecka looked at each other. "No," said Files. "No cell phone. Why?"

"I know he had one," said Alice. "A new one. He had it with him when we were out at the ranch that Saturday, to look at the rock art. He was proud of it. And I don't know why he wouldn't have had it."

"Well, he didn't," said Files. "And I didn't see it in the house or the truck, though maybe we need to look again." He glanced at Kubecka, who nodded. "Here's what he did have that was odd. He had two pocketknives. One was just a regular working pocketknife, small size. Kind everyone has. And it was in beautiful shape. Oiled, sharpened."

Alice nodded. That sounded like Ollie.

"The other one was gold, with initials and an inscription. But it was very beat up. Blades were corroded. Dirt in the hinges. Do you know anything about that?"

"No," said Alice. "What initials?"

"DBW. Date was 10-10-2000. Think it's Doyle's?"

"The initials sound right and that would be about when he and Mary got married," Alice said slowly. "Where was it? Was it with the other knife?"

"No, it was stuck down in his watch pocket. It's real small."

"Did you show it to Mary?"

"Yes. She said, 'How odd.' And when we asked why, she said it looks like one that Doyle has. That her dad gave him before the wedding."

Alice stared past them, thinking, then looked down at her desk, tapping her pen on a blank legal pad. An idea was slowly emerging in her mind—no, in her gut, which felt sick.

"Anything else that you can tell me about Ollie?" she asked. "I hope he didn't suffer too long. How far did he fall?"

Files glanced at Kubecka, who nodded.

"He took a bad fall. Broken legs, broken back, left arm too. Looked like he tried to grab something with his right hand; it had tree sap on it."

"Tree sap? But—"

He looked at her. "Yeah, we're trying to figure out what kind of sap. Medical examiner said it was resin like pine resin but that doesn't make sense for the hill where he was found."

Ah. "Can you tell me when he died?"

"Not clear," said Kubecka. "Could have been as early as late Tuesday afternoon. Definitely by about two on Wednesday morning."

"And everyone was gone, right?"

"Yes. Everyone was off the ranch. Doyle was in Houston on a site visit; Mary was in Dallas on business for the gallery; Allen was in Fort Worth."

"You're sure?"

"Yes, we checked on all three of them. Got Doyle's receipts, talked to Mary's Dallas contacts and Allen's dad, and so on."

They left, asking her to call if she thought of anything.

She was thinking of plenty.

Chapter Twenty-Three

Main Force and Awkwardness

At six on Friday, Alice was out on her deck with Jordie's old Steiner field glasses, staring at Orion. Lord, he was beautiful. She focused on the galaxy in his right leg. Unutterably lovely. The stars were bright, so bright, seeming almost magnified by the faint humidity. Alice made coffee and went back outside to sniff the air again. The dry weather was holding. Coffee Creek had not seen rain for over a week. If a hurricane stirred up the Gulf, though, Coffee Creek might get some weather, especially if the hurricane headed toward Corpus Christi or Brownsville. We could really use a little rain, thought Alice. Ever since the flare gun incident, she had worried about how fast the pasture caught fire.

Then she stopped, standing on the deck planks in her bare feet. Since Ollie had been found a week ago last Thursday morning, not a drop had fallen. But that couldn't last forever. What if Ollie's phone was outside, out on the ground somewhere? A wet cell phone would be dead as a dodo, or so Alice assumed. An extinct phone. Or would it?

Ollie's missing cell phone, and the little gold pocketknife, nagged at Alice all morning. She thought about them while she fed the donkeys and checked their watering trough. She thought about them as she drove in and unlocked the oak front door at the office. Finally, after an unsuccessful effort to work, she picked up the phone and called Red.

"What are you doing this afternoon?" asked Alice.

"The usual. No state trailer scheduled, which means I can work the horses a little and catch up on paperwork. But . . . I am a little bit bored and you sound like you have something wicked in mind. So, what's up?"

"I don't know if it's really trespassing," Alice started, "because he is my client, or was my client—"

"You want to go out to Ollie's ranch!" breathed Red.

"Yes. I think he lost something out there."

"His life, for example."

"Not just that. Oh, for God's sake, that sounds dreadful. Red, he showed me his new cell phone just before he died. And no one has found that phone. And I have this weird feeling I know where it is. And it might possibly be a little on the wrong side of trespassing, but I have got to go look for it. Will you go with me?"

"Sure," Red said promptly. "But why don't you just call Mary and ask her?"

"I don't want to put her in Dutch with her husband any more than I already have. Her husband does not like Ollie's documents, and therefore he does not like me. He doesn't like the will, the trust, or anything else Ollie hired me to do."

"Ahhh." Red said nothing for a moment. "So," she said, "this requires a little creativity. A little resourcefulness. You recall that is my specialty, Alice?"

"Oh yes I do," said Alice.

"Gate code?" said Red.

"Yes, I know the gate code, unless they've already changed it," said Alice.

"But you don't want to show up in the truck and broadcast your presence?"

"Exactly," said Alice.

"I am looking on the computer at a map of Ollie's ranch," said Red. "Where exactly do you want to be?"

"I need for us to get over to the north side, the steep ridges on the north side. Just a sec, now I have it up on my screen." She stared at the mixed satellite/map picture on her computer.

"Aha. The north side," Red said. "You will not be surprised to learn, given my wide social acquaintance, that I know the folks who ranch next to Ollie on the north side next to the highway."

"The McDuffies?" said Alice.

"Yes. Indeed, Doug and Annie McDuffie have invited me to come inspect their horses on several occasions. They bought one at an auction that needs some talking-to now and then. Perhaps I am due for a visit. Alice, can you ride a horse?"

"Oh come on, Red, you've seen me on a horse. I can sit up there if someone pushes me up there and if the horse doesn't smell my terror and fling me off in the tule bushes."

"I'm serious. Alice, of course you know there's a ranch gate between Ollie's and the McDuffies' place."

"Well, there should be." Every ranch had gates that neighbors could use in emergencies.

"What do you think about us riding into Ollie's ranch?" said Red.

"You are kidding!"

"No. I think we could come in on the north side through the ranch gate pretty close to the highway. Does that get us where we want to be?"

Alice thought. "If we come in fairly close to the highway, we have a pretty steep ridge to climb up and then go down. But we wouldn't cross the creek. Then we'd need to ride west along the foot of the ridge to where the cliffs start. I think we could be in cedar scrub most of the way so hopefully we wouldn't stick out too much."

"Okay, Alice. Boots and hat. If anything happens, you have to look like you are riding along with me to help try out these horses. That's the story, and the McDuffies will back us up."

"Okay," said Alice. "Blame it on me though. I'm going to say I was just so taken by the rock art I wanted to show it to you."

An hour later, Alice was at Red's, in jeans and boots and hat, trying not to get kicked while Red loaded a roan mare and a gray gelding into her red and white horse trailer.

"Let's roll," said Red. Unusually, Red was not wearing red. She had on a black shirt and jeans and hat. "Pirate outfit," she said. "For breaking and entering."

"Yikes." Wonder if I can be disbarred for this? Alice thought. Did this make her as bad as Treacher?

Red called the McDuffies from the road. "How would you feel about our exercising a couple of horses out at your place?" she asked. "Need to get them out on a little bigger piece of turf than the rescue ranch."

The McDuffies were delighted. They made Red promise to talk to their problem-child horse while she was there.

After they unloaded the two horses at the McDuffies, Red left Alice struggling to saddle both of them and walked the McDuffies' problem horse around the corral, talking to the animal the whole time. The McDuffies leaned on the rails and watched.

"Horse hasn't been that calm since it was born," said Doug McDuffie. "How does she do that?"

Red talked to the McDuffies awhile about the horse. Doug wondered if it would help if Red could give their daughter some supervised lessons.

"Maybe," said Red. "Worth a try."

Red checked Alice's cinch job on both horses, then swung swiftly up onto the roan mare. Alice clambered up onto the gray gelding. They headed slowly west through the McDuffies' pasture, then doubled back under the tree line that ran along the fence, to where Red had spotted the faded red ranch gate that abutted Ollie's property. Red opened the gate and led the roan through, then shut the gate after Alice and the gelding. "I'm not locking it; I'm leaving the chain off," said Red. "In case we have to leave in a hurry."

The ridge rose on Ollie's side of the gate. Alice led her horse at a slant up the ridge, mostly cedar scrub with a few hardwoods, then over the top and down toward the level of the creek. The horse slid a couple of times on the scattered limestone outcrops. Red trotted behind on the roan. As they neared the bottom, Alice slowed, fearful about stepping out into view. She tried to stay about ten feet back in the brush as they moved to their right, toward the spot where the ridge got steeper and steeper.

Finally Alice turned around in the saddle. "Red, we're cliffed to the right. So I think this is pretty close to where Ollie took me up to what he called the first set. I think we need to get off and walk the horses so we won't miss anything."

Alice walked in front, Red behind. They took their time, scanning the area along the base of the bluff, Alice glancing nervously west and south from time to time. Not a sound came from the south, the direction of the ranch house—no cars, no trucks, nothing at all. It was close to four o'clock; the sun was full in their faces as it slanted toward the horizon, turning Red's hot face even redder. Sweat trickled down Alice's neck. "We need to curve in some," Alice whispered to Red. "The bluff makes this big turn to the north, and that's close to where the cave is." For another hour they worked systematically back and forth along the bluff, Alice close to the tumbled rocks near the base and Red further out. Nothing. Red looked at Alice interrogatively. Alice knew Red was game—but was this a wild goose chase?

Alice closed her eyes and thought of Ollie—gray hat, steady eyes. Send me word, Ollie! Tell me where! Craning her neck, squinting against the low sun, Alice scanned the bluff. She thought she could see the shelf she had crawled along en route to Ollie's cave. They needed to move further into the curve of the bluff. But here the cedar scrub formed a barrier as determined as Sleeping Beauty's thorn hedge. Branches poked their eyes, poked their hair, snagged their clothes.

"Should we just tie the horses?" Alice whispered. They did, and edged into the cedar brake below the cliff, heads down, walking slowly, ten feet apart, looking for a glint of anything manmade. Cedar duff, dull blue cedar berries, and Spanish oak leaves covered the ground. Red was ahead now, closer to the cliff, her head moving methodically from side to side as she scanned the ground.

Alice moved away from Red into a break in the scrub. Her eyes were caught by an area on the ground where the cedar needles were kicked up, disturbed. Her stomach knotted. She could see two lines in the dirt, lines like boot heels being dragged away from the cliff. And other boot prints as well. Carefully staying to the side, ignoring cedar prickles in her arms and back, she followed the boot lines past the last piece of cedar scrub. The scuff marks ended at the edge of the pasture, but the tall grass, yellow in the fall sun, was flattened, as if a big truck had been parked there. Alice walked back toward where the scuff marks began. As she stood there, feeling the late afternoon sun pouring over her, she sniffed a faint resinous whiff of piñon. She looked around. On the ground lay a broken piñon branch. She leaned her head back, staring far up along the bluff. Was that yellowish gleam a broken branch end, high up?

"Red!" she hissed. "Red, I think this is it." Red reappeared through the scrub. "We need to look around here," said Alice. "Something happened here. Don't step on the scuff marks."

"Whoa," Red said. She pulled out her cell phone and started taking pictures. Alice looked up at the broken branch, her imagination sickened by the thought of Ollie falling from that height, trying to grab a branch, falling—right here? She shook her head, trying without success to erase the picture. She looked to her right. An enormous cedar had wrapped itself around a live oak. The cedar's spiky branches spread nearly to the ground. Alice tried to pry the branches apart, was poked in the armpit by a silver wooden cedar spike, and finally got down on her knees. Sweating, she peered into the shadows and saw a silver gleam behind the lowest branches. She leaned way in, yanked the bandana off her neck, covered the little silver phone, and stuffed it in her pocket. As she scuttled backward her eardrums almost popped. A sharp crack echoed on the cliff and cedar needles fell in her hair. Good lord! Someone's shooting! thought Alice. Red? Where was Red?

"Red!" she hissed again, crawling toward the cliff. She heard nothing. "Red!"

"I'm here," whispered Red. "Lying here under this bush. That was a rifle, Alice. Who the hell is shooting at us?"

"Let's get up the hill," urged Alice. "Let's get out of here!" Her heart pounded. If she got Red killed, she would never forgive herself, never. They panted up the hill, dodging behind cedar branches. Where were the horses? They heard a nearby snort, grabbed the horses' bridles and tugged them up toward the limestone outcrops as fast as they could. Alice put up her hand and stopped. "Listen!" she hissed. She heard a deep rumble. Diesel truck? "He'll have to go cross the creek, I hope," said Alice. "Come on! Surely he won't shoot at two people on horses!" They mounted, Alice sticking her boot in the stirrup, grabbing the pommel, and hauling herself up with main force and awkwardness. No style points, she thought, spurring the gelding up the ridge after Red. She could hear the truck now, coming from a different direction. She kicked the gelding hard. He broke into a trot, up over the rocks and across the ridge. Red was already downhill, off her horse, holding the gate, and Alice raced through and stopped. Red flung the chain around the gate and worked the clasp, panting.

"Hallelujah," said Red. "Let's boogie!"

"Wait," said Alice. "I want to see—no, Red, do this. You ride back to the

McDuffies so it's just me. I want to see—"

"You idiot!" said Red. "That guy had a rifle!"

"But I want to see—"

Red grabbed the gelding's bridle and pulled, and slapped him hard on the rump.

"Come on, Alice!"

Chapter Twenty-Four

Better Have a Good Story

Now what? thought Alice. How happy would Detective Kubecka be about this? Probably not very. And could she and Red drive the horse trailer past the entrance to Cloud Ranch without running into rifle man?

"Red," she said, "I've been thinking. Maybe you stay here and I just race for town with this stuff."

"Nope," said Red firmly. "We'll be fine. You aren't going by yourself. But you can call and tell them we're coming."

Alice waited to call until after she and Red had coaxed the horses back in the trailer, had said hurried good-byes to the McDuffies, had left Cloud Ranch behind, and were halfway back to Coffee Creek. After it was over, Alice thought it was the weirdest call she'd ever made, like something out of a movie. Kubecka didn't sound best pleased. He slammed down the receiver.

She and Red left the horse trailer in front of the sheriff's office and marched in. Kubecka, arms folded, was standing by the desk.

"Ladies, you better have a good story."

Alice and Red looked at each other.

"Well," said Alice, "it's my fault really, not Red's. Don't blame her. But it was such a wild notion I thought I should check it out beforehand, before bothering you."

"No you didn't," said Kubecka.

"Well, really, I did," said Alice. "There was no reason I thought about this place except that I'd been up there with Ollie, and for some reason the cave made me . . . well, it seemed like something could happen there. Or could have happened. So it was a wild hair. And it may mean nothing. But we did find Ollie's cell phone. And these tracks, that Red took pictures of. Here's the cell phone."

She took the bandana-wrapped object out of her pocket and handed it to Kubecka. "Red took a picture of where we found it," Alice said. "It was way under a cedar tree, a really thick one. We nearly didn't find it."

"Like someone threw it?"

Alice nodded. "Hard to see how it got there otherwise," she said. "And I know it's a reach, but Ollie was very intrigued by the fact that he could take pictures with his new phone. Now I don't know if he did or not, I mean take a picture or throw the cell phone, but I was afraid if this thing got rained on, I didn't think we would ever know if we didn't go get it." She took a breath. "Maybe you have ways to revive dead phones. If it's dead."

"Let's see," said Kubecka.

The phone battery was dead. He hooked it up to a charger that sprouted multiple tails for multiple brands. When it finally showed signs of returning to life, he pushed the photo icon. He bent over the phone screen, with Alice and Red and Files, who had joined them, peering over his shoulder.

He pointed. "What's that?"

Alice stared. "It's the ledge," she said, "the ledge to the cave."

"Well, where was he when he took it?"

"He's—he's at the bottom of the cliff."

"Where the hell is this?"

"Over on the north side of the ranch. Below the cliff where the rock art is located. And the cave where the major pictures are."

"So he took this after you were with him on Saturday, is that right?"

Alice nodded. "He didn't know his cell phone could take pictures. I showed him how when we were up on the ledge."

Kubecka looked at Alice and Red.

"Okay, tell me all about it. And I mean all."

Red got out her cell phone and showed him all the pictures they had taken that afternoon—where they found the phone, the twin tracks. "Honestly, we didn't step on them," she said. "Alice said to stay way to the side."

"And there's the piñon branch," Alice said.

"Piñon? Like in New Mexico, the little nuts?"

"Yes. They grow up high on that ridge. But this branch was on the ground."

Kubecka glared at them.

"Why didn't you call us right away?" he said.

"Well, that rifle shot. It hit the tree where Alice was reaching for the cell phone," Red said.

Kubecka shook his head. "Did you mention that on the phone when you called me? No, you did not." He leaned back in his chair, arms crossed on his chest, heaved an exasperated sigh. "Okay, where did this rifle shot come from? Did you see who it was?"

"No, we had to get the horses up to the gate and get out of there," said Red.

"Horses!" He looked at them in disbelief. "You went in there on horseback? Who do you think you are, the Cisco Kid and Pancho?"

"We were out for a ride at the McDuffies."

He stared at Red. Red stared back.

"You don't know if it was someone shooting at you, or someone just checking out the deer blind before deer season or what, right?"

"That's right. Alice wanted to go see who it was but I made her leave."

"Thank goodness someone showed at least a modicum of sense," Kubecka growled.

"True," said Alice. "We heard a truck come towards where we were, but we were out the gate by then. And it was only one shot."

"Only one shot," said Kubecka. "And how would you feel if it had killed your friend Red?"

"Hey!" said Red. "Hey! I came up with the horse idea!"

Alice said, "Look, officer, we were afraid it would rain, we knew it was a very long shot, excuse the pun, and we got the cell phone. And pictures of the area. You didn't have to go get a search warrant."

"Besides, the ranch is Alice's client's, or at least the conservancy's, now." Red gave Kubecka her best rodeo-queen smile. Alice did not correct the unusual attorney-client arrangement Red had suggested.

"Besides," said Red, "have you found out who rammed Alice's truck yet?"

He shook his head. "Too much TV," he said. "No, we don't know who rammed Ms. Greer's truck while driving a truck that might have been black, green, brown, or navy, with a black brush guard and a Texas license, that might possibly have had the letter G in it."

Behind, she could hear Adam Files organizing the crime-scene people to head for Cloud Ranch. Kubecka brought the ranch up on Google Maps and Alice and Red pointed to where they thought they had come down the cliff and where the cell phone had been found. Adam printed the page and made them mark the spot.

"So," said Red, "you need us." She grinned at Kubecka.

"I need you to stay alive and not complicate the crime scene, and not turn into some kind of traveling crime scene yourselves," he said.

"Right," said Alice. "We'll be good."

You don't know how good, she thought. Because Alice had a couple of ideas. And it was after she left that she remembered she had never mentioned Howie Randall to Detective Kubecka or Constable Files. Oh, but, she thought, I promised his sister I would tell her first. So it's all right. Then she wondered if Kubecka would agree.

Chapter Twenty-Five

Keep Driving

On Saturday morning, Alice steamed a mug of milk, poured in some exceptionally strong coffee, and stood barefoot out on the deck, looking at the creek and sipping the foamy coffee-milk. How wonderful to be alive, she thought, so long as there is really good strong coffee, and a deck to stand on, and a creek meandering along in the early sun, down there in its limestone bed.

Today she had an appointment for a facial in San Antonio. She and Red had back-to-back appointments with the Prague-born woman who had changed their lives—facially speaking. Gerda had some sort of sixth sense about what skin needed. She had met all kinds of skin and figured out the truth of each one. She was harder to get an appointment with than the Queen of England. "How old is Gerda?" Red asked once.

"A thousand? Sixty? A reincarnated Egyptian?" Alice had wondered aloud. At any rate, every two months, or as often as they could afford it, Red and Alice headed for west San Antonio to visit Gerda's tidy little salon. They emerged lectured, cleaned, encouraged, and glistening. "Makes me feel so taken care of," Red said.

Alice thought getting Nigel to cut her hair and Gerda to give her facials and life advice was all the luxury a good Presbyterian could stand, but she was not about to give up either. And today she had special plans for San Antonio. Still drinking her coffee-milk on the deck, Alice called Red. "Hey, pick you up at nine?"

"Why so early? Our appointments aren't until one and two!" said Red.

"Well," said Alice, "if we go a little early, we could cruise by US Security. It's on the north side of San Antonio, close to Loop 1604."

"US Security," mused Red. "Ah. I see. Okay, pick me up at nine, but let's leave your dented-up truck and take mine. Might not look so familiar if we see anyone, which we hope we don't."

"Done. But yours is pretty memorable." Red drove a bright red Suburban, once hailed by a Texas magazine as the Texas state car. Hard to miss, thought Alice. But hers was already too familiar to rammer man.

They grabbed coffee and tacos at their favorite Coffee Creek roadside stand before heading south. "One al pastor," Alice told the proprietor, "and one pork with verde sauce and avocado."

Red as always ordered one egg-chorizo and one bean and cheese with extra salsa.

"Yum," Red sighed, holding the steering wheel with one hand and dabbing salsa off her chin with the other.

"Yum."

"Okay, here's Loop 1604. You tell me where to turn."

Alice navigated while Red maneuvered through a light warehouse district just off the loop.

"There." Alice pointed. They were cruising slowly through an industrial park. A tan stucco building bore the green and black US Security logo out front. Two blank windows stared at an empty front parking lot.

"No one here, looks like," said Red.

"Just keep driving," said Alice. "Could you turn around in the next block? Come on back by? And turn into the driveway next door, at Wave Pools."

Red made a loop and parked. Alice got out.

"Where do you think you're going?"

"Just got to go look at what's out back," said Alice. "Don't leave!"

Alice walked around the back of Wave Pools purposefully, as if she knew what she was doing and as if she needed most urgently to examine the empty pool forms stacked up behind the building. She stalked around, staring earnestly at the pool forms, making a few notes in her little notebook. I look ridiculous, she thought. What would a real detective do? She sneaked a peek toward a fenced-off storage area that ran from the back of the tan stucco US Security building toward an alley. Beyond a ten-foot chain-link fence she could see an orderly row of large square crates, then another row of small travel trailers, with no distinguishing logos, then a large shipping-style container. And behind those, a Hummer, two black vans, and three pickup trucks. Two were white, both with the US Security logo.

And finally, there it was. Pulled in flush with the fence, all the way at the back, stood a big forest-green pickup, no logo, sporting a big black brush guard on the front. I must see that license plate, thought Alice. And I want to see that brush guard. An alley ran behind the storage yards of both Wave Pools and US Security. The US Security yard had a big padlocked gate on the alley side, next to the truck.

She angled back toward the rear of the Wave Pools lot, dodging behind a giant fiberglass shell. Now she could see the truck better. Yes, the brush guard was dented, on the left front side. Yes, there was a G in the license plate. She scribbled down the number, heart thumping, then sidled back around the Wave Pools storage yard, skirted the fiberglass pool shells, and trotted quickly around the other side of the Wave Pools building. She yanked open Red's passenger door and slid down below the window. Red raised her eyebrows. "I'm not cut out for this," Alice panted. "It scares the crap out of me."

"But nobody's there, right? What now?" said Red.

"Can we just drive to Gerda's?" said Alice, still scrunched down with her head below the window. "That was the truck, Red, I swear it was. And there was a G in the license plate."

"Can't be more than a thousand of those, honey," said Red.

"Well, it explains something. He didn't have to use his own truck," said Alice. "He could leave that big black SUV out front and just slide out to the storage lot and take that green pickup out the alley gate. Who would know? With his car out front, it would look like he was in the office the whole time."

Red wheeled away from the Wave Pools lot and headed for Gerda's. "Yes," Red said, "that could explain rammer man. And maybe skunk man. But wasn't Doyle in Houston the day Ollie fell? Isn't that what Kubecka said?"

"Humph."

"Still, you should tell Detective Kubecka."

Out of the corner of her eye, Alice watched Red checking the rearview mirror—often. But nothing interrupted their sybaritic trip to Gerda's. They were peered at, scrubbed, scolded, and patted, and then emerged into the fine San Antonio air, sunny and soft, in a state of high glisten. "Ahhh," they chorused, collapsing back into Red's front seat. "What did she tell you?" demanded Alice.

"She told me my eyebrows didn't look as moth-eaten as before." Red patted her eyebrows complacently. "And you?"

"She muttered about the crease between my eyes. She said, 'RRRRRRREEEE-LAX' those eye muscles! Blink more so you won't have puffy eyes!" Alice sang.

"Blink more?"

They headed north to Coffee Creek.

Chapter Twenty-Six

Use Your Eyes

On Monday morning Alice drove in cold, steady rain to the office. "Bender called," Silla reported. "Fieldwork project ended early. He wants to move the rock art assessment at Cloud Ranch up two weeks. Says his team can be ready tomorrow. Do I tell him it's okay?"

"Don't see why not," Alice said. "Call and tell Mary. And Allen, I guess, so he won't shoot them when they come down the ranch drive. What time will they get out there?"

"About noon, he thought," Silla said, disappearing back to the workroom. Alice heard her on the phone.

"Okay," said Silla, popping back. "Left a message for Mary, talked to Allen. He's in Fort Worth. Says he went to see his grandmother."

Alice turned back to the will she was working on. She looked up. Uh-oh. Shouldn't she check with Kubecka before letting a team tramp around up on the cliff? "Silla," she called, "could you call Kubecka's office and ask him to give me a ring?"

She left for Rotary. No Treacher in attendance today. The rain was letting up by the time she got back to the office. "Call Kubecka," Silla ordered.

"Yes ma'am." She and Kubecka played phone tag. Finally Adam Files called back.

"Detective Kubecka wants me to bring you up to date on a couple of things," he said. "First, that sap on Mr. West's hand—looks like it could be piñon, but the lab is still testing. Second, the lab did test his truck. There were some blood smears in the truck bed and some hair. Looks like he was in that pickup bed at some point after he got hurt."

"You mean someone moved him in his own pickup?"

"Looks like it."

"But you don't know who?"

"No. No prints except Mr. West's on the steering wheel, so maybe whoever it was wore gloves, or wiped the interior."

"So, Adam," said Alice, "is this a murder investigation?"

"Suspected homicide. He still could have just fallen by himself and somebody moved him for some reason."

"Are you going to go look up at the cliffs where the rock art is? Up above where we found the phone?"

"Already did. Detective Kubecka sent someone out over the weekend. But didn't find anything, apparently."

"Nothing?" Alice felt the flat sense of disappointment. And surprise. She had hoped—even assumed—that an answer lay somewhere by the little pool, or the piñons clinging to the edge of the cliff. "No footprints? No anything?"

"Apparently not," said Files.

"Okay," said Alice. "In that case, I guess you don't mind if the Rock Art Conservancy people go up there tomorrow? They're ready to start their assessment."

"Should be okay," said Files, "and I'll call you back if it's not."

Alice sat at her desk, staring out the window toward the street, drumming her fingers to some song. Her mental soundtrack was running a Béla Fleck banjo. Endless loop, like this: Still no answers as to why Ollie fell, or who moved him, bloody and broken, in his own truck. Allen, Mary, and Doyle all had alibis. She herself still did not know the identity of skunk man and why he had been under her deck, or why rammer man had tried to run her into the overpass. She thought rammer man was Doyle, but Doyle was out of town when Ollie died.

None of this, therefore, made any sense. Gunny Powell? No reverberation there. Surely not.

All she wanted right now was to be sitting in the lap of the cliffs at Cloud Ranch before the rock art team invaded with lights and measuring tapes and sampling kits and cameras. She wanted to make her way across the narrow shelf, and to stare up at the odd figures until she again felt herself rising, felt her arms become wings, felt the elevator rush of flying up, up, up toward the sun. She wanted to sit by the small, immeasurably rare spring, and remember Ollie, and, perhaps, Cassie. She would think of them both, she decided—Cassie who could look far and deep, Ollie with his steady eyes.

Okay, Alice said to herself. And that means getting to Cloud Ranch ahead of Bender and the team. With Allen in Fort Worth, no need to stop at the bunkhouse to explain where she was going or what she was doing. She would just beat them all there, and be with those rock paintings while they worked their magic. Before they were catalogued and photographed and made into research projects.

* * * *

Early on Tuesday Alice headed out once more to Cloud Ranch. "I see you, Mr. Jackrabbit," she informed a pair of twitching black-tipped ears in the pasture. "I see you." She bumped down her drive, trying not to spill her coffee and listening to a funky Austin public radio station playing music she'd never heard before. "Road trip," Alice said aloud. But this road trip felt so different from her first joyful early-morning drive out to Cloud Ranch.

To cheer herself up, Alice stopped west of Fredericksburg at Bet's Biscuits, for that usually delightful luxury: breakfast fixed by someone else. She slid into the corner booth and ordered sausage and eggs. The breakfast crowd had already thinned out on this weekday. But Alice found herself rushing through breakfast instead of enjoying it. She paid and left. She wanted to get up the cliff and down that shelf before she thought much more about it.

Ollie's gate swung open when she punched in the code. At the top of the ridge she jammed on the brakes. Cloud Ranch lay before her, silent. Nothing moved below. No trucks at the house or the bunkhouse.

She pulled her truck into the same place Ollie had parked his on their first visit. By nine thirty she lay panting on the rock platform before the golden dancers. So beautiful! But no stopping here: she wanted the little spring. Nothing for it but to tackle that narrow shelf. This had definitely sounded like a better plan yesterday afternoon. Alice thought remorsefully of John and Ann, left without their mother, orphans entirely, if she fell off this cliff. And no one even knew she was here. What a dunce I am. She hadn't called Silla, Red, Ann, John, Bender, or anyone at the sheriff's office, and coverage was weak here. She texted Silla and Red. "At Cloud Ranch." Not my best move, she thought. Vowing not to abandon her children by falling off the cliff, Alice took a deep breath and picked her way up the rocky slot. For the second time she climbed past the little trees until she came to the dropoff and had to turn right, inward, toward the cliff face. For the second time she leaned on the inclined rock and inched up onto the little shelf. For the second time she began inching along on her knees, across the fourteen-inch-wide ledge to the cliff garden below the cave.

There was her pool. She flopped gratefully by the water, touched her tongue to the water, touched her hand to the water and to her forehead. Made it, she thought. The ground was damp after yesterday's rain; her jeans were wet at the knees. The rain washed this place, she thought. If anything had been up here, the rain took it away. She sat back on her heels, looking around. Late October morning sun slanted from the shelf toward the pool, and lit up the figures on the rock.

Was Ollie here before he fell? Did she feel some trace of him, see some wavery hologram of Ollie shimmering in the air? He'd told her he hadn't been up here in years, because of his knees. But had he made a last trip? She couldn't reconcile the broken piñon branch and the sap on Ollie's hand with Adam Files's assurance that the sheriff's office found nothing out of the ordinary up here.

Stop, she ordered herself. Be a little Zen, Alice. You can't change whatever it is that happened. So, try to think for a moment of Ollie and Cassie. She tried to say a brief prayer for them. But instead she felt herself staring again at the figures—the black one, the white one, the snaky one above. The wind riffled the spring. She stared, transfixed, at the figures. She felt her head lifting, her hands floating, the sun lifting her hair, air beneath her arms. She was flying, up, up, up toward the arch of the rock, past the figures, up toward the top of the cliff. She felt like a new creature, a strong one, lifting on the wind, ready to rise up and up forever.

But a puff of wind rustled the grass, rippled the pond, blew her hair in her eyes. Whomp. She was back on the ground, a human staring at rock pictures. Just Alice MacDonald Greer again. How strange I feel, Alice thought. Like myself again, but more like an animal. She shook herself like a puppy. No, she thought. I'm . . . sleek and sharp-clawed? Maybe my shaman spirit has visited. She looked at her hands. Short nails. No polish. And no claws. A secret shaman with invisible claws and invisible fur, apparently.

A deep rumble reached her. Diesel engine, she thought, switching gears down the drive from the highway? But Bender couldn't already be here, could he? He was aiming for noon. Alice's gut knotted. She edged on her hands and knees toward the cliff, peering off toward her left, off to the south. If she leaned out just a bit she could glimpse the road. Oh, God. The dark green truck. Crouched rigid in horror, she saw it heading north toward her, then lost sight of it.

Where could she hide? Nowhere up here. The cave was too shallow, with that rockfall at the rear. Could she race back down the shelf and the rocky slot, get down to the platform and down the first cliff and get to her truck and get it started before he caught her? Or could she at least slip into the cedar brake? Run for the gate to the McDuffie place?

Alice started for the shelf. This time, she thought, no backing down it. She would go downhill, frontward. And because she headed down it on her knees instead of backing down it, she saw something she had never seen—had had no reason to see. At the end of the shelf, above the slanted rock she had to slide down to get to the rocky slot that led back to the first platform, there was a little rift in the rock—a sort of mini-chimney. Could she go up there? But I want to be off this cliff, Alice thought desperately. I want to jump off and hide in the cedar, creep to the faded red gate, be safe at the McDuffies'. I'll try that first.

So she took a deep breath and started down the shelf as fast as she could, heart pounding, knees aching, trying not to even look over the edge. She slid down the inclined rock onto the end of the rocky slot and peered down the slot—no one coming. Good. She raced down the slot and suddenly was on the rock platform below the golden dancers. She crept to the edge and looked over. Doyle was below. She stood frozen, sick with horror. He walked around her truck, staring into it. He opened the door of his green diesel and pulled out a short, sharp shovel—the kind Jordie used to call an entrenching tool. He pulled out a pistol, and a big olive canvas duffel. The duffel he rolled and put in a pack on his back, with the shovel point sticking out. The pistol he put in his pocket. He pushed his sunglasses up on his forehead. Then he glanced up and their eyes locked.

"Got you," he said. He smiled and gazed up at her—pale blue eyes, impassive. Sniper eyes, thought Alice. She had never seen such a menacing smile. He started for the cliff and Alice backed away, panicked. She couldn't go down. Couldn't go back to the cave. She turned and raced back up the slot, turned right, clambered up the inclined slab of rock to the beginning of the narrow shelf, and looked up. Oh, little chimney, she thought, oh, do not let me fall. She began inching up the chimney. It looked like she could get up ten or twelve feet—then what? Then where? Nowhere else to go. Alice braced her hands on small protruding limestone knobs, inched higher, panting, sweating. Up she went, leaning back into the narrow space, pushing her thighs against the rock, trying to be quiet, trying to be higher, trying to be invisible. A few fragments rolled down and bounced off the shelf into the air. Could not let Doyle see those. She remembered his sniper eyes.

But that was not really his way, was it? No, the deaths around him looked accidental. She shuddered and looked up, hoping for another grip, higher. The chimney narrowed, became just a crack, further up. She pushed up another foot. Here she was half-hidden, half-exposed, hands gripping the sides of the chimney, hiking boots wedged on tiny outcrops, thighs pressed to the sides of the chimney. Alice was not sure how long she could stay put. She shut her eyes, prayed, breathed. She could hear Doyle now. The shovel, or something metal, clanked on the rocky cliff of the slot. She heard him walking up now, rocks moving under his boots. If he would just keep going straight up to the cave, not lifting his head to see—her feet were at least twelve feet above where his head would be—he wouldn't spot her. But if he did? She had nothing, nothing. Clinging with her left had, Alice groped with her right around the side of the chimney. Her hand closed on a fist-sized outcrop. She pulled. Loose, like a tooth. She pulled again. It came free, a fist-sized piece of limestone, old seabed, in her hand. She clung to the edge of the chimney with her left hand, holding the rock in her right. Rocks crunched underfoot in the slot below. He was very close now, very close. Alice tried to still her thumping heart.

Below she saw Doyle's head. He climbed up the incline onto the little rock shelf, maneuvering his pack with the sharp entrenching tool. Fourteen inches was narrow for someone as broad and blocky as Doyle, with his pack. And he was too big for her chimney, she hoped. Alice tried not to breathe, not to move. Shhh, Alice, she warned herself. Let him just go on up the shelf to the cave. That's where he thinks I am. Let him turn and start up the shelf.

And Doyle did. But Alice's foot slipped, making a crunching noise. A pebble bounced onto the shelf. Doyle didn't turn at the sound. But the pebble bounced off the shelf and flew out into the bright air. His head turned to follow it. Then he carefully turned around and looked up at the chimney, and up at Alice.

She saw the calculation in his face. No bullet, no strangulation, no knife—just a fall for the lady lawyer, the meddling, interfering, officious lady lawyer, whose words on a piece of paper took away his right to run this ranch, his right to be jefe, his right to control every inch of this dirt, including the cliff where he stood. He showed his teeth. He stared at her while carefully shifting his pack from his back to his front. He reached in, pulled out a rope, reached in again, groped at the bottom, and pulled out two big carabiners. Staring at Alice, he put the pack back on. Then he tied loops in each end of the rope, attaching the carabiners so they slid loose. He gathered the rope into loops, like a lariat but with twin carabiners dangling.

Alice was paralyzed—pressed into the chimney, holding on with her left hand. Doyle began to swing the carabiners, and then suddenly flung them at her head. SMACK! The biners hit the rock, sending sharp splinters flying. Alice felt warm blood trickling down her eyebrow and toward her eye. She flinched, blinked. Doyle twirled the biners again, then cracked the ropes like a whip, aiming the biners at her left hand. She couldn't try to grab them—she'd fall. She pulled her hand into the slot just as the biners hit the rock. CRACK! More rock splinters. She squeezed her eyes shut. Then suddenly Alice was seized with fury. You bastard, she thought, you murdering bastard. This is what Ollie felt, isn't it? She watched Doyle. He was grinning. Thinks he's got his range, with his little homemade atlatl, thought Alice, furious. What'll it be this time? Crack my kneecaps? Try my head again? Put out my eyes? Break my nose? She clutched her rock. She tensed, with the same rising tide of "get ready" she felt back in college when serving for match point. In her head her coach was yelling, "Take dead aim!" And Ilka was saying, "Your eyes! Use your eyes!" Doyle started swinging the carabiners in a tight circle. Just as his arm took a bigger swing, ready to crack the whip, Alice made herself flick her eyes left, like she saw something. Doyle looked too and in that split second, as he turned back in scorn, she brought the rock up and flung it straight at his face. Doyle flinched in surprise, jerking his head just enough that the rock clipped his ear and the carabiners caught on a little branch behind his head. He leaned an inch too far out in space, then tried to pull back toward the cliff. He grabbed for the shelf but the heavy pack pulled him off balance. For a long moment he hung, one foot on the little shelf, one waving behind him in the air, while he grabbed for the little tree, whose sparse branches still entangled the carabiners and the rope. The tree couldn't hold him. Suddenly the tree broke loose in a shower of dirt and rock, and Doyle and the tree fell. Alice heard branches breaking, one after another, then a heavy thud. Oh God.

Alice was shaking so hard she thought she would never be able to start down the chimney. Palms sweating, she inched down, waving her boot like a clumsy antenna before each tiny step down, testing each outcrop before sliding her thighs down the next cautious inch. She nearly fell twice and had to grip with every muscle to stay wedged in the narrow rock jacket. Finally she was only a foot above the inclined rock. Careful, careful! her mind ordered. One slip and you are off the shelf! She begged her feet to stay put. When she got her feet onto the shelf, she sat and slid down the inclined limestone slab, gripping every handhold, groping with her toes for the scanty level inches that would mean she could slide around and be safe in the rocky slot below. I can't bear to look over the edge, Alice thought. But she finally peered down through broken branches. Doyle lay splayed nearly fifty feet down, carabiners wound about him, the pack sideways beneath him.

"Doyle?" she called. Did his eyelids move?

"I'm coming!" she called. Oh for God's sake. Why? He tried to kill me, tried to make me fall! she thought. But I'm an officer of the court, she argued. I can't try to make someone fall off a cliff. Yes, but didn't he kill Ollie? And wasn't he trying to kill you? Wasn't he trying his same old modus operandi out again, but this time on you? Knock you off the rock, leaving no mark—like he did to Ollie? Knock you off so you would die in a fall that would look like it was your fault . . . the way he made Howie Randall drown?

But I am not like him, Alice thought. Oh really? said her other self. Oh really? What about that spurting rage you felt when you hurled that rock—even though you only clipped him on the ear? Yes, but I didn't mean for him to fall off the cliff, she argued to herself. Oh, didn't you? Didn't you? What did you think would happen if you hadn't managed to hit him, or at least make him flinch? Do you think he would have just quit trying to kill you?

Suddenly she was exhausted. Oh, whatever, thought Alice. Numbly she stomped down the slot. And now, again, she heard a truck laboring up the hill toward the cliff. Again she reached the platform where the golden dancers arched and pivoted, oblivious to the murderous struggle that had just unfolded.

Wearily, Alice lay on her stomach and backed over the edge of the cliff as Ollie had taught her, moving down, left foot here, right foot there. Put your little foot . . .

Solid ground. She turned slowly and found Bender staring at her. "We need to call 911," she said. "We need an ambulance."

"What happened?"

"Doyle fell off the cliff."

"Who's Doyle? What's wrong with your head?"

Wordless, Alice turned and started around the side of the cliff, Bender following. Doyle lay where he'd fallen, unmoving. Only his eyes turned to Bender and Alice.

Bender said, "We can't move you. But we'll call for help." Doyle looked at him, then turned his eyes back at the sky. He didn't seem to be in pain. But he also didn't seem able to move anything but his eyes.

Bender punched buttons on his phone, shook his head, and walked off into the pasture looking for coverage. Finally he walked back.

"The EMS guys said to put a coat over him to keep him warm but not to move him," said Bender. "It's the Fredericksburg EMS—they'll be here pretty fast."

Alice nodded, watching Doyle.

"Let me look at your head," said Bender. He peered at Alice's forehead and parted her hair, prodding a bit. "Well," he said, "maybe a new scar, but it's pretty much stopped bleeding. How'd that happen?"

"Piece of rock?" Alice offered.

"And this bruise?" He patted her forehead. "Gonna be an interesting color."

"Carabiner?" she said. Then she looked at him and said, "Gotta sit." She sank to the ground, scattering cedar duff.

His face changed. "You were up there too?"

She didn't answer.

For a few minutes there was no sound. High above in the clear blue sky circled one, two, three birds. Vultures. Doyle lay motionless as a fallen statue, ten feet away, covered with their jackets. The late October sun warmed Alice's cold hands, warmed her hair.

Ollie, she thought. Ollie, hovering near her. And perhaps the other presence? She inhaled deeply. Cedar, sun on cedar and pasture and limestone, and—something faint and sweet? The smell of autumn? Alice thought.

La pourriture noble. Leaves, yellow and dry, then leaf meal. Golden grove unleafing, then the short, erratic Texas winter. She breathed in one more time, very deeply, remembering Ollie. And now suddenly the air was—just air. Normal outdoor Hill Country air. She got to her feet.

"What the hell was he doing with all this stuff?" asked Bender, pointing at the entrenching tool and the big duffel and pack, still underneath Doyle. "And what the hell is that? Was he roped and climbing? Or what?" Bender pointed at the carabiners and the rope draped over Doyle.

"That's—" Alice started, then suddenly realized Doyle was listening.

"Doyle. Can you talk?" He looked at her without moving his head, then shut his eyes.

Alice walked away and nodded for Bender to follow her. "That man," she began. "That man tried to kill me. I was hiding in the chimney above the slot and he was trying to make me fall, using the carabiners like an atlatl or something."

"An atlatl? No," said Bender impatiently. "Not the right thing. Not an atlatl. You must mean something else, like a bola. Trying to hit you with the carabiners? Like, popping them at you?"

"Yes. I threw a rock at him. He dodged but I got him on the ear. Then he caught his rope in a little tree and then he tripped and fell with the pack and the shovel."

"What was he doing here, Alice?"

"He didn't know you guys were coming today," said Alice. "I guess Mary didn't tell him."

"That's Ollie's daughter? The one we deal with on the conservancy stuff?"

"Yes. She's married to Doyle."

"But what is he doing with this stuff? The shovel? The bag? Where was he going, Alice?"

She could hardly talk, hardly think, anymore. "The cave."

"But why? He can't be digging in there! We've got to assess the cave, before anyone disturbs it! What else is in his pack, Alice?"

Alice stared at Bender. "Don't touch it," she said. "And don't talk to him any more about what happened until the police get here."

Bender looked blankly at her. Then his eyebrows lifted. "Oh.""

"Yes," Alice said.

"And . . . did he kill Ollie?"

"I think so," said Alice. "But don't let him hear us. Don't give him any more information. He's—he's pretty good at this. And don't touch his stuff. And could you call my office and tell Silla to call Mary and tell her about

Doyle?"

"Let's wait until the EMS folks get here," said Bender.

"No," said Alice, remembering Jordie. "No, she wants to know. She just doesn't know it yet."

Bender walked off. She could see him out in the pasture, on the phone. They heard the ambulance before they saw it, rumbling down the hill, lights flashing but no siren. Coming down the hill behind were a pickup and a big beige sheriff-mobile.

"Hey," Alice said. "Didn't you say you were bringing your team? Grad assistants and so on?"

"Yeah," said Bender. "Believe that's who's in the truck. I came out first because I just . . . wanted to see it first, without them."

He cocked his head at Alice.

"Is that what you were doing?"

She nodded. "I just wanted to sit up there and . . . you know."

He nodded. "I know."

In the pasture, doors were slamming, boots running toward Doyle.

"And did you fly?"

She slid her eyes toward Bender, then up at the cliff.

"Yes."

"And did you find your shaman spirit, Alice? Your spirit animal?"

"Maybe."

"Gonna tell me?" Bender pressed.

Alice looked at the cliff again, then at Bender. "Water-loving," she said. "The little pool up there. You'll see."

"Hmm," he said, watching her face. "I'll see the pool, or I'll see your shaman animal start coming out?"

Alice managed a weak grin. He grinned back. "Well, you're finally looking better, Alice. I didn't so much like the pale green look. Think you can talk now?" He cocked his head and glanced pointedly behind her.

"Yep," said Detective Kubecka, followed by Files. "We're here."

Alice pointed at Doyle. "Make them take pictures before they move him," said Alice.

"I did," said Files.

"How'd you get that?" said Kubecka, pointing at her head and the dried blood on her hair and forehead. "You okay?"

Alice said a silent prayer. Get me through this, Jordie. Then she gave her statement.

All talking stopped when the EMS team lifted Doyle and started for the ambulance. Alice turned to watch. The pack had spilled open when Doyle fell. Now Alice could see that a roll of silver duct tape had fallen out, and some black plastic behind it.

Files said, "Shovel, black bag, duct tape."

"You've got a dirty mind," Kubecka answered.

Alice said, "I've got to step aside for a moment." She pushed through some cedar until she found an out-of-earshot, out-of-sight spot, and she peed. An improvement.

When she came back (and she noted Files was watching exactly the spot where she emerged from the cedar thicket), Kubecka said, "We need you to show us where he was when he fell." Alice pointed up at the cliff.

"I mean, can you take us up there," said Kubecka.

"Okay," she said. They started through the cedar to the bottom of the cliff, where she remembered Ollie saying, "Now we've got to climb." She showed them the footholds up to the first set of rock art, on the little platform. She went first, Bender last. Once they reached the top, Files and Kubecka stood staring at the golden dance unfolding on the wall.

"Nice," said Kubecka.

"Nice?" said Bender. "These are superb! World class."

"This why Ollie wanted that rock art group to take this over?" demanded Kubecka.

"Oh, it's just part of it," Alice said.

"And this is where you were standing?" Files said, pointing at the platform.

"Oh no," said Alice. "We weren't here. We were up there." She pointed up the rocky slot. "You have to climb." The officers started up, cameras in hand. When they got to the end of the slot, Kubecka, leading, stopped dead.

"Now what?" he called over his shoulder. He was holding a piñon branch, right at the end of the slot, right at the dropoff.

Alice edged forward. She pointed over his shoulder, up the incline to the little shelf, and pointed where the shelf went, toward the little cliff garden. "That's the way to the cave," she said. "And the rest of the pictures."

"Good lord," Kubecka said. "And where was Doyle when he fell?"

She pointed up at the beginning of the shelf.

"Oh, yeah," Kubecka said. "Now I see." He stared at the dangling roots, the remnant of the tree Doyle had dragged down with him.

"But where were you?"

Alice silently pointed up above the shelf. From where she stood she couldn't quite see the rock chimney in the big slab of limestone that inclined up from the slot. "You have to get up higher on that shelf before you can see where I was."

She showed them how to inch up the slab onto the shelf. Kubecka and Files followed. Finally Bender crawled up the slab, muttering encouragement to himself, but then he paused at the top, gazing, horrified, at the length of the shelf that ran before him along the face of the cliff. With Kubecka and Files lined up on the shelf next to her, Alice showed them the chimney.

Kubecka, Files, Bender all stared at her. "How did you do that?" Kubecka said.

"Scared to death," Alice said. "I was scared to death. I was hoping when he came up that he would go all the way down the shelf to the cave and wouldn't see me up there and I could get down and make it back to my truck. But that didn't happen."

"He heard you?"

"No, I don't think so. I don't think his hearing is great. I accidentally kicked a little rock down. And it bounced on the shelf, and he saw it and turned and saw me."

"How high up did you get?"

Alice looked up at the slab of limestone with the little gap, the narrow chimney, facing out toward the shelf. Twenty feet up a fresh white spot showed on the weathered limestone. "See the place where the rock is chipped? Where it's white?"

They nodded.

"That's where the carabiners hit the rock. He was swinging them together at me, on the rope."

"That's what got your head?"

Alice nodded. "Both the rock chips and the biners. Then he swung at my left hand, the one I was holding the rock with."

Kubecka prodded. "And then?"

"I threw a rock at his face. He moved his head but I got his ear. But he was whirling the ropes and when he moved they caught on the little tree and he got off balance. And he fell."

They all looked at the dangling roots.

"Then I came down," said Alice. "And Bender showed up right then."

"Yes," said Bender. "I saw you coming down."

"But when you said all the way down the path to the cave," said Kubecka, pointing down the shelf toward the cliff garden, "you meant that thing?" He pointed back up the narrow shelf with the one protruding rock and the sheer drop.

"Yes," said Alice. "At the end there, that's where the cave and the really amazing pictures are. That's where Ollie fell from, I think. Didn't you send someone out to look at it?" She looked at Files, who looked at Kubecka. "Adam said you didn't see anything."

"Well, damn it," Kubecka said. "The officer I sent probably didn't see anything because he probably didn't go all the way out that shelf. I don't think I told him right."

"And now it's rained out here," Alice commented.

Kubecka grimaced, making a mouth like a frog. "We oughta go look," he said.

"Wait a minute," Bender objected. "That's a world-class scientific site. We have a team coming out here today to assess it. We've got to do that before it gets tromped all over." He waved his hand at the pickup they could see out on the road from the ranch house, moving slowly toward them. "Bet that's them in the truck."

Kubecka barked back, "It's a crime scene. Possibly. And that takes precedence."

Files put his hand up. "Sir? What was Doyle doing with that stuff? Shovel, duct tape, and all that?"

Silence.

They looked at Alice.

"Well," she said. "Here's what I think." And she told them.

And so began one of the oddest fieldwork experiences Bender had ever directed, and one of the strangest crime-scene investigations Files and Kubecka had ever worked. Bender's grad students made their way up to meet them, lugging lights, cameras, tape measures, calipers, sample kits, and GPS. The whole group, pulling along equipment and led by Alice, crawled like a cautious caterpillar along the little cliff shelf, with Bender roped for form's sake to an obliging grad student with some rock-climbing experience. Kubecka and Files made everyone stop on the shelf while the two of them first walked out onto the area below the cave and scanned and photographed the site, starting from the end of the shelf. Alice thought as she watched that they didn't seem to see anything worth comment, or else they were keeping their own counsel. With Bender sweating and swearing after being made to wait, roped in, on the narrow shelf, the entire group finally assembled on the tiny slanted patch of grass by the pool, clinging to the few slim trees and staring up at the cave pictures.

Bender, Kubecka, and Files held a muttered discussion; then the group moved up to the cave. Wearing gloves, two grad students carefully numbered and moved each rock in the rockfall inside the cave. Kubecka made the rest of the group stay by the spring. One grad student systematically photographed the rock art. Watching intently, Bender shook his head. "Alice, couldn't you tell this rockslide wasn't natural? Couldn't you tell someone had blocked up part of the cave?"

"No," said Alice. "I couldn't see that. But I thought I knew why Doyle would try to get back up here, before you."

The rockslide now had an opening at the top. "Sir!" called Files, hunched and peering into the gap.

Kubecka knelt, peering along the flashlight beam. He turned.

"Okay," he said. "It's a body. Buried sitting up but hunched over. Long hair, still."

Faces turned to Alice.

"I'm thinking it's your Cassie," Kubecka said. "And I'm assuming she didn't put herself in here and wall herself up."

"No," said Alice. Oh, no, she wouldn't have, wouldn't have left the air and sun and hills, and Ollie, and Mary. Oh, no.

For a moment the world darkened at its edges. She saw Cassie by the little pool, looking up at the beckoning figures, thinking to rise, to spread her wings, to fly for one precious moment. And then—turning at the sound of someone else, someone coming up the shelf. Not Ollie. Perhaps she'd invited Doyle to have a talk before the wedding, looking for reassurance about Howie Randall. Or maybe they'd had that talk already, and she'd gone to the cliff to think, and he had followed her up there.

"Ms. Greer?"

Alice walked slowly to the cave. She closed her eyes, then looked in. A folded skeletal heap, with hair. Pushed, leaning, sideways, against the solid rock of the inside wall of the cave, legs folded under what was left of her head. Files moved his flashlight, pointing it down into the opening. Alice said, "The bandana?"

Kubecka nodded.

"Her boots," Alice said. Caliche-dusted, cobwebby, but visibly a pair of Goodson Kells boots, with stitching still intact—and the bones inside.

Alice thought of Cassie in the photo Ollie carried, laughing at Ollie from the top of the corral fence. "Can you tell?" she asked. "If he strangled her? Or hit her head?"

"I don't know," said Kubecka. Files was already on the phone, calling for a technical team. "Everyone, let's stand down," said Kubecka. "Not going to rain, is it?"

"No, sir," said Files."

Alice said, for the second time that morning, "We must call Mary."

Kubecka made his frog-mouth face. "Yep."

"At least she's safe for the moment," Alice said.

"Meaning from Doyle?" said Kubecka. "Yes, I'd say so. But you do remember he had an alibi for the time Ollie fell, and for Cassie's disappearance too, if I remember. And of course she left that note."

"That note," mused Alice.

"Remember?" said Kubecka. "We looked all over Texas and Mexico because of that note."

"And now what do you think?" Alice asked, interested.

"Convenient, that note," said Kubecka. "Maybe we look at it again." He looked back at the cave, where Cassie's hair was visible. Alice averted her eyes. Kubecka said, "You go home. I'll be in touch. In fact," he ordered Bender and the grad students, "you all need to leave."

Obediently Alice and Bender and the grad students made their way down the shelf. Alice crawled. Bender did too; he refused a rope this time but was pale and sweating by the time he and Alice were back on the ground, in front of their trucks. After hovering over her, muttering and peering into her eyes ("My pupils look fine!" she insisted), Bender finally agreed that Alice could drive home by herself. And she wanted to be alone. In her own house.

Silently, they dispersed. Doors slammed and trucks pulled away from the cliff. Only Kubecka and Files remained, with the medical examiner and a team to bring out Cassie's body.

So we found Cassie, and we all got into our own trucks and drove away, thought Alice, as her truck bounced across the dam and headed up the limestone ridge to the highway. If we were riding horses, we might ride together and talk. About Cassie. Ollie. Doyle. Mary. Rock art. What those pictures have seen, what they might mean. Now we're all alone again in our metal cocoons.

But Bender turned off the highway when she did and followed her home. When she pulled up, a cloud of dust behind her slowly covering the truck, he stopped in the driveway and got out. "I'm just checking," he said. "I just want to be sure you're okay."

"I'm okay," Alice said automatically.

"Just wanted to check that no more baddies were out here lying in wait."

"But Doyle's in the hospital!"

"Kubecka said he had an alibi for when Ollie died, said he had an overnight trip to Houston for his company. Their accountant showed Kubecka his travel receipts and the parking receipt from the San Antonio airport where he left the car. So that still means somebody else offed Ollie."

Alice felt tiredness wash over her. She couldn't stand to think another second.

"What are you going to do now?" Bender asked.

"Hot bath."

"Sounds good. Okay, Alice. You look like you'll make it."

Of course I'll make it, Alice thought indignantly. But her face was muffled in Bender's plaid flannel shirt. Quick hug and a kiss on the top of her head, as if she were ten years old.

"See you." And he turned and headed for the truck.

Exhausted, she headed for the house.

Chapter Twenty-Seven

On the Threshold

Alice reached for another grape and slid back deeper into the hot water. Steam rose around her. Perfect bliss—a paperback mystery in the bathtub with a bunch of grapes perched behind the faucet of the little claw-foot tub. She would wash away all thought of the day, the flying carabiners, Cassie's hair behind the rock wall. Cassie's boots. Cassie's bandana.

She turned on more hot water. A great vice, thought Alice, popping another grape into her mouth. Hot bath, new mystery set in Venice, by one of her favorite authors. Temporarily she would abandon her battered tub-side stack of Sayers mysteries, read and reread, leaving Lord Peter Wimsey forlorn in London, and travel instead to Italy. She tried to keep the paperback dry but it was already damp. Like Venice. As the water cooled she ran in a little more hot, feeling her leg muscles relax. Her mind strayed to Venice, to the basilica of San Marco, music echoing high in its dome, candles lit before saints in the chapels along the walls. Centuries of painstaking work, of art, of beauty in the face of wars and destruction and rising waters. Gilt, mosaic, oil. Human effort to rise above the darker side of human nature?

Warm to the bone, she wrapped up in her robe and a blanket and dragged the blanket like a coronation train behind her, trailing out on the deck to look at the stars. She leaned back, back, back, starlight falling in her eyes. Orion was still chasing something with Sirius scurrying along beside him. Ollie, Alice said to the stars, we're getting there. We found your Cassie at least.

Inside the phone rang.

"Alice?"

Mary's voice.

"Alice, I hate to call so late. Can you come down?"

"To New Braunfels?" The kitchen clock said 10:00 p.m.

"I know. I would never call you this late but . . . I know I won't sleep at all tonight. I found some things in Doyle's desk. If you don't look at them—I don't know if I can bear to wait until morning."

"Are you okay, Mary?"

"No." Long pause. "I've been . . . I've been . . ."

"Okay," Alice said. "Let me get jeans on. I can be there in about forty-five minutes." Need to give Mary something to do. "Hey, Mary, will you make some coffee?"

"I will," said Mary. "Thank you, Alice. I'll be watching for you."

At least I shouldn't run into rammer man, since he's in the hospital, Alice thought, racing out to the truck and heading south down the creek road.

Devil's Backbone, Purgatory Road—she met no troopers and set a personal best record for shortest time to New Braunfels.

Mary opened the door when Alice was still wheeling into the driveway.

"Good grief," Alice said. "When did you last get some sleep?" Mary's face, hollow-eyed, was pale as death under the porch light.

"I need you to come see," she said. "Oh. I mean, after you have your coffee. It's all ready."

Worried, Alice followed Mary into the kitchen, watched her trying to fill a coffee cup. "Hey. Let me." She poured a cup and looked at Mary. "What about you? How about some coffee? Or tea?" She looked harder at Mary. "A glass of wine?" Mary nodded. Alice rooted in the refrigerator and found a half-full bottle of wine. When Alice handed her a glassful, Mary's eyes spilled over. "Honey, what is it?" Alice demanded.

Without a word Mary turned and headed down the hall. "Doyle's office," she said. Alice stopped suddenly on the threshold, remembering how Doyle had warned her off the day of the funeral. Mary looked back at her and nodded. "I know. He didn't like me to come in here. Said this was his room. But when I got back from the hospital, Alice, something made me come look in here. I've been so worried. Look."

Alice followed her around Doyle's huge dark mahogany desk. The cabinet door to the left of his chair stood open, key still in the lock. On the floor were several small stacks of paper.

"Was it locked?" Alice asked.

"Yes."

"Where did you find the key?"

"Computer bag. Look," Mary said again. "This is what . . . this is why I called."

She picked up a stack of greeting cards—beginning to fade, a little creased—and handed them to Alice. The first one was folded open. "Darling Mary," Alice read, "Thanks so much for the sweet Mother's Day present! I love that book, but you are the best Mother's Day present of all. Love you. Mama." Alice furrowed her brow and looked at Mary.

"Look at all of them."

Alice looked at the stack. There were six cards, all to Mary, all from Cassie, all folded open to the handwritten message. "See you when you get here! Can't wait to celebrate and make wedding plans!" read the next-to-last card in the stack. The last card was to Doyle, still in its envelope, but folded open to the message, still vivid in Cassie's spiky handwriting. "August 1, 2000—Happy birthday, Doyle! Hope you enjoy this book. Love, Cassie and Ollie."

"They gave him a copy of 'Lone Star' for his birthday, when we were engaged," Mary breathed.

"I understand keeping his own birthday card," Alice began. "But the rest of these were to you from your mother."

"Right."

"And you found them locked up in Doyle's desk."

"Yes, way back on this side." She pointed to the open door.

"These were cards you saved?"

"Yes, I kept every card and every letter she ever sent me, in a box in my closet."

"But then how come these are in Doyle's desk now?"

"Look at them," Mary commanded. "Don't you see? He has them folded back. And look how the writing is doubled, like he went over it."

Alice turned on the desk lamp and brought the top card up six inches from her eyes. The letters Cassie had written looked engraved, as if someone had traced over them repeatedly. On the card to Doyle, blue ballpoint ink overlaid black ink.

"He was trying to copy your mother's handwriting?" Alice guessed. "For that note, the one he left at the ranch. The one about going to the border for flowers." She looked at Mary's stricken face. "This is what you were afraid of?"

Mary nodded.

"What's this other stuff?" Alice pointed to the floor.

"Look here," said Mary. On her knees, she handed up to Alice a little order pad like the one the waitresses used at Bet's Biscuits and the Camellia Diner. Several pages were torn from the front. Next she handed up a paper-clipped group of credit card receipts. "ABIA Parking," Alice read on the first one. Austin-Bergstrom International Airport? "Hobby International Parking," she read, flipping to the next. "San Antonio International Airport Parking."

Still kneeling, Mary handed Alice a small roll of blank white paper, the same width as the parking receipts. "Found this in the cabinet too," Mary said flatly.

"Huh." Alice got on her knees, peered into the cabinet, groping at the back with her fingertips. She pulled out a gray plastic device. "Mobile three-inch receipt printer," she read. She groped around again and pulled out an old-fashioned adding machine with a roll of paper tape. "Receipts. Did he need to print receipts as a US Security employee, Mary?" She fingered the airport parking receipts.

Mary shrugged, staring at her.

"Where is his computer?"

"Usually locked up in his SUV," Mary said. "But I drove down to his office tonight and got it. His car was still parked in front." She pointed to a black laptop bag under the desk.

"Meaning he left it there and drove the green US Security truck to the ranch today," Alice said.

Mary nodded, tugging the computer out of the bag.

"Let's take it to the kitchen," she said, shivering. "I don't want to be in here."

Alice was astonished when Mary typed in a password and the screen promptly opened on Doyle's computer.

"He told you his password?" That didn't sound like Doyle.

"Of course not," Mary said. "I guessed it. 'Eljefe1.'"

"El jefe one?" Alice tried to visualize.

"What he always wanted, I think. Not me . . . the dirt out there. Be the big boss. Own Cloud Ranch."

Alice nodded slowly. "Can I?" Mary nodded and Alice tapped "Start" and then tapped "Programs." Up popped the usual list of applications for email, fax, accessories, spreadsheets, web browsing—and an extra: "Homeoffice 3-inch Receipt Software." Alice started to open it and then thought, No. Good grief, I'm messing with evidence.

"Mary, we need to stop. We need to give this to the police. We shouldn't mess with the computer any more." Alice remembered one case she worked on where the outcome turned on the mirror image the judge had ordered of everything on the defendant's computer—every data entry, every date, every save-over. "We can't open this."

"Do you think Daddy knew? Do you think he knew what happened to my mom?"

"Are you assuming that Doyle killed her?"

Mary nodded. Alice tried to imagine being Mary at this moment, the pain echoing in her brain.

"I think he guessed, that last day," Alice said. "He had put the little gold pocketknife way down in his jeans watch pocket, and it was still full of dirt, like he'd just found it. I think that happened when he was up at the cave, thinking about Cassie, and that . . . someone . . . found him up there. And then—that he fell from up there. And then was moved from where he fell."

"Oh God." Mary crossed her arms on her chest and rocked back and forth.

"Maybe when Doyle saw him up there—these are all maybes—he leaped to some conclusions about what Ollie had figured out." A vision of Ollie kneeling near the pool, thumbing the dirt from the little gold object, and looking toward the cave with a growing surmise, growing certainty, rose before her. And then a vision of Doyle, coming quietly up the shelf and watching Ollie look toward the cave.

"I should tell you something," said Mary. "When the police asked me about that little gold knife, I told Doyle. And he got this expression on his face like he was . . . oh, assessing what I said. Evaluating it. Calculating it. And his eyes went blank like he was looking right through me."

Alice had a sudden vision of Doyle with the entrenching tool, the plastic bag, the duct tape. She had told Kubecka and Files of her guess that he had decided to remove Cassie's body before the conservancy people could start investigating the cave. He just hadn't known precisely how soon that would be.

Oblivious, Mary went on, staring at her hands in her lap. "I always had this feeling that even though Daddy was very 'hail fellow well met' with Doyle, he was still a little . . . watchful. Even after ten years. You know, he'd let Doyle put up a deer blind, or talk to him about what he might do with the cows, that kind of thing. Didn't let him make any real decisions but treated him in that manly way. One Christmas he gave Doyle a horse so we could both ride out there."

Alice imagined Doyle up on a horse and felt zero at the bone, thinking how she had exposed Red to his rifle.

"He loved it," Mary said. "Couldn't ride very well, jerked the bridle too hard, horse didn't like him. He just loved being up on his high horse. But what he really got off on was shooting out at the ranch. He wanted Daddy to let him high-fence it and raise big trophy deer, then let him bring his business friends out to shoot them."

"I don't remember any high fence," Alice said.

"Right. Daddy did keep a boundary on those ranch decisions. He just looked at him and said, 'Not gonna do that. Animals can come, animals can go. If it keeps my cows in, it's enough fence.' Daddy hated that some people fence out all the native deer just so they can breed some big ones and then shoot them."

Alice kept quiet. She felt the same way about her own place, though she knew hunting leases were the only reason some ranchers could afford to keep their ranches intact, and keep the Hill Country from turning into a sea of subdivisions.

"I think I'm talking this out to myself," Mary said, "because I've had this cloud of worry in my mind for the last ten years. Just a cloud of worry. Never knowing what happened to my mama or where she was. It's been like being in a fog."

"One thing, and I know you know it," Alice said. "Your mother and Ollie wanted so much to be sure you were happy. And safe."

"I know, I know," Mary said, rocking herself again.

"And they weren't sure, and they didn't want to ruin Doyle for you."

Tears rained down Mary's face. Alice handed her a dish towel.

"I was starting to worry too," Alice said. "After Ollie died, I was very worried about you."

Mary looked up. "You mean, once he got the ranch . . . ?"

"My guess is, your dad wasn't sure, wasn't sure about Doyle, so he put the ranch and the money where your death would not benefit anyone but an orphanage. I think he thought that was safe."

Mary wiped her face with the dish towel. The kitchen clock ticked away the minutes—nearly midnight. Outside, a branch touched the kitchen window, and the wind sighed in the trees. Alice cocked her head and looked at Mary. Why did her face look different?

Ah. Ollie's eyes. That's what she saw now. Mary wasn't wearing her usual anxious expression. She was staring out the kitchen window into the night. Her eyes were narrowed, but with Ollie's crinkles at the corner. She didn't look anxious.

She shifted on the kitchen stool, straightened her shoulders, took a deep breath. "I'm free. I'm free now. I don't care what the police find in there." She nodded at the computer.

"Well, we should call. You should call," she corrected herself. "Want Kubecka's number?" That number was etched in her mental contacts list.

Mary punched in the number and walked off. Alice heard her in the dining room, pacing back and forth, bumping into the dining room table. Apparently Kubecka asked about Doyle. "The nurses say he's stable. I'm home right now." Pause. "Alice is here. I called her because I found some things. She said you should know." Mary came back into the kitchen. "He wants to talk to you."

Alice told Kubecka about Mary's call and what they'd found.

"I'll be there in an hour," he said.

Alice said, "You don't want to wait until tomorrow morning?"

"Nope. On my way."

Another long night, after a very long day. "Let's make some more coffee," Alice said. "Before Kubecka gets here."

Chapter Twenty-Eight

Distant Bell

Time seemed to collapse and accelerate. On the Thursday morning after Alice's Tuesday-night run to Mary's, and Kubecka's midnight appearance there, Kubecka asked to meet again with Alice and Mary, at Mary's house. When Alice opened the front door, Mary's house smelled different, somehow. Alice sniffed. What?

Doyle remained in the hospital, with a broken neck and paraplegic prospects. A sheriff's deputy sat outside his room. Alice wrestled with conflicting emotions—horror that she had put him in this condition, and pride that she'd saved her own life.

Sitting in Mary's living room, Kubecka told them that tests on the dirt in the little gold knife indicated it likely came from the cliff garden, not the barren limestone rockfall where Ollie was found. "It had piñon pollen in it," said Kubecka. "Who knew we'd be doing pollen tests?"

"Like the archeologists do," Alice said.

Kubecka also told them there were signs Cassie had been strangled, given how tight the bandana was around what was left of her neck, but at this point the cartilage was deteriorated and they couldn't be sure. "Still, like I said, she sure didn't put herself in that cave and wall herself in," he said.

"What about the receipts?" Alice asked. "What about Doyle's alibi for the day she disappeared?"

"We checked the expense accounts at US Security. They only go back seven years and then the company destroys the records. So, I don't know if we can figure out anything except from the little gold knife."

"It means he was up there, before my wedding, and I never knew it," said Mary. "And I knew he'd lost the knife by the wedding because he couldn't find it to wear that day."

"How do you know that?" asked Kubecka.

"We were living together. He couldn't find it when we were packing to come to the ranch for the wedding. Told me he'd misplaced it. And I know he replaced it, because after the wedding, I found a receipt from the same jewelry store for the same knife and when I asked Doyle about it, he said he'd apparently lost their present and was afraid they would be upset if they found out so he ordered a new one. At the time I just thought . . . how thoughtful."

She looked at Kubecka. "It was the Meier jewelry store on Congress, where we got our wedding rings. I was in there a lot just before and after the wedding. Old Mr. Meier is not in there now but his sons are."

"We'll look at that," said Kubecka.

All pretty circumstantial, Alice thought. "What about the receipts from the day Ollie fell? When Doyle said he was in Houston?"

"Now that is interesting," Kubecka said. "He did turn in a real receipt from a motel out north of Bush Intercontinental Airport. The security job was in the vicinity of the airport. The motel's records show a late arrival, around midnight. Doyle also turned in a dinner receipt for that Tuesday, with an adding machine tape stapled to it, indicating he gave cash and got change back. Same kind of receipt you'd find in a barbecue place—not even the name on it. And he told his company it was from Woody's BBQ, also way out in north Houston by the airport. Sonny's confirms they use that kind of setup. But the way the paper is torn from the tablet exactly matches the torn top of a missing page from one of the tablets in his desk. We'll get the handwriting analyzed. The lunch receipt is similar. And it matches the tablet too. We think he faked those two meal receipts. In fact, his computer has that program in it for printing receipts on three-inch paper and you saw he had that little three-inch paper printer. We found a dummied up receipt still in the computer.

"On the other hand," he went on, "Doyle turned in a parking receipt for the San Antonio airport, for entry on Tuesday morning and exit on Wednesday afternoon. It looks genuine."

"What about airline tickets?" Alice asked. "How could he fake that on his expense report?"

"He didn't, apparently. He gave his office the confirmation showing the credit card charge for a flight over on Tuesday morning and a flight back the next afternoon. Airline says those do check out. So Adam started checking rental car companies at the Houston airport. Found where he rented a car on Tuesday morning—which you would expect, since he would need a car to do his site reconnaissance for his Houston client. But according to the rental company, he put nearly six hundred miles on it."

"That's a lot of miles to drive to check fence line on an airport operation," Alice commented. "But how do you prove where a rental car has been? You can pay cash for gas."

"So true," said Kubecka. "Maybe he got cocky. Didn't reckon with Adam Files, who found his rental car's picture in the Department of Transportation camera records for the tollway shortcut you can take between Houston and Austin. Funny thing is, that rental car plate appears on the stretch heading west, nearly back in Austin, early Tuesday afternoon, on the Elgin part of the tollway. And the same car shows up on the records again heading back to Houston, about ten at night."

"Which means," said Alice, "that he could have left Houston right after he flew in, picked up a rental car, driven straight back to the ranch, then turned around and returned to Houston Tuesday night, done his work Wednesday morning, and flown back."

"Right. It's about 275 miles to the ranch from the airport in Houston. Could do it in, say, four to four and a half hours, if you didn't get messed up in Houston traffic. It's doable. You could still check in by midnight."

"What does Doyle say?" Alice asked.

"We're going to talk to him tomorrow. He retained counsel."

They looked at Mary. "I don't know who. I haven't talked to him," she said.

Alice thought about that. If it had been her own husband, and she learned he had murdered her parents, what would she do? Go to the hospital and spit in his face?

"I didn't want to say anything until I knew exactly what I was going to say," Mary said, almost as if she had heard what Alice was thinking. "When I do say something, it will be forever."

"Also," Kubecka went on, "we talked to Mr. Treacher. By the way, first we called Ventopoder about him. He did have some sort of contingency arrangement with them if he could get the whole tract leased, but they claim he was not their lawyer or their employee. Anyway, Treacher admitted he tried hard to get hold of that power of attorney. Doyle apparently got a glimpse of it in your truck, somehow, when you were out at Cloud Ranch, but couldn't figure out what it was about. So Treacher tried to get somebody else to get hold of your briefcase, out at your place."

"Skunk man." Alice felt rage creeping back at the thought of someone invading her property.

"Yep. Skunk man failed. Then after Ollie died, Mr. Treacher apparently tried to find it himself in your office. He's still clamming up, but our guess is he was trying to figure out how to get Cloud Ranch leased, figure out who he would have to deal with. We don't know yet if he talked to Doyle about the will."

"What did skunk man look like?" Alice demanded. A vision of Treacher's red-faced companion at the Beer Barn rose before her.

"Just some ol' boy from Blanco. Show you a picture if you want, later."

"But skunk man wasn't rammer man, was he?" Alice said. Again she saw the murderous pickup, trailing her, crossing the highway median to try a second time to slam her truck into the concrete abutment. That was more Doyle's style.

"Don't think so. Still checking on that," said Kubecka. "Well, I need to get back. Want to be sure we have more of the loose ends tied up. I will talk to that Meier jewelry store, Mary." He checked his notepad. "Whoops. Another item. There was one real odd thing on Doyle's computer. Adam told me not to forget it. That kid keeps me in line, I tell you."

"What?" said Mary.

"Did Doyle ever complain about air bags? Was he one of those guys who thinks he has a constitutional right not to have an air bag?"

Mary stared at Kubecka, eyes puzzled, shaking her head no.

But a distant bell rang in Alice's brain.

Kubecka went on, "His computer has elaborate instructions for disconnecting an air bag. Really precise instructions. The weird thing is, they aren't for your Morris or his SUV or that green truck, Mary. They are for a late-model Buick sedan. Did you ever hear him talk about disconnecting an air bag?"

"No," said Mary.

"But you know," Alice said slowly, trying to formulate the sentence properly, "Allen's mother's air bag supposedly didn't inflate last year, when she had an accident."

"Debard's mother?" Kubecka narrowed his eyes. "Nobody told me that."

"Accident happened in Coffee County. Not Gillespie County," Alice answered. "But maybe talk to Coffee County about it. I hear they ragged on Allen for awhile, trying to figure out if he disconnected his mom's air bag."

Kubecka rubbed his face with his hands and shook his head. "Too much stuff," he said, hoisting himself to his feet. "Okay. Later, ladies."

After he left, Mary looked at Alice. "Why would he do that?"

"Do you mean, if Doyle messed with Leanne's air bag, why would he have done it?"

Mary nodded.

"I wonder if he was trying to get rid of anyone that he thought might wind up with some claim to Cloud Ranch?"

"Ah," Mary said. "I see. It was Allen who usually drove Leanne around, I recall. So you're saying that wasn't really meant for Leanne."

"All supposition," said Alice. "Could be. But how it would ever be proved I'm not sure." So circumstantial. Would any of this amount to proof beyond a reasonable doubt, to a jury?

Mary nodded. "Yep. He was very clever, covering his footsteps, wasn't he."

"Covering them for a long time. Cassie, Ollie, maybe Leanne," said Alice. "Maybe Howard Randall."

"Howard Randall? Who is that?" Mary asked.

"Um. That's another story, from long ago. And you know what, Mary?

Maybe you too would be in that list, if Ollie hadn't changed his arrangements the way he did."

She looked at Mary. Mary shivered, shook her head. And Alice looked around at the paintings in Mary's living room. Mary followed Alice's glance, and nodded.

"You are right," she said. "Time to paint. I already started." She unfolded her fingers and waved them at Alice.

That's what that smell is, Alice realized. A faint little hint of turpentine. "Oils?"

Mary smiled. "Yes. For my dad. I'll show you when it's done."

Chapter Twenty-Nine

All the Way

Driving home from New Braunfels, Alice felt a hole in her heart, a gap, an empty place. She called Mary. "I want to go up one more time to the cave," she said. "Do you mind?"

Of course Mary didn't mind. Alice turned west instead of heading for Coffee Creek. This time, she promised herself, no one would wreck her visit. Doyle was still hospitalized. Sure enough, when she came over the ridge above Cloud Ranch, the ranch lay quiet and still below.

Once again Alice scrambled up the rock, up the slot, up the inclined rock. Once again, the narrow shelf lay before her. She dropped to her hands and knees and inched across, to the safety of the cliff garden.

This time the pictures took her almost immediately. The white figure, the black figure, the snaky shape. She felt her eyes close and her mind open, as if she were somewhere very high, very far away. She saw Ollie, receding, his back to her, walking toward Cassie, far off on the horizon. And as Ollie neared Cassie, the two of them seemed to fly up, fly away.

She felt a presence near her, a fur-covered, large presence. Like a bear. A bear, but Jordie. She could feel the warmth. A bear could maul, could move faster than fast, could swipe with a paw, eat blueberries, dive into water, catch fish—could stand on its hind legs in terrible height, eyes aflash, like Jordie.

The bear stood near her, not moving. She felt that the bear planned to stay put. Hair rose on the nape of her neck. Her ears and fingers tingled. Her eyes were shut so tight, yet she could see so far. The bear ambled slowly off and sat in the middle distance. She was not a bear, but she knew this bear.

The bear waited, and would wait.

Birdcall. Cardinal, finch, titmouse. Alice opened her eyes. High up, silent, a hawk circled, free as the wind. Alice's neck, shoulders, arms felt limp and loose, as relaxed as if she'd had a massage.

So, a bear would wait for her, like Cassie waited for Ollie. When she passed through that parted curtain . . . a bear would be there to lead her on. Meanwhile, the bear stood aside. She had clients to worry over, friends to enjoy, donkeys to brush and talk to and feed. And children to visit.

Alice stood, still feeling light and loose, and faintly as if she too were fur-covered, with claws. Those decorations, though, were invisible.

She had seen past the invisible barrier, had risen into the dark rose beyond the cliffs, had felt the onrushing air of the world beyond. New Alice, she mused. Alice. An odd name for a furred creature with claws. She must have a new name, but no one had mentioned it to her.

Alice was halfway down the narrow cliff shelf—nearly to the little obtruding boulder—when she realized she was not crawling. She was walking on the fourteen-inch shelf, fifty feet above limestone outcrops and cedar trunks.

"Damn sure-footed little animal I am, I must be," Alice muttered. She counted the distance. Ten more steps to the safety of the inclined rock leading down to the slot. She walked all the way.

Chapter Thirty

Many Stories

Alice stood by the curve of creek, its water glinting in the late November sun. She shivered a little when the breeze picked up out of the north. Cassie and Ollie, bodies finally released by officialdom, were being buried together, in the pasture west of the ranch house at Cloud Ranch, across from the curved bluff with its old Indian midden, where the creek undercut the cliff and bent toward the west.

"Took a rock saw to get through the limestone," Mary had said on the phone, "but I know they would want to be there, and want you there. They would, I mean. And I do."

So Alice stood by the curve of blue-green water with Mary and Allen and a host of Ollie and Cassie's friends—Ilka, Bryce, Miranda, Silla, the Men's Wild Game Committee, and others Alice didn't know.

Mary looked different—tired, but no longer anxious. She looks at home, thought Alice.

Stepping forward, Mary turned to the group and took a long breath, then began: "My mother and father loved life, and loved Cloud Ranch, the sky, the hills, the water. They'll be here, and now they are free to wander. But they would most of all have loved to celebrate again with you, their friends. So let's let them be, here by the creek, and then laugh and cry and tell stories again, up at the ranch house."

Then Allen and Bryce and the Men's Wild Game Committee members lowered two plain wooden coffins into the single rectangular excavation. Cassie's box looked light as a feather, light as a cotton bandana.

A woman minister Alice didn't know stood next to the excavation. Without a word she looked around, collecting them all, and then said, "We lift up our eyes to the hills. From whence does our help come?" Again she surveyed each of them. Alice looked back, interested.

"Cassie and Ollie. For each of them, we would have wanted a peaceful farewell, with no fear, no pain. But think of their spirits, their fierce determination to act from love, to care for Mary and all around them. Think how they took themselves up to the high places, up the narrow way"—Alice saw in her mind's eye the narrow cliff path, and marveled—"to the cave, to a spring in the rock, a spring in the wilderness, always and ever the place of mystery, the place where humans are drawn, seeking to touch that mystery, to reach beyond—beyond—into all the ends of creation, and perhaps to find, if only for a moment, their full, true selves."

Silence. Alice flexed her fingers, recalling that sense of claws, of fur, of flight, all mixed. Rising up, past the drawings, past the cliff top, up—

"So we bless Cassie and Ollie, their bodies here, and we think of their spirits, freed now and beautiful. We say thanks for their driving desire to protect life, to seek love, to feel the beauty of this sweet world, with all its perils. We say thanks for life. And into the dirt and rocks of Cloud Ranch we commend their bodies."

Mary walked forward and put a bunch of late wildflowers, purple and yellow and dusty green, into the joint grave, and everyone took turns with the shovels, adding dirt to the excavation. Then the procession wound back to the ranch house. And late into the evening Alice heard many stories and saw many bottles poured.

Chapter Thirty-One

New Ventures

On the Saturday before Thanksgiving, Alice put on some Celtic music, turned it up loud, dragged one suitcase and a carryon onto her bed and started packing madly. Her flight to Scotland left the next afternoon. It wasn't clothes that required planning—that was simple. She needed wool socks, hiking boots, wool sweater, hat, gloves, and a warm windbreaker, for expeditions with John and Ann up Arthur's Seat and, leaning into the winter wind, to the Sheep Heid Inn in Duddingston. What took careful planning was the food. For Gran's planned Thanksgiving dinner in Edinburgh, Alice had been assigned the ingredients for cornbread stuffing, canned pumpkin for the pies, and cranberry sauce. Plus, the children had begged for corn tortillas, jalapeños, chorizo (which Alice had frozen), and chipotle chili powder. Try sniffing that, she mentally ordered the drug-sniffing dogs who (she imagined) were edging around her suitcases. Just try.

Again she picked up the email from Ann, which she had printed out to tuck into her purse. Ann had forwarded a snapshot someone had taken of her and John in the university commons. Ann was studying urban history but also taking voice lessons, and John was studying history of science. In the picture, Ann was grinning very fondly at the photographer (Who was that person, to get such a flirtatious smile? wondered Alice) and wearing charming boots with ribbons in the top. John, waving a sandwich, wore a yellow muffler. "Here we are having lunch," Ann wrote. "I am virtuously eating salad because I have a voice lesson this afternoon and can't have anything cheesy. As you can see, John is busily studying for the history of science seminar. But tonight he promises he will bring his fiddle to the jam at Sandy Bell's!" Alice grinned, thinking of John looking at a skeptical audience, taking a deep breath, and bravely bowing the downstroke on a Scottish jig for an audience that knew precisely how each note should sound. But, she thought, they'll soon learn: John can flat play that fiddle. And I will get to hear him soon, and maybe Ann will sing too.

There. Both bags were done, except for the frozen chorizo. Now, to go or not to go? Because also on the bed lay the printed invitation from Ben Kinsear, to the grand opening that night of The Real Story, his Fredericksburg bookstore. Alice was of two minds. No, more than two. One, go; two, don't go; three, dither and fret.

Oh, stop it. She would go to Fredericksburg, stop at the five-and-dime for bandanas for the tribe in Scotland, and just pop in to the bookstore. Surely David and Isabel Frohbel would be there—she wouldn't be all alone. We should celebrate all new ventures, she had decided. Somewhere off in her mind, the bear nodded.

Leaving her bags propped by the door, she pulled on velvet jeans and a wildly embroidered rodeo jacket that Red had given her for her birthday. And her own Goodson Kells, just finished. She looked in the mirror. Good heavens, all that glitter and rickrack. Was the barrel racer look really her?

But then how many barrel racers have barely escaped murder? she thought. Probably a good many, her brain answered, but that's a story for another day. Sporting the embroidered jacket, all yellow roses and glitter, and swaggering a little in the new boots, she headed to the truck.

The Real Story blazed with lights. Kinsear had opened the bookstore in a classic little German stone house. A band in cowboy hats played Texas swing music on the porch. Laughter rang inside. Alice stood still on the sidewalk, looking at the door. Then she walked in. Kinsear was right at the entrance.

"Alice!" He waved at a waiter who inched through the crowd, resplendent in cowboy regalia but carrying a silver tray of champagne flutes. "Alice! I was afraid you wouldn't come!" He hugged her sideways, careful not to spill her champagne. "Come look around. I especially want you to see the Alamo section."

Alice let herself be tugged into what looked like the old dining room. "That whole wall," he said. "Can you believe it? That much stuff about the Alamo?"

Alice grinned. "Of course I believe it!" she said. "It's our foundation myth!"

Someone yelled at Kinsear and he dodged off into the crowd. Alice looked around for Kinsear's wife. She needed to go say hello. Instead, Isabel Frohbel materialized at Alice's elbow. "Darling," she said. "I was hoping you'd be here." Alice sighed in relief and fell into intense how-are-your-children discussion with Isabel, who had two sets of twins. Isabel's husband shouldered his way through the crowd with a Dos Equis for Isabel and champagne for himself. Alice laughed.

"Can't get the woman to drink anything else," he said. He glanced at Isabel. "He seems to be holding up fine, don't you think?"

Alice furrowed her brow, questioning. "Kinsear? What's wrong?"

"Well, of course it's only been a year. But I think he's doing fine."

Sinking sensation. "A year?"

They both stared. "Don't you know?" said Isabel. "His wife died last year. Riding accident. She was trying to jump her horse. I thought you knew."

"Yeah," said Frohbel, "I thought you knew that when you and I were sitting there at the Altburg with Kinsear. I mean, I handled the will, Alice!"

How could I not know this, wondered Alice.

"How could you not know?" scolded Isabel. "It was in the alumni notes!"

"Guess I wasn't vigilant," said Alice.

They both looked at her in horror. "Oh, Alice, we're sorry. I mean, it's only two years since Jordie died, isn't it. We are just heathens. Heathens with no class."

Frohbel snatched her empty glass and fled to the waiter, still swanning through the room in his cowboy boots with the silver tray of champagne flutes held aloft.

"Well, so, now you see why we wanted you to be here," said Isabel. "Not just so we could catch up with you. But you and Kinsear were . . . were pretty good friends, before Jordie."

"We were," Alice said stiffly. "But that was a long time ago and in another country."

"I hear you," said Isabel. "But life is fragile and life is fast, and we should keep all our friendships."

Alice thought about that.

"We should," she said. "Okay, I have to head back. Flying to Scotland tomorrow to see the darling John and Ann." She hugged both halves of Frohbel & Frohbel and edged toward the front door, where she turned, surveying the crowd. Kinsear was against the back wall, but looked up. Their eyes met. Alice took a deep breath, smiled and waved, and headed out the door, leaving the happy music on the porch for the quiet of the street, and then the dark drive back to Coffee Creek.

Two days later it was morning in Scotland, and her connection from Heathrow had curved west and was bouncing atop the clouds over the Firth of Forth. The pilot's British accent announced, "Ladies and gentlemen, we are making our approach into Edinburgh. As you may have noted, with the headwinds, the flight in will be a bit tippy. Please fasten your seat belts, and welcome to Scotland."

Below her, the clouds parted, showing sun glinting momentarily on the waters of the Forth, the Castle, and Arthur's Seat. It felt like a homecoming—arriving in this Scotland to which she was tied by such strange, strong bands. But a homecoming without Jordie. Still, there would be her children. Time to wrap her scarf around her neck, grab each child by the hand, and head straight to Sandy Bell's, for music, for stories, and a glass of Talisker. With one teaspoon of water.

The End

AUTHOR'S NOTE

"To lose one parent, Mr. Worthing, may be regarded as a misfortune; to lose both looks like carelessness."
Lady Bracknell, Act 1, Part 2, The Importance of Being Earnest.

After rooting around in Psalms, Alice decided that Ilka must mean Psalm 32.

THANKS AND MORE THANKS

This book would never have happened without the collaborative brainstorming, insightful suggestions and constant support of Larry Foster, Fritz and Sydney Foster Schneider, Drew and Amanda Foster, and my sister Grace Currie Bradshaw. Heartfelt thanks to you, who were there every step of the way.

Nor could this book have hatched without the generous comments and encouragement of Alice's tales from all the following friends and family: Carol Arnold, Ann Barker, Megan Biesele, Bill Bradshaw, Boyce Cabaniss, Pat Campbell, Elizabeth Christian, Ann Ciccolella, Keith Clemson, Susan Conway, Ken and Pam Currie, amazing Austin pianist Floyd Domino, Gretchen Weicker, Suzanne and David Wofford, Martha Wood, Virgil Yarbrough and Stephenie Yearwood. What friendship.

For the superb expert advice (any errors are mine) and support from Bill Crawford, Diana Borden, Natalie Bidnick, Dr. Mark Currie, and Aaron Hierholzer (*editor nonpareil*), and for Bill Carson's cover, layout, craftsmanship, web design and sheer professional brio, thanks and more thanks!

ABOUT THE AUTHOR

Helen Currie Foster writes the Alice MacDonald Greer Mystery series. She lives north of Dripping Springs, Texas, supervised by three burros. She is drawn to the compelling landscape and quirky characters of the Texas Hill Country. She's also deeply curious about our human history, and how, uninvited, the past keeps crashing the party.

Find her on Facebook or at www.helencurriefoster.com.

CPSIA information can be obtained
at www.ICGtesting.com
Printed in the USA
LVOW12s0219051017
551235LV00001B/40/P

9 781505 414301